"With a whiff of orange spices, the flipping of some Tarot cards, and a sip of herbal tea, reporter Alexandria Vilkas is off and running again, investigating a murder mystery that makes for one hell of a wild night at the opera. Silvia Foti has created a real winner.... You'll laugh, you'll cry, but above all, you'll love it." –Michael A. Black, author of *Melody of Vengeance*

"Tarot cards, murder, and a reporter with a box full of incriminating evidence lead the reader to a magical world where the paranormal proves more powerful than traditional crime solving methods. ...a fun-filled story with plenty of action and vibrant characters. ...witty, suspenseful and an all around terrific read!" –Scarlett Dean, author of *Invisible Shield*

"*The Diva's Fool* casts a powerful spell impossible to break until the last page is read. Magical, yet grounded in reality, the book takes the reader behind the scenes of Chicago's Lyric Opera, into the mysterious realm of the occult and the gritty world of gunrunning." – Gail Lukasik, author of *Destroying Angels*

"...a window of delight on backstage at the Chicago opera world. The well-paced novel mixes intrigue with sharp characterizations all around the last performance of Macbeth by the title's aging diva....highly recommended." –Robert W. Walker, author of *City for Ransom*

Skullduggery

"A fast-paced fictional tale of mystery that just about any Chicagoan can enjoy. It's a serious suspense with a good dose of humor added. I recommend Skullduggery." –Joe Kulys, *Southwest News Herald*

"New Age philosophies and murder mix when the first Mexican mayor of Chicago dies of poisoning ...and a supernatural crystal skull goes missing. ...suspects include uppity aldermen, a treacherous billionaire, and several cuckolded husbands. A highly appealing, up-front heroine and a novel look at Chicago politics make this an attractive first mystery." –*Library Journal*

"A crystal skull that may have supernatural powers, Chicago politicians, a dead mayor, and an astrologist combine to make Skullduggery a fun brew. A humorous romp with a good bit of mayhem included." –Barbara D'Amato, author of *Authorized Personnel Only*, and winner of the first annual Mary Higgins Clark Award

The Diva's Fool

By Silvia Foti

Silvia Foti

Echelon Press

Publishing

The Diva's Fool
The Order of Tarot Chronicles
Book Zero
An Echelon Press Book

First Echelon Press paperback printing / May 2007

Cover Art © Nathalie Moore

Echelon Press
9735 Country Meadows Lane 1-D
Laurel, MD 20723
www.echelonpress.com

ISBN 978-1-59080-506-0
10-Digit ISBN: 1-59080-506-2

PRINTED IN THE UNITED STATES OF AMERICA

10 9 8 7 6 5 4 3 2 1

To Franco, Alessandra, and Gabriel

A Note from the Author

By way of research, I placed several books on opera and the Tarot in a God Jar, then shook gently. This rich material fertilized my dream world and brought this fictional cast to life. All the characters are products of my imagination with personalities and frailties that are exaggerated not too greatly. Every book draws from others before it, adding to the stream of knowledge and entertainment, and I owe much to those who have written about the Tarot and raising consciousness.

In addition, I have the following to thank: Paul Thurman for his expertise on Tarot cards; Joel Ostrander for his mastery of guns; John Binder for his know-how on organized crime; Nijole and Arnold Voketaitis for their authority on opera; and my mother, Dalia Kucenas, for instilling a love of classical music. Several friends and colleagues lent their editorial encouragement, including: Chris Smith, Mary Harris, Robert Walker, Michael Black, Joan Hadac, Jill Sherer, Carol Tessler, Susan Weisenburg, Keri Clark, Rebecca McIntyre, Beth Ann Sabo, Sharon Wildwind, Liz Dolinska, Mary Rose Dallal, Jerry Cleaver, Hanley Kanar, Karen Syed, Betsy Baird, and Kat Thompson. For being there at the beginning–Robert Gover. For camaraderie–Sisters in Crime and Guppies. For one of the most inspiring mystery writers' conventions that bolster fledgling authors–Love Is Murder. For babysitting–Franca and Carmelo Foti, the best in-laws on the planet.

Overture

The doorbell tinkled as I entered, but The Wizard acted as if he hadn't heard it. I wasn't offended or surprised–I'd gotten used to his moments of focused concentration. He lifted the woodsy perfumed broom, its knobbed handle gleaming, and swept about three to six inches above the floor, leaving crumbs and dust behind. He remained intent on finishing his task, whistling a gleeful melody as he brushed the air with a whoosh to right and left. After observing him for several moments, I still could not figure out why he swept in such an odd fashion.

Gemstones, herbs, incense, and Tarot cards crammed the studio's shelves. Cinnamon spice laced the air from a fat, red candle flickering in the corner next to the blazing fireplace. The place held an aura of high-mindedness mixed with whimsy, and I loved the incorruptible way it made me feel.

Slowly, methodically, The Wizard swiped the space above the well-worn wooden floor. Absorbed in his work, over and over he sang in a deep tone, "Be gone…away…fly…leave." When he had swept the last corner with a curlicue swirl, he approached the center of the room, lifted the broom waist-high, parallel to the floor, and rotated his body, eyes closed, muttering a prayer.

Suddenly, his eyes popped open. "Alexandria Vilkas," he cried. His joy charged me like a mug of steaming tea. "Come in, come in."

"Hello, Master." I stepped forward and quizzically looked at him.

With indigo eyes and a snowy beard trailing to his heart, he wore jeans and a thick ivory wool sweater. Dots of perspiration rimmed his brow, and when he wiped his clammy forehead, he mussed his stiff, white hair. He upended the broom, holding it like a pitchfork. "It's the New Moon, time to clear away the detritus from the last cycle and usher in our new desires. Your timing is impeccable–I've just cleared away the negativity."

I smelled dust bunnies. "Cleared away the negativity?"

"From clients, mostly. Dump every problem! By the end of the moon cycle, it's an astral mess." Breathing deeply, he spread his arms and looked around. "Much better, isn't it?"

"If you say so."

Looking me over from head to toe, he lamented, "You are a wet undine, aren't you?"

My hands flew to my hair, drenched all the way down to my waist from the heavy snow outside. I could imagine how terrible I looked, but I shoved those thoughts aside to talk about this momentous occasion.

"It's March 4th," I said. "The big day."

"*Hmmm.*"

"Please, you're not going to put it off any longer, are you?"

He motioned toward the leaping flames in the brick fireplace that engulfed two crackling logs in an orange blaze. "Very well. Take off your coat and dry it by the fire."

Once we settled on his zebra-patterned couch, he showed me his new ten-inch crystal ball set atop a pewter stand that an artisan had sculpted into a trio of jesters.

"Oh, how beautiful!"

"Ordered it by catalogue."

From my past year of studying with my master, I knew the crystal ball did not contain any magical properties. All the hocus-pocus, if you want to call it that, came from The Wizard's mind, trained with rigorous study and capable of sustained concentration.

I nodded, regarding the folds of a black velvet, hooded cape hanging next to a wall-mounted sconce of a dragon. The Wizard had added those to the decor since my last visit seven days ago. He always added something new…last week he hung ornamental flower fairies in front of the window. The week before, he rearranged his essential oils into a pyramid.

"It's March 4th," I said again, as if that would make The

Wizard hurry.

"You must be patient. Tell me all you have learned this year."

I could tell he was fishing for a certain answer by the way his forehead creased like an accordion; but I had no idea what he wanted to hear. "We've been working with Tarot cards, their aspects of astrology, elementals, symbolism, numerology, colors, reversals, dignities, and correspondences–what they mean individually, and how they interact with each other in a spread."

"And what else?"

"We've covered ritual work and meditation, fortune-telling versus divination, and path-working. You also had me shooting guns and picking locks."

The Wizard folded his hands together and looked me over. "I'm sorry, but I don't know that you're ready."

What did I say wrong? "But you promised!"

"Initiation is not an exact science. It's true that we've been studying together for 365 days, but you are not ready. Not yet."

He may as well have pricked my hope with a needle and deflated it until it crumpled into a rubbery puddle. "What else do I need to do?"

The Wizard massaged his chin. "You must pass a test."

The acids in my stomach whipped my breakfast of Baltic rye bread and farmer's cheese into an acrid soup, but I swallowed hard because I trusted my master. He would give me a test I had a chance of passing. "What sort of test?"

"Tell me about the story you are working on."

He often assigned me spiritual exercises that applied to my occupation as a journalist. As a reporter for *Gypsy Magazine*, a bimonthly in Chicago, I covered paranormal happenings such as haunted houses and ghost sightings. I'd had this job for three years, and I had earned a challenge. "'Tarot Cards and the Celebrities Who Use Them.' Is this story going to be part of my test?"

"If you are ready to live a life of service."

Our lessons always came back to the topic of service and

helping others. I knew this. Why did he repeat himself?

"The story is always more than just about your byline, Alexandria Vilkas. It is about how readers will benefit from the information. By the same token, entering the Order of the Tarot will not make your life easier. Your own needs and wants must be subjugated for the betterment of someone else."

I heard only "The Order of the Tarot." "The Order of the Tarot? That's the first time you uttered the name of the secret society."

The Wizard nodded. "It goes by many names, but that is the one you will know it by."

"What does it do? How many members does it have? Are you going to let me join today?"

The Wizard held up his right hand. "All in good time. First, you must pass the test. Oh, and there's one more thing."

"What's that?"

"Since the Order of the Tarot is a secret society, you are not to discuss it with anyone, not your mother, not your friends, not your boss, not your boyfriend. No one. Do you understand?"

I nodded, wondering if he weren't being a bit overdramatic, but I swore to keep my promise. "I don't have a boyfriend."

"Never mind that."

The Wizard glanced at his crystal ball, polished it with his sleeve, and picked off an imaginary piece of lint, perhaps one that contained my negativity. Then he leaned in, as if pulled by an invisible force. "Oh, my," he gasped and he looked at me in awe.

"What? What?"

I focused on the three jesters holding the crystal ball, as they stood frozen in their dancing positions.

"Your test is two-pronged. Do you want a reading on what you can expect?"

"Yes, please."

The Wizard smiled. "Very well."

He reached into a nearby wooden cabinet and pulled out a

deck of Arthurian Tarot cards wrapped in a black silk scarf. He made a big show of unveiling the cards…shuffling, whispering a petition, and asking me to cut them into three piles using only my left hand. With a flourish, he flipped over the top cards from each of the three piles onto the black silky folds.

The Page of Swords (The Adder) appeared first, followed by the Ten of Spears (The Green Knight), and the Three of Cups (The Dressing of the Sacred Spring). From my previous year of studying the Tarot, I knew the meanings of these cards, but I was curious to hear my master's interpretation.

"After this story, your life will never be the same," he announced. "You will become a servant to those in jeopardy of malevolence…supernatural and mundane. Shall I continue?"

Gulping, I nodded.

The Wizard drew his eyebrows together and proceeded in a clinical monotone. "You are the Page of Swords, an inconspicuous witness to important events, a clever spy to make sense of unexpected plot twists, an active person with a sharp mind and a gift for learning secrets. You endure a ten-day struggle, an awesome task of life over death that demands courage and diplomacy. During that time, a handsome married man seduces you, presenting you with an item as a gift. If you suppress personal desires, you will be positioned to help victims of cruelty, immorality, and ruin. When your mission is complete, pay homage to the spirit of the spring."

Despite the warning I sat back and grinned, like I'd just discovered a special present on my lap left by one of the flower fairies hanging near his window. The Wizard had been grooming me for this moment all year long, and now I hovered on the threshold of enlisting into the elite, secret society that fought supernatural evil forces. I'd heard rumors about it shortly after I started working for *Gypsy Magazine* and made it my mission to find out more so I could do a story on it. I remembered being surprised to hear The Wizard admit he was in a position to help me gain entry into the clandestine organization, but that I could never write about it.

"Wow! Sounds like the story is everything I've asked for.

And for ten days!"

The Wizard studied the spread, gazed into his crystal ball, and shook his head with a "*tsk, tsk.*"

"Do not underestimate your attraction to the married man. You have known him in a previous life; that is why his pull is so strong."

I inhaled sharply, now beginning to appreciate the test that lay ahead. I knew exactly which married man he was foretelling–that's what filled me with dread. Bruno Scavoro, a trustee of *Gypsy Magazine*, had enough magnetism to flip-flop the earth's poles. I just hoped he didn't have the capacity to derail me from what I wanted most–membership in the Order of the Tarot.

"You said this test was two-pronged. What did you mean by that?"

"Earning the degree of the Fool involves two challenges. The one with the married man is the easier of the two. The other you will recognize when you see it. See me after it manifests itself."

Chapter One

Day One: Sunday, March 23

Carmen Dellamorte lay on her stomach, her nude body covered only by a large pink towel. She gripped the end of the table with such intensity that her knuckles turned bone white. "Miss Diva, *por favor*," Jorge, her masseur, purred. He warmed peppermint oil between his hands and rubbed her shoulders. "You must try to relax."

"Relax?" murmured Carmen into the donut-shaped face pillow, her olive skin glistening. "This opera is bad luck, I tell you."

I sat at her side taking notes on this Sunday afternoon, doing writer's research on her passion for Tarot cards. In two hours, the diva would give her final performance at the Chicago Lyric Opera House as Verdi's Lady Macbeth. Her nerves were as frazzled as the fringe on her opera costume hanging nearby. In the center of the dressing room stood a three-foot tall cardboard box, taped along its seams with wide packaging tape.

I fidgeted in the plush burgundy armchair and looked around Carmen's dressing room–wigs rested on foam skulls, along with several dozen long-stemmed red roses in glass vases wrapped in wide crimson ribbons. Fruity perfume and peppermint oil laced the air. I lifted the foam skull lying next to me, and placed it on Carmen's vanity table.

"Miss Dellamorte," I began. "About your interest in the Tarot cards."

"Not now, *cara mia*," she said. "I am ordered to relax by this madman."

I had no other choice but to watch the massage with the hope that she'd allow me to begin the interview soon. I spotted the diva's Tarot deck on the ledge of the upright piano…she had flipped over two cards, the Fool and the Hanged Man, and

15

I wanted to ask her about that. How strange that she displayed these two particular cards.

She looked at me sideways and said, "You know about the ancient curse on this play, don't you? The one that forbids you from saying the name of the production?"

I nodded. It was one of the reasons my editor, Alyce, sent me here. She hoped I'd witness something supernaturally ill fated during this cursed opera. "It's not just an article about the Tarot cards," Alyce told me three weeks ago when she first gave me the assignment. "It's about the Macbeth opera, the curses that surround any production of The Scottish Play. See if you can interview cast members on their feelings about performing in a show with a 400-year-old curse."

To help Carmen relax, I spoke slowly and calmly. "During its first production as a play in 1606, a castrato playing Lady Macbeth—because women weren't allowed on stage—was stricken with fever and died. Since then a curse forbids anyone to pronounce the performance's title while in production."

Alyce would love that Carmen was worried about this curse before her last performance, and I poised my pen, ready to take down her every word.

"Don't you see?" Carmen asked Jorge as she skooched herself up. "If someone says the name of this opera in the next few hours, somebody from the cast will die."

Jorge glared at me and I stiffened. He seemed to want to protect Carmen from any thoughts that threaten to disturb her, and he treated me as her enemy. He moved over to the other side of the table, so that his back faced me, and helped Carmen to lie back down.

For my part, I wanted to pursue the conversation in the same direction because Carmen might offer something colorful about the curse that would be perfect for the story, a quote that would grab my readers. At the same time, I wanted her to start talking about her use of the Tarot cards.

"It doesn't mean anything," Jorge said to Carmen. He moved back to the other side of the table and faced me again. "Don't let it rattle you. Why don't you let me finish your massage?"

"I suppose you're right," she said, but her tone of voice suggested doubt. She pursed her lips and closed her eyes, although she did not look relaxed. Jorge rubbed her slowly and sensuously. A silver and black pendant bearing an image of a cat hung from his neck.

"Does she have to be here now?" Jorge asked Carmen. "This massage is not going to work in front of *her*."

I hoped Carmen would come to my defense, but she lay silent on the table, allowing him to rub her. I realized I wouldn't get very far with Jorge in the room. He wanted her lying down and quiet; I wanted her up and talking.

Jorge chop-chopped on her thighs. He took a bottle of warmed rubbing alcohol and freely poured the clear liquid on her back.

"*Mmm*," said Carmen. "So what are your questions, Alexandria?"

I avoided making eye contact with Jorge. I rearranged my notebook and pen, cleared my throat, and asked, "How long've you been working with the Tarot cards?"

"It's been at least ten years," she said, stretching her arms forward. "I have a collection of Tarot cards, at least seventy different packs."

"So that's not just a rumor."

"Oh, no, it's true. Every morning I meditate on a card."

"What card did you pick today?"

She closed her eyes, as if to focus on the card she'd drawn for that day.

"The Fool, one of my favorites. I love it when I draw this card. The Fool is a trickster, the one no one takes seriously, yet the Fool always says wise things." She opened her eyes and sent a coy look. "Some people are really scared of the cards. Have you noticed that?"

I nodded, eager to capture more quotes.

"When I say I like playing with the Tarot cards, I rather like the reaction I cause, shock and outrage sometimes. It's all rather fun."

She looked sideways at me as Jorge continued to wear his set-jawed expression.

"The Tarot is misunderstood by many people. It can take a long time to get over one's natural fears of its power," I said.

Jorge glanced uneasily at me.

The Diva rolled to her side, careless of her nudity. "Would you mind finishing up, dear Jorge? It's time for me to get ready for my final performance."

"Are you sure? You're still full of knots. And this interview right before your last performance...you have enough to worry about, if you ask me." As he scrutinized me, he looked like he wanted to kill me, and the hairs prickled on my neck. I sat quietly, waiting him out. As I held his gaze, I feared he might lift me by the scruff of my neck and toss me out. After what seemed like a long moment, he lifted his hands off Carmen's body and wiped them on a towel.

"How silly of me to think I could relax before a performance," Carmen said as she stood up and stepped to her vanity mirror. In the meantime, Jorge gathered his supplies.

The mirrored closet door squeaked as Carmen opened it to remove her first costume. "You're a writer, aren't you?"

"Yes, reporters are usually writers."

She either missed or ignored my sarcasm.

"Why, just three weeks ago, you called me for this interview, and I thought you'd be perfect. I confirmed it with my Tarot cards." She dressed in front of Jorge and me with no shame. It left me feeling uncomfortable, but I couldn't help evaluating her body. She had an ample figure, well proportioned, but with three rolls of olive-toned flab on her waist. A thin ribbon held her long brown hair in a knot at her nape, and her dark chocolate eyes set off dramatic high cheekbones. The press called her *La Tempestua*; I assumed because of her temperament on stage.

"Why do you need a writer?"

"I need help with a special project I've been working on."

I looked at my watch. In less than an hour, Carmen would be on stage, and then off to Florence. If I didn't do this interview now, I'd never meet my deadline. Alyce had been complaining about the magazine's dip in subscriptions, and any misstep on the part of a writer caused her to fly into a rage. About six months ago she'd fired one person for missing a deadline, shocking the rest of us into punctual compliance. On the other hand, I found myself torn with curiosity over what Carmen, this world-famous diva, wanted from me.

"What sort of project?"

Her expression hardened. "For years, I've been collecting material on my father, and now I want to write a book about him. It's all there." She pointed to the box. "Every time I start it, I'm interrupted, and I just haven't been able to..."

"Ah, the box." I approached the box and touched it, attempting to gauge its weight; it looked quite heavy.

"To begin. I need someone to put it into some sort of order."

"You want me to write a book on your relationship with your father?"

"Of course I'd pay you handsomely. Name your price."

Jorge and I exchanged glances as he folded up the massage table. I sat back down and crossed my legs. This morning, I'd slipped on black sheer pantyhose with shiny black patent leather pumps. Now I studied a scuff in the area of my left big toe as I contemplated my dilemma. Alyce didn't like her writers freelancing on the side. She said it caused them to lose focus on her magazine. The only problem with that line of thinking is that I always come short of paying my bills, and here was the diva asking me to *name my price*.

"My price?"

Carmen sensed my hesitation. "What is it they call it? Ah, for...ghost writing. I'm prepared to deposit $20,000 into your bank account, and give you this material on the spot."

Never in my life had anyone offered me that kind of money for anything I could do. Something about Carmen made her appear desperate, and I couldn't believe she would give me so much money without knowing me better. Fear, mixed with excitement, surged through me. I tried to move the box–it was so heavy I could barely slide it two inches.

"It's such an unusual request. Can't you tell me anything else? Like why me?"

"Of course you couldn't possibly carry this box alone. We'll get a messenger to do it, how's that?"

She didn't answer my questions, and that bothered me.

"Why me?" I asked again.

"Because of your timing. I'm ready to write a book about my father, and you're the writer who is in front of me. Call it an accident or fate."

I sat back down on my chair and arranged my notebook and pen, both of which promptly dropped from my lap onto the floor. As I bent over to retrieve them, my head began to spin. Logic and desire battled within me–I wanted the money, yet my boss didn't want me to take on side jobs. Carmen offered me more money than I'd make in the next five months at *Gypsy Magazine*. I thought about paying off credit cards and having enough for a down payment on a condo on the North Side. It would be hard to refuse all that money, but could I do it? On the other hand, no story worth that kind of money could be easy.

"Who is your father?"

"I can't talk about it right now. There's not enough time. I need you to accept this material. Please. You've got to do it."

"I just…I don't know anything about him."

"It's all in the box." With shaking hands, Carmen pulled an appointment book out of her purse. In that moment, she resembled a frightened schoolgirl. "What's your address?"

Jorge moved into the restroom with a garment bag, apparently to change his clothes.

I didn't know what to make of her plea. Why did she want to give me so much money for a book about her father? Why didn't she just write it herself? Yet the figure of $20,000 danced before my eyes, jiggling and wiggling, until I could barely resist. I knew this story would bring me trouble. I had to say no.

"No, really, I couldn't."

"Nonsense."

"Can't we talk about this after your performance?"

"You need to accept this now. There's no one else. Please."

A feeling of fireworks mixed with foreboding hit the pit of my stomach when I knew I couldn't say no. All my life I wanted a story that would pay me bundles, and that could take me straight into the mainstream. Maybe this was my break, the one that would get me away from *Gypsy*, away from Alyce's tirades, and onto something bigger.

"All right, I'll do it," I said, surprised at the elation washing over me.

"Oh, that's wonderful! I'll have it sent to your home tomorrow morning. I'm off to Florence for a couple of weeks, so let's talk about this when I return."

As she took my address and called a messenger to pick up the box, I thought about what I'd tell Alyce. Maybe I wouldn't tell her anything, I'd just work on this project on the side. That extra $20,000 would eliminate several of my troubles, give me a cushion to think about my future, and be enough for a down payment on the condo. Then I wondered what The Wizard would think about my taking this job. I had a feeling it was part of my test, and that he would approve.

During this conversation, Jorge had changed into a black turtleneck and slacks and was now ready to leave.

"Good-bye, Mademoiselle."

"Did you get the tickets for this opera, Jorge?"

"Oh, yes," he said. "Thank you. I look forward to your last performance."

Just as he walked out the door, Carmen said in a low voice, "If anything should happen to me, I want you to keep the box, and I don't want you to talk about it with anybody else. There's something in there only you would understand."

Before I had a chance to respond, someone knocked on the door. "Who is it?" asked Carmen.

"Teresita. I'm here to fix your nails."

"Oh yes, hold on." To me, she added, "It's a deal then,

right? You'll take this assignment and not talk about it to anyone, no matter what happens?"

I nodded as Teresita barged in.

"You're so late," scolded Carmen, back into her role as the commanding diva. "What in heaven's name took you so long?"

Teresita, a beautiful woman with a commanding presence herself, one I didn't normally associate with manicurists, looked at me with surprise, regarded the box with raised eyebrows, and a puzzled expression. Then she looked at Carmen.

"That's Alexandria Vilkas, a reporter," said Carmen. "This is Teresita, my manager at Parsifal's Beauty Spa and chorus member at the Lyric."

Ah, she managed a business and had a voice good enough for the Lyric. That accounted for her self-confidence. After we both said hello to each other, Teresita dug into her pocket and pulled out a bent three-inch carpenter's nail, which she offered to Carmen. "I found a nail on the floor for you."

Carmen sighed. "Just put it over here, next to the others." She pointed to a corner of her white vanity table, which held three such carpenter's nails already. Oddly, they all looked similarly bent.

"Keep them for me. You're the only one I trust with them."

Teresita smiled. "Okay, let me see the damage. We don't have much time."

Carmen held out her right hand, revealing a horizontal split on the nail of the ring finger. Teresita proceeded to fix it so it looked like the others, painted with an intricate black and white art deco design.

Silence filled the room as Teresita worked intently on the diva's fingernail.

"Why are you collecting nails, Carmen?" I asked.

"They're good luck tokens. I'll tell you about them another time."

Teresita worked on Carmen's nails some more, and I worried Carmen wouldn't continue our interview on the Tarot cards. I still had to write that article for *Gypsy*, my first priority. My story would be ruined without her, and I knew Alyce would threaten to fire me for missing this chance. I noticed how Teresita kept glancing at the box.

"I know it's none of my business, but what's in that box, Carmen?" Teresita asked.

"Some material I'm giving to this reporter."

"Oh?"

Carmen locked eyes with me. "About Tarot cards, how they are symbols and speak using their own special language."

I felt she was trying to tell me something, but couldn't with Teresita there. The contents of the box contained material for the book about her father, yet she talked as if they contained material about the article on Tarot cards. Perhaps she didn't want to talk about the book in front of Teresita. I tried to help Carmen.

"What do you like most about the cards?" I asked.

"Every card tells a story, but in a spread, they unlock hidden truths. Sometimes it takes time to interpret their mysterious messages; other times, they come across loud and clear. Trust them. They can connect you to your Inner Guide."

I wrote down the diva's words in my notebook and wondered if she wasn't sending me some sort of a code about a mysterious message in the box. Teresita kept looking at Carmen and me.

Someone knocked. "I have more flowers for you," said a man's voice from the other side of the door.

"Come in, Felix," Carmen replied.

Felix Vasilakis, the assistant conductor, strode in with a plant wrapped in white paper. A tall, thin man with wisps of black hair brushed across the top of his head, he wore a black turtleneck and dark slacks.

Carmen stiffened her back and angrily looked at Felix. "About this opera…"

"What about it?"

"Too many leave before the second act. You know how I hate that! Chicago's opera crowd is so damned conservative."

"It happens when an opera is modernized," Teresita said. "They dislike progressive sets or singers wearing contemporary costumes. They prefer Shakespeare's Renaissance."

Felix turned to me, smiling. "They are fools, conditioned to think one way."

"Then give them what they want," shouted Carmen, obviously enjoying what looked like a well-worn argument. "Next, you'll be tinkering with Verdi!"

Felix put up both hands, saying, "It's pointless to argue over our final performance. Besides, modern costumes and settings speak to today's audience."

"Nonsense. It speaks to cheap designers!"

They both doubled over in laughter. I felt like an audience member watching two actors rehearsing their parts. They had obviously talked at length about modern opera, and always ended up on opposite sides of the argument. They looked like good friends.

"We really don't have much more time," Felix said.

"I know." Carmen sighed. "I can't believe it's the last one. Tell me who sent the flowers."

Felix turned to the potted plant and unwrapped it. "Oh my, this is belladonna! It's poisonous!"

"What? My God! What will happen next? Who sent it?" Who would send a poisonous plant to the diva during her last performance? The assistant conductor looked around for a card.

"I don't know. There's no card. No, wait...here it is. That's strange. It looks like a card from a deck. It's the Fool's card from the Tarot deck. It says, 'April Fool!' That's ten days away. This must be a sick joke. Oh, this cursed play!"

Carmen swayed and looked ready to faint. "Was this somebody's idea of a prank? Did anybody else know I was going to be interviewed on Tarot cards?"

"My editor and other staff members at *Gypsy Magazine*," I said.

Felix rushed over to calm her. "Now, now, don't give this another thought. We'll get to the bottom of it right after this afternoon's performance, and I promise you this, whoever sent this plant or that card will never work in Chicago operatic circles again."

Someone else knocked on the door. The messenger had arrived to pick up the box. He strolled in pushing a dolly and hoisted the box onto the cart, promising to have it to my address the next morning.

"Oh, I almost forgot," he said to Carmen. "Someone sent you a bottle of champagne."

He pulled out the bottle from a canvas bag slung on his shoulder. Because no one leapt forward to take it from him, he set it on the piano.

After the messenger left, Carmen sighed with relief.

"Who's the champagne from?" Teresita asked.

Carmen sat at the vanity applying make-up at the mirror, so I stood up to find out. It was next to her Tarot cards, and I wanted to ask her about the Fool and the Hanged Man, but first had to read the note. The bottle had a gold string wrapped about its neck, with a small note attached that stated, "To help the poison go down easier, darling. Love, Dad."

When I read it aloud to Carmen, she laughed shrilly as if holding onto her last nerve. "That's my father."

Teresita rolled her eyes and said, "He would do that."

"I don't understand," I said. "How could he send his daughter a note that tells her this champagne will help the poison go down easier?" I was almost beside myself at the strange humor and worried over the project I had accepted from Carmen. What kind of a relationship did they have? Nothing made much sense.

"You will," the diva said.

Carmen's understudy, Donacella Dimitriano, stepped in with a black and white kitten in her arms. The messenger had left the door open, allowing the understudy to arrive unannounced.

"I know it's your last performance and I wanted to give you a parting gift. We all know how you love your Tarot cards and I thought you must love cats too."

Carmen looked at Donacella and the kitten with such

loathing; I wondered what elicited her hatred.

"You've been waiting for just this opportunity!" Carmen sneezed as she hysterically attacked Donacella.

I watched, confused, not understanding her reaction. "*Ah-choo*! Get out, get out, and take that nasty beast with you!" She flashed her brown eyes, chiseled in her face like a Greek sculpture.

Standing still and doing her best to maintain her cool, Donacella stroked the piebald kitten, although she seemed shaken by Carmen's harsh reaction. "You know, Carmen, I just wanted to give you a gift on your last performance. Of course, I had no idea you are allergic."

"Like hell you didn't," screamed the diva. "Did you think I'd help you launch your career by letting you sing my last role? You did this to ruin my voice." She looked around the room. "Will somebody get me a tissue?"

Felix moved swiftly as Teresita handed him the box to pass to Carmen. I looked at both of them for a hint of what was really going on, but they each bore a stoic expression.

Donacella's face, in the meantime, crumpled and her eyes watered. As she stepped back to leave the room, the kitten bounded out of her arms and ran toward Carmen, hissing. The diva grimaced and kicked at the kitten, but the creature bolted. Fortunately, Carmen missed. Had her aim been better, the kitten would have flown through the air like a wobbly football.

"Ha," huffed Carmen, as she regained her balance.

"How dare you," cried Donacella, who scooped up her kitten and nuzzled it against her cheek. "There, there," she purred to her pet, looking back at Carmen with disgust.

Then she spat, "Macbeth! Macbeth! Macbeth!" and darted out.

Felix, Teresita, and I gasped. Donacella had done the unthinkable.

The diva screamed after her, "I will remember this!" Then she grew quiet and covered her face. "My God. It is the end. I can't take much more."

A voice outside the door yelled, "First bell. Places

everyone!"

Carmen's face had gone ashen, and her right hand went to her heart as she shook her head. "Let's just get through this last performance, shall we?"

"You'll be stellar, as usual, Carmen," Felix said in a reassuring tone. "You always are." He picked up the plant on his way out.

"Second bell! Places everyone," someone shouted on the other side of the door. "Miss Diva, now!"

I took that as my cue to exit.

Chapter Two

The Chicago Lyric Opera House closed its doors at the rise of the curtain, strictly forbidding anyone to enter during the show. I rushed from the diva's dressing room to an exit, down a corridor into the lobby, with four minutes to spare. The grand foyer's gilt cornices glittered beneath sparkling Austrian crystal chandeliers and elaborately stenciled ceilings–its design a hybrid of Art Nouveau and Art Deco, its color scheme a palette of salmon pink, rose, olive, gold, and bronze.

Just as I feared, ushers shut the doors to the auditorium with firmness, and I stood on the wrong side. My mother sat waiting for me in a front row seat, and I knew she'd be furious even after I explained. I also hated missing the live performance, not just because I loved this particular opera, but also because I looked forward to seeing Carmen Dellamorte, Chicago's reigning diva, in her last performance as Lady Macbeth.

Swallowing my disappointment, I checked my coat and oversized bag after retrieving a tiny black purse that carried the barest essentials–a pen, small notebook, lipstick, and cell phone. Holding a glass of red wine, I walked to the wide-screen TV on a northern wall to watch the opera in progress. Carmen's roommate, Roberto Andretti, known in the opera world as Castrato, played one of the witches who warn Macbeth of his doom. Instead of the traditional Elizabethan costuming, the witches wore black leather. The stage design was a modern subway station–grimy, dark, and rife with danger. Carmen had been right in her argument with Felix, the assistant conductor. The design didn't sit well with many in the traditional audience. They wanted their Shakespeare the old-fashioned way. During previous shows, I'd read in the *Chicago Tribune* that several left after the first intermission.

A movement on the staircase across the foyer caught my

eye. Descending the east flank of the red-carpeted double staircase came Bruno Scavoro, the diva's manager. He stopped midway when he noticed me, his hand resting on the gleaming brass railing as he flashed his irresistible smile. He continued his descent, each step an eternity, as my pulse quickened. Bruno was old enough to be my father, but the way he looked at me with a slow up and down scan of his eyes and a half-smile on his lips, blanked out all sensible thoughts. For days after seeing him at the office, I'd ruminate over his deep-set eyes and the dimple in the middle of his chin, until mercifully his image faded. But now he'd come to Chicago again, leaving his box seat in Peacock Alley, named after the way people dress in the choicest section at the Lyric.

Bruno reached the landing and turned directly toward me as he crossed the foyer's marble floor. His right eyebrow arched in a frame over a bemused expression. Rendered powerless under the explosive feelings surging through me, I gripped my wine glass and gulped half of it down. I wanted to feel only esteem or friendship, but couldn't control the butterflies blooming in my belly whenever he stood near me. My reaction to seeing him again had scaled to a full-blown, knock-me-over-with-a-feather crush: The Wizard's test had begun.

"Hello, Alexandria," he said. "Did we miss the opening act?"

His question, his voice, made my stomach spiral. He stood about a head taller than me, with wavy hair, almond eyes, and a wide jaw. Sporting a thick turtleneck sweater, he slung a black, soft-leather bag over his shoulder. Since Bruno was on the editorial board of *Gypsy Magazine*, I had consulted him several times for story ideas over the past year. Although he lived in New York, I called him for the silliest little reasons, and had noticed, with pleasure, that he never seemed to mind. Nevertheless, neither of us has ever spoken about the unmistakable attraction running between us. With a wife and four daughters, ages nine to twenty-one, Bruno was an extremely married man.

"I took your advice, Bruno, and was just backstage interviewing the diva for our story on Tarot cards and celebrities who use them. We ran longer than I thought we would."

"How fortunate for me. I have you all to myself."

Oh my, that doesn't sound very married to me. How would his lips feel against mine? "So you do," I said instead. I smiled as I turned toward the screen to collect my thoughts. Would he dare to ask me out? Yet I hoped he wouldn't make a pass at me because then I'd have to deny what I felt for him.

I thought of Shakespeare's line that Lady Macbeth says to her husband as she plants the seed of murder: "Look like the innocent flower, but be the serpent beneath it." That line said it all about Bruno–an innocent flower on the outside, but a serpent underneath who, with one kiss, could stop me from joining the Order of the Tarot.

"How did it go?" Bruno asked.

"I'm sorry. What?"

"The interview with Carmen. How did it go?"

He stood so close to me, I could feel his warmth. It took all my restraint not to reach up and rub my fingertip along the line of his jaw. I just kept repeating to myself, "Order of the Tarot. Order of the Tarot. Bruno is my first test."

"Fine. It went fine," I answered, my eyes back on the screen.

"The role demands considerable artistic maturity, don't you think?" Bruno asked. "She drives the entire plot with her ambitions."

Carmen launched her first aria, *Vieni, t'affretta.*

"She certainly has fire in her voice," I said. During her aria, I slowed my breath to calm my mind and heart. Nothing could happen between Bruno and me; I just had to get through this moment alone with him. I became a journalist and steered my mind toward the story, planning to start a conversation about how Bruno felt about losing one of his stars and, I assumed, lots of his income. I could inquire what he thought about Carmen ending her career tonight. Feeling composed enough to face him again, I asked, "Would you happen to know her father?"

"Funny you should ask. Why?"

"A messenger delivered a bottle of champagne while I was interviewing her. It had the strangest note: 'To help the poison go down easier, darling. Love, Dad.'"

Bruno chuckled. "And Carmen?"

"She laughed, like you." I shook my head. "You both have a strange sense of humor."

"You have to know Adriano Capezio to understand the note. An eccentric, well-connected man who created a spoiled little diva."

Bruno loved gossip…everyone in opera did.

"What do you mean?"

"Oh, I don't want to speak out of turn, of course, but whatever the diva wants, Daddy always provides. For a price. The diva wanted to be an opera star. Imagine who arranged that for her."

"But she has a beautiful voice."

Bruno smiled. "That's not enough. In the opera world, many stars get to where they are by bringing along wealthy sponsors. This is Carmen's last performance, a bitter poison for her to swallow. Even with his connections and all that he's given to the Lyric, Adriano can't create a new voice for a diva past her prime."

Much of this came as news to me. I knew this performance was Carmen's last opera and that she was upset about it, but had no idea her father had played such a big role in her career. I now wondered how much financial support Adriano Capezio had given to the Lyric Opera House. My story on Carmen's use of Tarot cards would deepen if I could discover how her departure from the opera stage had affected the important people in her life.

Bruno grazed my hair with his fingertips and my skin shimmered with electricity. The reporter in me shriveled, leaving only a woman with feelings for this man. I took a step back, reminding myself that Bruno was married.

"What are you doing?" I asked.

Bruno stepped forward to close the space between us. "Isn't it obvious?"

Oh, God help me–he was making a pass. "What about your wife?"

"What about her?"

"She...You...I..."

"She's in New York, and I'm here with you. That's all that matters."

"It's just that...I...You're married."

"Oh, Alex, I want to see you after the show to talk about this. Please come visit me at the Four Seasons."

"Bruno, I couldn't." Yet, I wanted him to persist. I turned to face the screen and tried to concentrate on the show. I groped for a way to talk about something else, but the reporter in me couldn't be roused. "Too bad I'm missing this."

"Is it really all that bad, Alexandria? How red your cheeks are."

My breath quickened. He made my visiting him in his hotel room after the show so natural. But if I were honest with myself, I had to admit I only wanted to be alone with him with hours of unhurried time ahead of us.

A thunderous applause sounded on the other side of the doors; on the screen, I saw the red curtain drop.

Bruno's presence now both frightened and excited me. He had invited me to be with him after the show! Of course I wouldn't go. That would be taking my fantasy too far.

"Have you ever wanted something badly enough that you would kill for it?" he whispered in my ear as he rested his hand on my arm.

I would have killed for the power to control my feelings for him. I knew I shouldn't be attracted to him because he was a married man. Why didn't that fact alone clamp the valve in my heart that released rapture toward him? "What a question," I shot back. "No, I can't say that I have."

Bruno roared. Oh, the way he laughed. "Of course not, dear sweet Alexandria. How could you? Your world is still black and white. You're one of the good guys–or gals–or something like that, right?"

I feigned nonchalance, but felt out of my element. It wasn't every day that an older, married man asked me to his hotel room, but I had to convince myself I shouldn't go. Bruno stood like a king before me. He could wave a wand in any direction and I'd follow like a fool.

The doors from the theater opened and the sea of Chicago's cultured filled the lobby. The groundswell of noise from people coming out of the theater stopped the conversation between Bruno and me. Two women walked past, toward the coat check, rolling their eyes and groaning about the avant-garde aspects of the production. They weren't the only ones; I noticed several more heading out the door, grimacing and swearing they'd only "sit through a traditional performance." Nevertheless, the majority would stay to witness Carmen's last act. I swirled the wine in my glass and thought about Bruno's last question.

"No, I've never wanted anything badly enough to kill for it."

That's when Mom approached.

"Alexandria Vilkas! How nice of you to finally make an appearance," Irene Vilkas's blonde hair was pulled into a chignon, her bone-white skin glowing from a fresh flash of anger. "*Where* were you?"

"Hi, mom. Great to see you too."

Her gaze raked over Bruno. In a black knit dress that hugged her trim figure, she twirled a gold and silver bracelet on her left wrist. Just as I was about to introduce him, a woman who seemed to carry a lot of authority approached us with an urgent look on her face. She said something to Bruno, which I couldn't hear because of all the noise around us.

Bruno nodded, then introduced her to us. "This is the Lyric's administrator, Denise Johnson," he said.

She wore a sparkly black gown that didn't fit her comfortably fit her wide figure. She seemed worried and spoke rapidly. "I'm so sorry to interrupt, but Bruno is Carmen's agent, and I *must* talk to him." She tugged at his elbow. "Please hurry."

"Would you excuse us?" Bruno asked.

"Yes, of course," I answered.

"I enjoyed our conversation," he said. "We will talk more after the show, won't we?"

I shook my head. "I...I don't know."

Bruno nodded, then turned to my mother. "So nice to have met you," he said. "You have a lovely daughter." Then he headed toward the exit with the Lyric's administrator. As he cast one more glance at me before the crowd swallowed him up, I wondered if I dared to see him later. Perhaps after the opera I could spend an hour at the Four Seasons–in the lounge– and listen to what Bruno had to say. But no, who was I kidding? If I opened my heart's door to Bruno even a teensy crack, I didn't know how far I'd let him in.

Chapter Three

"Was that Bruno Scavoro?" Mom asked.

I flinched. When I was a child, she used that same voice as a reprimand just before she spanked me for spilling milk or failing to wipe dirt from my shoes. "The mayor of Chicago gave us front row seats, and you miss the first act because you were talking to him?"

"I…It's just work. And how do you know him, anyway?"

"He's been in the mayor's office a couple of times. Is there anything between you? He's married, you know."

I almost crushed the empty glass in my hand. I wasn't sure of my feelings for Bruno, and her insinuating an affair with him only made matters worse. Besides, in at least one way she was responsible for my meeting Bruno–she had gotten me the job at *Gypsy Magazine* through her connection with her boyfriend, the publisher.

"Stop…just stop! It's bad enough you got me this job, but as far as my love life goes, you are banned from pulling your strings. Do you understand?"

She pondered this for a moment. "Oh, never mind!" She stepped closer and embraced me. "I am glad to see you. Let me look at you." She took a step back for the inspection. "Have you ever tried some purple to highlight those lovely green eyes? You're a beautiful girl, Alex; you just need to put a little effort into it." She brushed a long strand of hair behind my left ear as I rolled my eyes…it felt embarrassing to have my mother groom me in public.

"Please, will you stop fussing?"

"Oh, all right. We still have a few more minutes," she said. "Let's catch up with each other. How did your interview with Carmen go?"

Grateful she had changed the subject from Bruno, I told Mom about Carmen's love for Tarot cards. "I'm writing an article on Tarot cards and celebrities who use them. Carmen relies on them heavily...uses them every day."

"You're kidding. Tarot cards? Is that what you're working on? You don't actually believe those silly images on the cards actually mean anything, do you?"

"Uh...well..." I never felt comfortable talking about my Tarot lessons with The Wizard to my mother. This time I'd let my guard down with her about this story. In her mind, Tarot cards and anything else related to the supernatural was nonsense, a gimmick for charlatans to make money off desperate people. She'd only gotten me the job at *Gypsy Magazine* because she thought it would be a stepping-stone to a more legitimate career in journalism–she had never imagined I'd stay for three years. Anyway, I gave her the line that always settled her down..."I'm an objective journalist. I only quote what other people say about Tarot cards."

Mom smiled with a look of relief. "That's my girl. You just wait. The perfect job is around the corner for you."

Before I had a chance to respond to her, the first bell rang, warning us of the end of the intermission. "Maybe we should find our seats," I urged.

Mom nodded and waved at some friends across the lobby, then hooked her elbow into mine as we walked to our seats. "Tell me what the diva's like. Is she really as catty as everyone says?"

"Worse." I smiled, knowing how much Mom would relish my conversation with Carmen. I filled her in on how the understudy cursed the production as we settled into our seats.

"No!" Mom gasped. "She kicked a poor little kitten?"

"Yes, can you believe it? Luckily she missed, but the understudy was so upset she cursed Carmen by uttering the name of this show three times just before she walked onstage." I couldn't even say the name "Macbeth" out loud for fear of adding to the jinx.

"My, my, my," Mom said, shaking her head. "That must have rattled Carmen."

"It did. She was quite upset."

We ended our conversation as the opera resumed. It opened with three witches wearing punky black leather in a New York subway station stirring their cauldron and chanting: "Boil, boil. And you spirits black and white, red and blue, stir again. You who know well how to mix, stir, stir." This was considered to be the scene that fed the superstition of "The Play," the one that caused cast members to die mysteriously. "Double, double, toil and trouble; Fire burn, and cauldron bubble."

The link between the witches' curses in this opera and The Wizard's test to enter the Order of the Tarot didn't escape me. Had he chosen this story as part of my test because he knew the opera had these supernatural elements? As I watched the witches stir their poison in the bubbling cauldron, I thought of Bruno stirring his poison of unbidden love in my heart. What if I couldn't resist his charms? Where would that lead me?

The apparitions appeared, warning Macbeth of what lay ahead, how he would lose his kingdom and his life. Lady Macbeth sang her drinking song, "The Brindisi." It was Carmen playing her role to perfection as the conniving, double-faced hostess doing her best to cover up her husband's weaknesses. She was the consummate diva and her performance enraptured me, leaving me lost in the moment of her artistry and beautiful voice, forgetting all worries, fears, and upcoming tests. Sighs and gasps were anguished as Lady Macbeth futilely tried to impose gaiety on a macabre spectacle. Slowly the characters onstage went mad from overwhelming guilt, fleeing for safety from the apparitions they had conjured.

I looked forward to the diva's sleepwalking scene, when she would sing *Una Macchia*. While hearing bells and ill omens, Lady Macbeth wonders whether it was worthwhile–a throne for the price of murder.

Carmen completed her aria with a thrilling "*fil di voce*," just a thread left, ending in a bleak D flat.

"The voice of the devil," my mother whispered.

Finally, the last scene of the opera began, where Macbeth's enemies decapitated him and grimly paraded his head on a pole. I flinched at that scene; the production spared no amount of blood and gore. I wished they would have been less graphic, leaving more of the horrific scene to my imagination. Malcolm, the new king, sang the last song, explaining how Lady Macbeth took her own life.

Lady Macbeth staggered on stage and clutched at Malcolm during his last aria. But she wasn't supposed to be there! Maybe her appearance was part of the modern interpretation. Malcolm looked confused, with a puzzled expression, as did everyone else on stage. Was the diva's presence onstage another avant-garde addition to the production? No one had talked or written about the conclusion of this show being changed so drastically. I looked at my mother, but her gaze remained glued to the stage. Lady Macbeth dropped to her knees and Malcolm, bending down to help her, stopped singing. Moments later, the orchestra stuttered to a stop, section by section, first the horns, then the percussion, then the strings. I feared Carmen was in danger. Had her understudy's curse really affected her? In the front row, we could heard Malcolm whisper, "Carmen, are you all right? What in God's name is going on?"

Carmen clutched her throat as a poisoned Lady Macbeth, then doubled over in pain. Now she lay rocking back and forth in a fetal position. But her suicide was supposed to happen offstage! What was she doing here?

"Help! Help! Something is wrong with Miss Diva," Malcolm screamed.

This was no *au courant* staging of the opera, this was really happening. No! It must be part of the act.

Carmen stopped moving.

"Miss Diva! Miss Diva! Please, somebody help!" Malcolm cried out again. A man in the sixth row stood up. "I'm a doctor!" He ran to a side door which I knew led to the stage.

I sat in shock. I had just interviewed Carmen. She *couldn't* be dying. I looked at the conductor. He tore at what little hair he had and the musicians looked at him, as if pleading for direction. Felix Vasilakis, the assistant conductor, walked across the stage and stooped over Carmen. The doctor had arrived at her side and began examining her, as the other cast members gathered round. I turned to see the audience. One man bit at his nails; the woman next to him sat open-mouthed, aghast. Their horror matched my own. Were we witnessing the death of Chicago's reigning diva? A murmur spread wavelike, increasing in intensity. My mother clenched my arm. I cried out in pain. I couldn't believe this was really happening.

"This can't be," Mother whispered. "This can't be! Oh, my God!"

As the doctor knelt beside Carmen performing CPR, we all watched in silence, too horrified to speak. My terror rose by the second. Could he inject something in her to revive her? There had to be something in his black bag that could help her. He searched for her pulse at her wrists and neck. He felt for her breath. Was she still alive? Wasn't there a chance she'd be saved?

My mother's fingernails dug deeper into the flesh of my left arm. The doctor pounded Carmen's chest and blew into her mouth, repeating these motions over and over.

"For God's sake, doctor! Please tell us the diva is all right!" bellowed an audience member from the back of the auditorium. He couldn't see, but I felt he spoke for all of us, as we vainly hoped she'd be okay. Please Carmen, get up. You can't die, not like this.

The doctor passed his hand through his thick brown hair and started again with another round of CPR.

My God, this was happening right on stage in front of all of us. Was this the curse, the wretched curse?

Castrato appeared, still dressed in his Hecate leather outfit, his make-up streaked by tears and fear. "Carmen, honey! Carmen, please! It's me! Please be all right! Oh, Carmen!" He crumpled over her and cried.

The understudy, Donacella Dimitriano, rushed onstage, holding her kitten. "No! I'm sorry! I didn't mean it!" she screamed. "You weren't supposed to die! Not like this!" Her long black hair flowed past her shoulders and her face contorted into a look of agony. "I didn't mean it! I didn't mean it! I take it back! Oh, please."

What was she doing? How bizarre. I huffed in indignation. She was the one who uttered the curse of Macbeth in her face right before she walked on stage, and now she was trying to capitalize on it? Wait until everybody else finds out, I wanted to scream out at her. How dare she? Who did she think she was? At that moment the understudy turned to face us, shocked to see the curtain still up.

The director took charge, barking orders for the cast to move back. "Will someone bring down the goddamn curtain?"

The famous fire curtain made of fifteen tons of steel and painted with 100 opera characters descended, along with the hearts of 3,500 people watching. Oh, I just wanted to cry. There was no escape for Carmen–death could happen anywhere, even onstage like this.

Chapter Four

One man in back stood up and began to clap. "Bravo," he yelled. "Bravo!" I sat still, attempting to absorb the shock of it all. As people powered up their cell phones, I closed my eyes and took a deep breath, trying to decide what to do next. I came here to do a story that became infinitely more complicated than just a feature on Tarot cards. How much further should I get involved? Pulling out my own cell phone, I called my editor, Alyce Brownlee, to find out.

After I explained what had happened, she asked, "And you're in the front row? Get up there, before the police arrive! See what's going on backstage, then go into her dressing room, and call me back in twenty minutes with whatever you find out."

"But it could be a crime scene, Alyce," I said.

"Crime shmime," she guffawed. "This is big-time, big-ass news! Get up there!"

I looked at my mother. If I told her what I was up to, she'd try to talk me out of it. I decided to go forward without explaining. After living on my own and paying my own bills for the past three years, I'd finally learned to stop asking her permission.

As I stood up to move toward the stage door, my mother yelled, "Where do you think you're going? You're not just going to leave me here, are you?"

I paused, fighting the urge to move on without saying another word to her. "You practically run the city of Chicago, Mom. I'm sure you'll figure something out. I'll see you as soon as I can, okay?"

Without waiting for her response, I ran to the side door and up the steps to the stage, steeling myself for what lay ahead. I had to find out the truth about Carmen. As I entered the area behind the curtain, I looked down to the floor and saw a bent nail, the kind Carmen collected. I picked it up and placed it in my purse, then I walked onstage.

Carmen still appeared beautiful, although she looked like she was having a nightmare in her frozen sleep. Furrowed brows and tight lips suggested she suffered in her last moments. In her right hand, she gripped a carpenter's nail, the sort that people kept dropping off before her performance as a token of good luck. I wanted to stoop down and smooth her forehead, pat her hand, and see her smile again, the way she did just before this opera. The doctor continued the CPR, but did so in vain. A circle of singers and stagehands surrounded her, peering down with anguished faces, all shocked. The understudy stood with the lifeless kitten in her arms. How did her poor kitten die? Donacella kept muttering, "I'm ruined. My kitten is dead, and so is my career."

I circled them all, pacing nervously, took a step back for a wider look and tripped, bumping into Felix Vasilakis.

"I'm so sorry," I said to him.

He swallowed hard, his dumfounded expression on a pasty white face. He mumbled something incoherently.

"I'm sorry?" I asked, but he looked toward Carmen and stepped toward her, his arms outstretched.

"Carmen, oh Carmen!" he sobbed.

Within moments, emergency technicians surrounded Carmen. The team brought monitors, a defibrillator, and an oxygen tank. I heard a nurse say quietly to an EMT, "She won't make it." Yet they placed her on a gurney and wheeled her out, trailing all sorts of equipment, as if clinging to a shred of hope. Seconds later, I heard someone say she had stopped breathing.

I had used up about half the time allotted to me by Alyce's estimation and decided to spend my last ten minutes in the diva's dressing room to take another look. The poisonous plant was back in the room, and I noticed that several leaves of the belladonna, sent by an anonymous admirer, had been nibbled, which most likely explained the kitten's death. The bottle of champagne from her father sat partially empty; it seemed strange that Carmen would drink alcohol during a performance.

Perhaps a celebration? Her tea mug was completely drained, the tea warmer cold.

I flipped through the pages of her appointment book to see what else I might learn, worried that the police would be coming any minute. I hoped to find some clue quickly, before they arrived, something useful I could tell Alyce. I looked down at today's date, taking heed of the information Carmen had inscribed from our earlier conversation–my bank account number so she could make a deposit. Oh, God! This wasn't going to look good. They'd think I killed her right after she deposited a fair sum of money in my bank account.

My first urge was to rip out that page and stuff it in my purse…I knew it would require a lot of explaining to the police and anyone else who asked. I picked up a corner and yanked at it, but then stopped myself. I couldn't alter the crime scene.

I looked around the room again, noticing the item that drew me into this story in the first place–Carmen's Tarot deck, The Fool lying face up next to The Hanged Man. The first card of the Major Arcana, next to the fourteenth. Although Carmen had drawn these cards for herself, they also spoke to me since I was the fool in this cast who had witnessed her death. The Wizard's test had taken a sharp turn. Not only was I to overcome my desire for Bruno, I also had to become involved in solving Carmen's death. I'd discovered my two-pronged test to enter the Order of the Tarot.

Lieutenant Joe Burke from the Violent Crimes Unit walked in. We knew each other and didn't always hit it off. About a year ago, we had worked together on the murder involving Chicago's first Hispanic mayor. By the time the case was solved, Joe was on his way to a promotion and he and I had become friends. Joe was always more cop than friend, though, and if anyone I cared about was in trouble, I'd want Joe to be the cop on the scene.

Passing by the mirror, I caught a glimpse of myself, pale and drained like a wilted rose, frayed at the edges, my long brown hair disheveled, and a caramel silk shirttail hanging out from the waistband of my black velvet skirt. I quickly rearranged my blouse, tucking the shirttail neatly back inside the skirt, then used my fingers as a make-do comb.

"Alex?" Joe's face was pockmarked as ever, his hair worn in a crew cut, and his fingernails bitten to the quick.

"Joe, I...I..." I was at a loss for words.

"What are you doing here? This is a crime scene. You're not actually thinking about getting involved, are you?" He glared right through me.

I wanted to explain, but his tone offended me. I didn't expect his reaction to be so sharp, especially with all we'd been through a year ago.

"And what if I am?"

"Tell me you haven't taken out a P.I. license to practice in Illinois."

"Look, Joe. I didn't plan on this happening. If you must know, I've been interviewing Carmen and her interest in..."

"Wait, don't tell me. Astrology?"

I glared at him.

"Uh, those goofy lights that people see around other people? What are they called again?"

"Auras? And no, it's not about auras."

"Wait, wait, I'll get this. She channeled dead opera singers before every performance, right?"

"Oh, Joe, so unoriginal. My mother has already used all those punch lines."

"All right, Alex. I give up. What was the diva's special interest?"

I looked again at the Fool and the Hanged Man lying next to her appointment book. Without thinking I shuffled the cards nervously into the pack.

"What the hell do you think you're doing?" Joe grabbed my wrist as I held up the deck.

I suddenly realized my foolishness, but could only sputter out, "Th-these are Tarot cards. I...I was writing a s-story about Carmen's interest in Tarot cards."

"Put them back down," he said as he steered my hand none too gently until I released the cards. As a result, they

44

fluttered down to the floor. "Jesus Christ, Alex! Don't you watch television? Don't touch anything in here. We're going to have to fingerprint the place, you know. Unless, of course, you already know who the killer is."

"So you think it's murder?"

Joe raised his hands. "I just got here. I have no idea. Police do it the old-fashioned way, without crystal balls. Anyway, you can't go anywhere yet. I'm going to have to question you."

I held my head high, but became worried he'd accuse me of murdering Carmen. What would he think about my bank account number in her appointment book?

"But I'm sure the questioning will just be a formality," he said with the tiniest smile. "Of course, you've managed to be in the wrong place."

I bristled at his words. He didn't want me to get any further involved. However, I knew The Wizard had called me to this case as part of my test to enter the Order of the Tarot, and no matter what, I would do all I could to help solve the murder. I thought of Bruno at the Four Seasons; I couldn't meet him now even if I tried. I took solace in that decision being well out of my hands.

I exited the dressing room, going in search of Mother. "I'll be back."

"You'd better be, Alex–I mean it!" Joe shouted after I gently closed the door.

Chapter Five

Day Two: Monday, March 24

All night long the rain pattered against the windows, tap, tap, tapping a message I couldn't decipher. I tossed and turned in my bed, worried about how I'd promised to write a book about the diva's father and how The Wizard's test had begun. A crash of thunder coincided with the orange numbers on my clock radio flipping to 7:00, cueing classical music to flood the bedroom. In an effort to erase the request that Carmen had made of me during our interview, I burrowed my head under the pillow, but it didn't help.

What was in the box? And what possessed me to keep it a secret from the police yesterday? They kept me for nearly two hours in the lobby of the opera house, asking me to go over my interview with Carmen. I told them about everyone who stopped by–Jorge, the masseur; Teresita, the manicurist; Felix, the assistant conductor; Donacella, the understudy; and the messenger who dropped off the bottle of champagne from her father. I gave them most of the details of my interview, except for the box, but I also kept to myself how Carmen asked me to write a book about her father.

Carmen wanted me to have the box, and I wanted to examine its contents before the police did. Carmen had requested I tell no one about the assignment, no matter what happened. I wasn't planning to keep the box a secret from the police forever, and besides, they never specifically asked about it.

Of course, I wanted to visit The Wizard for further instructions, but couldn't leave home before the box arrived.

I swung my legs out of bed, slipped on my gray yoga pants and shirt, and launched into my morning stretches and poses, but I was unable to turn my mind from Carmen's last request. Why had she asked me to write a book about her relationship with her father? Who was he? I knew he owned the Italian restaurant Il Pagliacci on Taylor Street and that he sat on the Board of the Lyric. I discarded the next thought...just because he was Italian and wealthy didn't automatically make him connected to the Outfit. Besides, hoods weren't typically opera fans.

I swung my arms high toward the ceiling, arched backwards and then forward until the palms of my hands lay flat on the floor. I remembered how Carmen looked when she died and couldn't get that image out of my mind. Who would have killed her? During my interview with her, I could tell by the desperation in her voice that she wanted to tell me more, but too many people kept stopping by and interrupting us. Did she know her life was in danger?

I swung my right foot forward and leaned into my knee, raising my arms to the sides, then up. That box sat between Carmen and me as we talked. A huge box, a three-by-three foot cube of brown carton and wide packing tape. She had it all prepared, down to its delivery to my home by a courier service, and it contained, she said, everything I needed to start writing the exposé on her father.

Once I broke out in a sweat, I jogged in place for two minutes, then cooled down with more yoga stretches. After my shower, I tried my morning meditation, but it was impossible. I did my breathing exercises. I closed my eyes, inhaled deeply, held my breath for twelve seconds, then breathed out as slowly as possible. I attempted to bring my mind to a blank receptacle. Usually this prepared my mind to receive answers to my questions, but today I found no success. After ten minutes, I gave up.

While deciding what to do, I committed myself to reading the paper. Within the hour, I'd drunk my second cup of lotus tea and read two sections of the newspaper with my cat Siddharma rubbing against my legs. I devoured the stories on the unlucky opera and the diva's sudden death: "Curse of Macbeth Dooms Production from Beginning–Costumes Lost, Stage Set Collapsed During Rehearsal, and Death of La

Tempestua."

The paper quoted a drama professor from Northwestern University: "Carmen's understudy did the unconscionable. After a heated argument with the diva, the understudy uttered the curse. This woman will be vilified by the operatic and theatrical communities." A photograph of Donacella Dimitriano graced the front page with the caption, "Understudy utters curse against this town's former reigning diva."

I put down the paper to contemplate the furor over the curse. That scene remained etched in my memory. After La Tempestua kicked at the kitten, Donacella's face contorted with righteous anger. Yet I couldn't believe she meant her curse to kill the diva.

It's true we all shuddered in that dressing room when Donacella unfurled her curse. As much as I believed in the magical power of words, I couldn't convince myself that the curse supernaturally killed Carmen. No doubt the city paper's editor didn't believe it either, it just made good copy.

"What do you think about that, Siddharma?" I inherited the longhaired, white angora from The Wizard last year, after he discovered his wife's allergy to cats. A stroke on Siddharma's back produced an appreciative purr. She sat on my kitchen table and we stared into each other's eyes.

"Yes, you're absolutely right," I told her. "I should keep reading the paper."

The more I read about the diva's death, the more worried and scared I became. This was no easy test The Wizard had given me, yet I wanted to please him. If I begged off from getting further involved, not only would I disappoint him, I'd return to the despair I experienced throughout the last year in living a life without a meaningful purpose. That thought alone sent me into a panic. No, I still wanted to enter the Order of the Tarot, to live a life of service. If that meant helping to discover the truth behind Carmen's death, then so be it. I could barely wait to see The Wizard to make sure he expected me to solve this murder.

Again, I turned to reading about the curse. Could the

understudy's words really cause the death of Carmen? I knew from my own research into the paranormal that curses do have power and could lead to destruction. Usually, though, the events don't coincide so closely, not with this much immediacy.

To top it all off, now the future of the Chicago Lyric Opera House teetered on the brink of financial ruin. Another headline read, "Curse Tumbles Opera House." The Lyric Opera House's administrator lamented, "Big-name sopranos and tenors have already cancelled upcoming appearances, and the next season is practically decimated overnight. No one wants to perform in an opera house where a star dies onstage because of a ghostly curse."

The article continued to quote her on the superstitious nature of opera people. Not only had the curse killed La Tempestua, it was now eating away at Chicago's opera house.

A cloak of sadness descended over me as I contemplated a future without the Lyric. I had so many happy memories there, particularly with my father who insisted to my mother that I wasn't too young to go to the opera at eight years old. With him, my love for opera blossomed, yes, even as a child. As an adult, the Lyric helped me connect to his spirit.

I finished the paper and put it down. "Curse the curse." I also knew from my research on the paranormal that curses could be reversed, that their power could be diminished. Before this curse's power gained any more momentum and did any more damage by instilling irrational fears in those involved in the opera, I had to think about Carmen's death in a rational manner.

The image of Carmen lying onstage floated to me, how she clutched a nail in her fist. Maybe that meant something. The Wizard always told me to think about a problem with what was at hand, and perhaps I could start my investigation with the nail. I dug into my purse and found the nail I had picked up from the stage floor, and examined it from all angles. It was three inches long, without rust, and slightly bent. Siddharma meowed and approached the nail, sniffing it, then pawing at it.

"What do you think this means?" I asked her, lifting the nail higher and watching her stand on her hind paws to snatch it. I rolled it back into my fist. Siddharma shouldn't be playing with nails.

I reached into my purse again and pulled out Carmen's phone number, wondering if I'd reach her roommate. After three rings, someone answered.

"This is Roberto Andretti," said a husky, feminine voice.

He was just the man I wanted. "You don't know me," I said, "but my name is Alexandria Vilkas and I was with Carmen Dellamorte working on an article about her just before she died."

The voice sniffed and coughed. "Oh, God. Yes, she mentioned it, about Tarot cards, right?"

"Yes."

"I'm Carmen's roommate. Most people know me as Castrato."

Hecate in black leather, stirring her pot. I wondered how he had gotten that name. Had he really been castrated?

"Castrato! Oh, I loved how you played the witch yesterday. It was mesmerizing."

"Did you see me? How kind of you to say so."

"I know this is probably a difficult time for you, and I'm sorry to bother you. It's just that–" Turning over the nail in my palm, I continued, "I don't know who to turn to. I was hoping you could talk to me about Carmen."

"For your story?" The honeyed voice had turned sharp.

"Yes."

"I think you should let Carmen rest in peace. I have more important things to do than talk about Tarot cards. Really, the nerve of some reporters!"

"That's not what I meant. It's not just about her Tarot cards anymore. It's about how she died. I was thinking… She was gripping a nail in her hand. It might mean something."

"Oh, those nails." Castrato's voice cracked and I heard him blow his nose. "I…I just can't believe what happened yesterday. I'm a wreck."

"I'm so sorry to intrude at a time like this."

Castrato exhaled loudly. "She read an autobiography of Luciano Pavarotti. He used to pick up a bent nail on the stage floor just before starting a performance, for good luck. She naturally had to copy the idea. Thought it would help her sing better."

"But what's with them? What do they mean?"

"Italian superstitions–metal for good luck and bent like horns to ward off evil. Finding a nail right before a performance brings good luck–not that it helped her any."

We sat in silence a moment.

I said, "Right before the performance, she received about four of them from people popping into her dressing room."

"Happens all the time. She's got a whole jar full of them in her bedroom. Now if that's everything–"

It wasn't nearly enough, but I couldn't force him to talk longer.

"Hold on," he said. "I've got another call."

Siddharma crouched under the table, her tail up high.

Castrato came back on the line. "Someone just told me Carmen gave you a box yesterday. Is that true?"

Goosebumps appeared on my arms. Although I knew I couldn't keep the box a secret forever, I hoped I'd have more time. Did Castrato just speak to Teresita? If he did, I couldn't deny Carmen gave me the box. Perhaps I'd have nothing to lose by telling Castrato something about it, and I could gain his trust. He lived with her, after all.

"It is true. Carmen gave me a box of information about a project she wanted me to work on."

Castrato laughed. "Don't tell me she got you to write a book about her father. That's it, isn't it?"

I didn't want to say anything.

"You don't want to talk about it, do you?" Castrato asked. "I think Carmen wanted you to expose who her father really is. Am I right?"

"I promised Carmen I wouldn't talk about this project, and I'm trying to honor her wishes."

"So it is about her father," Castrato said, as if I'd just confirmed it. "My God, she does have balls. He's powerful, you know. Has all kinds of connections with the Chicago police too. You wouldn't want to get on his bad side."

Of course, I had feared this all along, and the thin layer of denial peeled away to expose my anxiety. "Is he…is he…with the Mob?"

"The Mob? No."

A wave of relief washed over me, although I worried that Castrato knew about the box and Carmen's assignment.

"But he might as well be. The only difference is he likes to work alone. A lone-ranger type. I don't want to scare you, but this man collects guns. Does he know about the project?"

I still didn't want to betray Carmen's confidence without first seeing the contents of the box.

"I bet he doesn't," Castrato said after a moment of silence. "Look, I want to talk to you in person. In light of what happened yesterday, perhaps you should return that box to me."

The box would arrive sometime today, so I'd have a chance to look over the material before I spoke with him. I wanted to see where Carmen lived; so I agreed to speak with him, although I wouldn't give him the box.

"That would be fine," I said. "How's tomorrow afternoon?"

"Perfect."

After writing down his address and saying good-bye, I waited for the box to appear. Every quarter hour, I looked out the window for a sign of the messenger.

The fourth time I looked out, I saw a big, black Cadillac across the street.

Chapter Six

During the next hour, the car never moved. A dark figure remained in the driver's seat. Was he waiting for the box to arrive too? Would he try to intercept it? Perhaps it was just my imagination, and he had nothing to do with the box after all. I felt stuck. If I called the police, I'd have to tell them about it and wouldn't have a chance to see what was inside. It had to arrive soon!

Back in the kitchen, Siddharma stepped out of the pantry, her head cocked in a way that meant mischief. I leaped up to see what she had done. A ten-pound bag of potatoes lay mutilated, clawed, and scratched, the contents scattered on the floor, the spud eyes bulging.

"Oh, Siddharma!"

She looked up at me, then at the potatoes.

"Kugelis? I'm supposed to make kugelis?"

I bought the bag more than a month ago to make my favorite dish, but couldn't find three free hours to peel, grate, and bake the potatoes. Perhaps while I waited for the box to arrive and worried about the black Cadillac, I could keep my hands busy. The Lithuanian recipe was handed down through generations of our family, my mother being the first in her clan to make it in Chicago. When my father returned from a concert abroad, Mom would fill the house with the earthy smell of kugelis. He always joked that the lure of my mother's kugelis would never keep him away from home long. After he died, Mom never made it again.

"I suppose while we wait for that box, we could make the kugelis," I said to Siddharma.

She meowed.

I turned on the television and proceeded to wash and peel twenty-two potatoes. A live press conference on the diva's death featuring the police commissioner began.

"Carmen Dellamorte died of poison found in her champagne," stated the Commissioner. "We found a bottle of rubbing alcohol in her dressing room used for a massage. Rubbing alcohol is a common household item that can cause death when ingested. The task now is to find the person who poured the rubbing alcohol into the diva's champagne. We are confident we will get to the bottom of this soon."

So it *was* poison in her champagne. Had the poison been there when her father sent the champagne or was the rubbing alcohol poured in after someone opened the bottle? It would be difficult, if not impossible, to inject poison into a sealed champagne bottle. No, the poison was most likely poured after the bottle was opened. While excising a dark bruise from a potato, I recalled how the door to the diva's dressing room was practically a revolving door. Just about anyone could have entered her room, noticed the open bottle, and poured poison into it. Of course, it wouldn't be easy, but a funnel might have been used to pour the rubbing alcohol into the bottle.

As the press conference continued, a reporter asked, "What about security in the dressing rooms? Wasn't there anyone standing guard by the door?"

The police commissioner answered, "Unfortunately, no guard stood by the door, and we've discovered that singers often failed to lock their doors. This was the case with Carmen Dellamorte."

After he answered questions from the media that didn't reveal any new information, the press conference ended.

The next potato had an eye that had grown to two inches, so I snapped it off. Rubbing alcohol? I remembered how Jorge, her masseur, poured the stuff over her body while he massaged her.

Poor Carmen. I pictured her singing her last aria, then walking offstage. She had enough time to go to her dressing room, freshen up, and return for the curtain calls. While in her dressing room, she may have sipped the champagne laced with rubbing alcohol. Perhaps someone poured it for her and then slipped in the poison. Assuming she drank the champagne, perhaps after several quick gulps, she returned to the wings to wait for the curtain call. She must have felt the effects minutes later. Not knowing what to do, in a panic, she staggered onto the stage, begging for help. But, of course, it was too late.

Was there something in the box that would tell me more about her life and who resented her enough to kill her? I walked to the front window and looked out again. The black Cadillac still stood there. Did the diva's killer find out about the box and send that black Cadillac to watch me?

I wished I could talk to The Wizard for some reassurance. This was all part of the test; to pass it, I had to calm myself and think clearly. As soon as the box arrived, I could leave my apartment.

I turned on the oven at 350 degrees and grated the potatoes. By the nineteenth, my right upper arm turned sore and I stopped for a moment to rest. My mind wandered to Bruno, the way the light cast a shadow on his face at the Lyric Opera House, the way he brushed his hair back. *Grate...Grate...*I couldn't stop thinking about him, yet I knew I had to. He was part of my test, and I was supposed to fight his advances. *Grate...Grate...*If only he weren't married. Despite my best efforts, my fantasy about Bruno soared. The Wizard said we knew each other in a past life, and perhaps we did something wrong together that caught up with us in this life...*Grate...Grate.*

Perhaps Bruno and I were supposed to endure this period of separation, his marriage to his current wife, my murder investigation, before we reunite. Goddess, what was I thinking? Why couldn't I stop this train of thought? I knew it was wrong, very wrong. He was terrible for me, a bad, bad boy...*Grate... Grate.* I would have to make sure I would never see him again, never talk to him. That would be my best defense against him. Out of sight, out of mind...*Grate... Grate.*

I fumbled with the grater, the slicer edge ripping into my right index finger. "Ahh!" My finger! I pressed the injured finger to my mouth, sucked the blood and ran it under cold water, then wrapped it in a paper towel. After a minute, I shoved the two pans of kugelis into the oven.

The door buzzer sounded. I ran down the indoor staircase from my second-floor apartment and unlatched the front door with my left hand, my right index finger still wrapped in the paper towel

"Delivery, ma'am," said a man standing behind a big box. He held out a form resting on a metallic clipboard for a signature.

"You don't need any help with that, do you?" He took a step backward.

"No, I'll be fine."

Just then the black Cadillac moved off, much to my relief. Perhaps the Caddy person had confirmed the box's delivery and would leave me alone now. Or perhaps the Cadillac had nothing to do with the box after all. Speaking of which, the three-foot cube of a package was way too heavy to lift alone. I knocked at my landlord's door on the first floor of our two-story building. Fortunately, Mindy Noreika had retired from his city job and was always home. Mindy was short for Mindaugas, a common name on the southwest side of Chicago, home to thousands of Lithuanians.

"Mr. Mindy, it's Alex."

"One minute please," said Mindy as he opened the door. "What the hell you have that fron' door open for? Doan you know it freezing outside? Just because I include heat in your ren' doan make it for free!"

"I can't close it," I explained. "That's why I need your help. To lift this upstairs."

"What's in that big box?"

"Material for a book about someone."

Mindy scowled, then sniffed deeply. "What that smell?" He wore faded blue jeans, an old red plaid flannel shirt, and brown vinyl slippers frayed at the edges. "Kugelis?"

Mindy was grumpy, but always upfront. With him, everything was for something, and nothing came free.

"You want some?"

"Okay, I help you."

Mindy lifted one side of the box and I the other. Slowly, we climbed the staircase, me walking backward, and Mindy carrying the brunt of the weight. We maneuvered through each step, grunting and sighing. When we reached my apartment, I left Mindy and ran to the kitchen to get a knife.

Rummaging through a drawer, I found a seven-inch cooking knife, then ran back to the living room. I knelt in front of the box, stabbed the knife into a seam to rip open the tape, and folded back the lid to reveal four white three-ring binders filled with papers, newspaper clippings, and photos. I took them out slowly, only to see three more binders, a handwritten diary, two photo albums, and a few bestsellers on The Outfit.

Mindy picked up one of the books, then let out a long whistle. "A mobster, huh?" He was always nosy, and I didn't want him to get any further involved because I wasn't convinced it would be safe for him.

"No, it's just background material," I said.

"This person you write about–is he dead?"

"No."

Mindy scratched his head. "Alex, you crazy young lady. Before you die, I want kugelis."

I laughed, despite the tension I felt. "It should be ready soon. How about I serve you a piece in the kitchen?" I also thought it would be a great way to get him out of the living room, so I could spend some time alone with the contents of the box.

Mindy stood up, walked to the front window, and peered out. "God damn, that car is back! I called police to tell that man to move. I no like him sitting there for so many hours."

I looked out the window at the Cadillac.

"I going to call police again," Mindy huffed. "He selling drugs, car like that. Not in fron' my house. Believe me, I know trouble, and this car trouble."

Mindy dialed the phone while looking out the window.

"Huh!" He put down the phone before he said anything. "Car drive off again."

"Maybe he figured you were calling the police again."

"Maybe."

Mindy reluctantly stepped away from the window. "You sure you doan want my help with all this?"

"Yes, I'm very sure. But I will give you some kugelis." I led him into my kitchen and sat him down, while I took the kugelis out of the oven. I served him a huge square of the potato cake along with sour cream. I had a bottle of vodka in my pantry, which I kept just for Mindy and poured it in a glass for him.

"Ahhh," he said, as he dug into his favorite meal.

I left him to go into the living room, to pull everything out of the box onto my living room floor. Siddharma perched on the arm of one of the couches, near the shelf that held my father's violin.

Soon the life of Adriano Capezio lay scattered around the living room, like bone fragments in an archeological dig. I didn't know where to start, so I chose a notebook at random and opened it to a recent newspaper article about the diva's father. Adriano Capezio stood in front of his restaurant, Il Pagliacci on Taylor Street, holding a box of pasta in one hand and olive oil in the other. The photo caption read, "Capezio brings Italy to Chicago." If the rumors about Adriano being a criminal were true, I wondered what else he brought to Chicago.

Then I leafed through her diary, eager to read her last entries. I skimmed through her last pages, pausing briefly over a passage that said, "If anything should happen to me, I need to leave my suspicions in a safe place. But who shall I trust? I am surrounded by villains. Until I find someone I can depend on, I'll bury my thoughts in a special chamber, a prop that someone dear to my singing heart could unlock."

I wondered what special chamber she referred to. She must mean the depths of her heart. Perhaps she had a chance to confide in someone before her death. As I continued thinking in this vein, I was startled when I noticed Mindy peering over my shoulder. He had snuck up on me, and I wasn't sure how long he'd been standing behind me.

"What are you doing?" I asked.

Mindy pulled the tip of his nose.

"Does your mother know about this?"

I had the feeling my mother often called Mindy to check up on me and had instructed him not to tell me about their private conversations. What else could I think when he asked me a question like that?

"No, and you don't have to tell her about it."

Mindy raised his hands like I was arresting him. "No, no. I just ask."

"You're not her secret spy, are you?" I asked.

"Aach!"

In the next instant, Mindy stuck his arm into the box, pulled out a book on the Mob, and flipped through the pages, then put it down and did the same with three more paperbacks. I couldn't help but think Carmen suspected her father of being involved in organized crime and she wanted to expose him in her book.

A sheet of paper, a bookmark, fell out of the last bestseller.

"Oh, look at this," Mindy said, as he picked it up.

"Please, you shouldn't be going through all this. It's confidential." I began to place the contents back in the box.

By this point, I wanted Mindy to leave. I feared him becoming too involved, but he wasn't taking the hint. Instead, he began reading the note.

"March 4. This living hand, now warm and capable of earnest grasping, would, if it were cold. And in the icy silence of the tomb, so haunt thy days and chill thy dreaming nights. John Keats"

I looked at Mindy. "Give me that, please."

He handed it to me. It was written in Carmen's hand–it matched the handwriting in her diary.

"March 4th," he said. "You know what day that is, don't you?"

"Of course I do. It's St. Casimir Day, the patron saint of Lithuania."

Silvia Foti

"Aha! Maybe a Lithuanian killed her."

I laughed, knowing that even Mindy didn't believe that. In fact, it was rare that ten minutes would go by without him mentioning his heritage. He had lived in Chicago for well over forty years, yet every single day he reminded me that he was born in Lithuania, that my parents escaped when the country was under Communist rule, and that I should always remember my origins.

Yet to me the date meant something else. March 4th, now three weeks ago, remained etched in my mind as the day I visited The Wizard to enter the Order of the Tarot; and he said my test would begin that day. The date on Carmen's note stood out like a neon sign, confirming that the diva's death was all part of my test.

But what did March 4th mean to Carmen? Why was that the date she realized something terrible might happen to her? As Mindy fingered the materials in the box, his frown deepened, and I worried over his health. At his age, he shouldn't be thinking about how he might inadvertently be involved in something sinister.

"I think it's time for you to leave," I said pointedly.

"One thing you can never have is too much kugelis," he said, heading back toward the kitchen. "Or vodka!" He started to sing a drinking song in Lithuanian.

I headed him off. "Why don't I give you a pan to take home?"

"You really want me to leave, doan you?"

I sighed. "I have a lot of work to do. I hope you understand."

Before he could answer, I ran to the kitchen and returned with a pan of kugelis wrapped in aluminum foil.

He took the pan and headed to my front door. First he looked through the window. "Damn that car. It back again." He ran down the stairs at top speed for a seventy-year-old and headed out into the street.

I looked out the window, and saw Mindy standing beside that Cadillac. I wanted to open the window and scream,

60

"Don't!" but it was too late. What if Carmen's father had sent the driver, a thug, to keep an eye on me and the box? Wouldn't that thug think Mindy was involved in my story about Carmen's father? I could only watch his agitated gestures and worry over what he was saying. The driver said something. Mindy responded by spreading his arms out about three feet wide by three feet high. Was he telling him about the box? Mindy shrugged his shoulders and stepped away from the car as the driver rolled up his window and drove off.

Now I ran down the stairs and accosted him before he could enter his apartment.

"What just happened? What did you tell that guy?"

"I ask him why he park in fron' of house. He say he leave an' no bother us if I tell him about special delivery here. He say he think it belong to him. I say, 'No, impossible. It belongs to my renter. I was just there in her apartment. Box is yay wide and yay high. It have material for story she working on.' Then man say thank you and drive away. Summovabeech. I hope he no bother neighborhood again."

Did Mindy really believe the man thought the package was an accidental delivery? But I didn't want to scare him or get him any further involved.

"That's good," I said. "You let me know if he returns."

"Aach! Next time I call police."

He had set the pan of kugelis on the stairway before he ran outside. Now he grabbed it and deeply inhaled its fragrance. "I can't wait to finish this. I have some now, some more tonight, maybe with vodka. I give you pan back when I done."

"Sounds good, Mr. Mindy. Enjoy it."

After Mindy entered his apartment, I climbed the stairs back to my own place. Mindy had just confirmed that the man in the Cadillac was watching me and waiting for that box. What kind of a story had I gotten myself into? I had no more time to waste; I had to see The Wizard to find out exactly what my test entailed. I hoped he would give me answers to my questions about the Cadillac, the box, and Carmen's death.

Chapter Seven

After I placed a fresh band-aid over the gash on my finger, I threw on my coat and rushed out the door. By the time I arrived at the South Side Psychic Studio, the rain had subsided but the clouds crawled above, like gray sentinels eavesdropping on Chicago. I pressed my hand against the wooden oak door bearing a half-moon shape of stained glass in a rainbow. When I entered, a tinkly bell sounded. A stick of Patchouli incense burned on the counter, its ash falling into a wooden tray.

The Wizard looked expectant, with a controlled sense of worry that dwelled just under the surface of his calm. Today he wore a multicolored sweater with braided rows of threads. He was dusting his crystals, and said, "Something tremendous is happening to you."

"Yes, my test has begun." I unbuttoned my orange mackinaw and threw it over the couch where I sat. He put down the feather duster on the shelf and sat beside me.

"There is a new man in your heart," he said.

I arranged the coat on the couch, grabbing the sleeves, pairing them up, and folding them together.

The Wizard waved his right index finger. "Love is easy to spot, Alex, but this is not true love."

I concentrated on the swirl of dust particles in the air.

My master raised his right eyebrow. "Your instincts are correct with this one. Trust them."

"That's not why I'm here."

"No?" he asked. "How did you cut your finger?"

"Grating potatoes for kugelis. No big deal."

"And were you thinking only about potatoes when you were grating them?"

How did he know I had had Bruno on my mind?

He said, "It is inevitable. This man's pull is strong. It is because of wrong thinking about him...be more careful in the future."

His words stung me, but I knew he was right. Nothing happened by accident. It made sense that I cut myself precisely because my mind needed to shut down its erroneous thoughts of Bruno, and I chastised myself for not paying attention to this.

"Let us talk about the other half of your test."

The words poured forth like a torrent as I explained how I was interviewing Carmen Dellmorte and her passion for Tarot cards in her dressing room. "Nearly three hours later, she died on stage, murdered by poison."

The Wizard stroked his chin and did the accordion thing with his forehead. "The time has come for you to get a gun," he said.

Whoa! For nearly six months, I had been begging The Wizard for his permission to get a gun, and his response had always been, "It is not time yet. Continue your practice. When you are ready, I will let you know." My weekly lessons with The Wizard focused on Tarot cards, yet I had also been receiving lessons on shooting and lock picking. Of course, I sensed The Wizard was grooming me for a task that would involve these skills, but no matter how often I asked why, he would always answer cryptically, "It is not time for you to know." Just three weeks ago, he told me I was about to enter The Order of the Tarot, and now I could get a gun. Events were moving fast.

"Now?"

"Yes. This test demands you pursue a gun."

I nodded, feeling the weight of this new development. Part of me was excited that I could finally own my own gun, but a bigger part felt nervous about what the rest of the test would entail.

The Wizard asked, "Why do you need to solve this murder?"

I shook my head. I knew he sought an answer that went beyond 'Because I want to join the Order of the Tarot,' or 'My editor said so.'

"You do know why?"

"Carmen asked me to do something for her."

"What?"

"Write a book about her father."

The Wizard nodded. "But that's not the real reason, is it?" His gaze penetrated mine like a drill into the center of the earth, digging, rumbling, twirling down deeper and deeper until it hit the core.

I suddenly understood. "It's about my father."

His forehead turned as smooth as a saucer of cream, and I knew I was right.

"He died when I was ten."

"Yes."

"I keep having a dream about him. I'm about to meet him at the opera, but when I turn the corner, he's not there."

"Go on."

"I've always been searching for my father after his death. With this test, with you, I believe I'll be rewarded with a visit from him. Yet…that doesn't make sense."

My master nodded. I wished he'd deny my absurd reasoning, shake me out of an illusion I couldn't destroy on my own, put a stop to this fool's paradise. Is this what he wanted me to admit? "Would you like a reading, Alex, to prepare you for what lies ahead?"

"Sure."

"Relax. Take three deep breaths."

I closed my eyes and fell into a light meditation, focusing on each breath.

"The Tarot will always give answers by giving you the big picture–bigger than perhaps you realize. Human incarnation is a test. There is no escaping the challenges."

When I opened an eye to peek, I saw The Wizard walk to an antique oak cabinet and open a drawer. He dug inside and pulled out a small red cedar box, sat across from me again, and placed the box in the center of the table. He opened it and pulled out the deck of cards, carefully wrapped in black silk, which he slowly unrolled.

"You can open your eyes now," he said solemnly. "Today, I'll use the Universal Waite Tarot. I know you are partial to it."

There were more than 300 Tarot decks created over the last 600 years, an accumulation of an impressive amount of insight. The Universal Waite Tarot was a derivation of the Rider-Waite Tarot deck, named after Arthur Waite, an original member of the Hermetic Order of the Golden Dawn. Waite worked with illustrator Pamela Colman Smith in 1910 to create the first tarot deck that appealed to the world of art and became the most popular 78-card tarot deck. Most Tarot decks have been based on this one.

The Wizard tilted down his head while keeping his eyes on me. "I'll work with just the Major Arcana today." He slowly shuffled the cards. "From a seventy-eight card deck, that eliminates fifty-six."

"Isn't that rather limiting?"

"They're the most important cards in the deck. And they signify the degrees you must pass as you move through the Order of the Tarot."

"Are you going to tell me about the Order?"

"Not yet, but soon. The time is close."

The Wizard placed the pack on the table, asked me to shuffle the cards, then cut them.

"Form your question. Pick up the cards and shuffle again as you feel the force of your question. Ask the spirit world for help."

I shuffled the cards as instructed.

"Ask your question."

"How am I supposed to solve this case?"

The Wizard closed his eyes, slowed his breath, and deepened his relaxation. A sense of peace pervaded. He took up the cards, dealt them with methodical leisure. He placed one card in the middle, crossed it with another, laid four cards around it, then placed another four cards vertically next to them, the Celtic Cross.

"Ah, a very interesting spread! Do you believe what you see?"

I saw the images of the cards before me, feeling the impact of their message. My mind raced through the meanings. "Yes."

"You are an excellent student," he said. "One of the purposes of the Tarot is to help the user combine her conscious and subconscious selves, to become more whole. Most people are fragmented, acting one way in one situation and another under other circumstances. You have an army of 50,000 horses–your thoughts in a day–but they all go in different directions. Align your horses so they all run in the same direction. Do you understand?"

"I'm trying."

The Wizard nodded. "You will. In the meantime, you've got a murder to write about, don't you?"

I nodded, anxious to hear his counsel.

The Wizard analyzed the spread for the next few minutes.

"The first card is the Fool, and this represents you in relation to the question. You are at the Fool's degree. Notice this zero card with an image of a colorful fool. The colors of his dress represent undisciplined emotions. You aren't looking where you're going. The card shows a dog, but in your case, you have a wolf on your left side."

"Vilkas means wolf in Lithuanian."

"That's most appropriate because the emotions of the wolf are driving you along. You carry a bag of treasures on your shoulder. Do you know what's in that bag?"

"Yes, my tools–the pentacle, sword, cup, and wand."

"Very good. Look in your bag. Study what you have. Be prepared to move in a new direction. The Fool is one of the most powerful cards in the Tarot. It implies an unusual intersection of forces at work, producing a rare opportunity for synthesis. It will require all your skill, understanding, and insight to harmonize them."

"Goddess," I said softly.

"The knowledge you have gained on guns this past year will come into play."

Perhaps this had something to do with the black Cadillac

and the box. I sat still, thinking about Adriano Capezio's well-known hobby of collecting guns. Right now, he looked like the prime suspect, and in my mind, he sent the man in the black Cadillac to keep an eye on me. After all, Carmen had asked me to write an exposé on him and had given me a box of material about him. I could only guess that Adriano wouldn't hesitate to use one of his guns on me to get the box. That's why I needed a gun to protect myself. I had become adept on the range this year, but knew I needed time to get used to my own gun. Why did The Wizard wait so long to give me his permission?

"What is this Order of the Tarot? You're asking me to join something I know nothing about, and now I'm to put myself in harm's way."

The Wizard bristled, his forehead crunching up like a foldable fan. "You can leave at any time. Remember, it is you who came to me. You insisted I teach you. Do you think I work with just anybody? Do you think your needs, your wants, your desires are more important than the opportunity you are being given? Yes, you will go in harm's way. Your life will be in danger, but you are well trained, more than you believe. It is not yet time to tell you of the Order of the Tarot, but this much I can tell you. You will experience glory in serving mankind with justice and in saving humanity from evil."

It was one of the few times I had seen The Wizard turn this angry, and I felt ashamed for questioning him. I couldn't leave him–no matter where he sent me, I would follow.

The Wizard placed his hands in a prayer pose and closed his eyes to compose himself and become calm again. When he opened his eyes, he asked, "Do you want to continue?"

"Yes," I whispered.

"Very well. You have something else to tell me."

"I saw a black Cadillac sitting in front of my apartment. The man inside was spying on me. Carmen gave me a box of material about her father, and I wasn't sure if I should tell the police about that box. I wanted to talk to you about it first."

The Wizard nodded, as he stared at the Fool card. "Yes. You must let the police know about the box's contents. That man in the Cadillac in front of your apartment *is* a danger. You are correct to be worried."

"What should I do?"

"Proceed as you have been. Solve Carmen's murder. Do not get further involved with the married man. In the seventh position, you have The Lovers, which in your case is a fool's love, beguiling and maddening."

I clenched my jaw. It was easy for The Wizard to say I should control my thoughts and emotions about Bruno, quite another for me to dominate fantasies that crept in like stealth spirits intent on possession.

The Wizard leaned forward to scoop up the cards and shuffle them back into the deck, wrapped them in the black silk scarf, and inserted them into the red cedar box. "I am giving you this Tarot deck as a gift."

"You are?" He had never given me a gift before, not a material kind.

"I know you have many other Tarot decks, but use this one to solve the murder. I have consecrated it three times—during the full moon, the waning moon, and the most recent new moon on March 4th. Work with it on a daily basis, and it will soon speak to you."

I held the cards in my hands, appreciating their weight and the significance of The Wizard's gesture. He believed in me, and I wouldn't let him down.

"They will help you sort clues and provide possibilities, but they will leave the final decision to you. The Tarot is a tool of the divine that will guide you on your path by developing your intuitive reasoning."

"Does the Tarot know who killed the diva?"

The Wizard smiled. "Yes, but it is for you to find out."

Chapter Eight

Day Three: Tuesday, March 25

The next day I woke up early. I rushed to look outside the living room window and felt relief to see the black Cadillac hadn't returned.

The Wizard's final words echoed in my mind. I've written about Tarot cards, interviewed experts and users on them, even had readings by psychics, but never considered using a deck to help solve a murder. Last time, I had to rely on luck and logic as I tried to piece together the information on the Mayor's murder. The very thought of it, though, excited me because it made so much sense. The images on Tarot cards unlock new thinking patterns in a user, and often that is exactly what is needed for reporters writing about murder.

After I did my yoga exercises, showered, and meditated, I headed toward the new deck of Tarot cards in my studio. When I pulled the cards out of the box, fanning them before me, I felt like a child standing on the threshold of a giant toy store wondering which toy I'd select. Seventy-eight cards lay waiting to tell a story. It had taken me all year with daily practice to master their meanings and interpret the various combinations.

Because there were twenty-two cards in the Major Arcana and that many degrees in the Order of the Tarot, The Wizard instructed me to work with Tarot cards every day for twenty-two minutes. I fingered as many cards as I could, searching for a message, a way to harness the deck's power, but felt like we spoke two different languages. This always happened to me with a new deck. I knew from experience, however, that in a few days I would feel a stronger connection to these cards. When I slid the cards back into their box, I thought about the material on Carmen's father in my living room.

Last night, before I fell asleep, I had pored through its contents, reading over Carmen's diary and fingering the photographs of her family. She had a stack of receipts from vending machines in Chicago held by her father, as well as contracts with JKL records. I assumed these would show a discrepancy with Capezio's income taxes, but would it prove his involvement in organized crime? I also read over a stack of papers related to a gun factory in Paraguay. What did all of this mean?

I kept looking for clues about Carmen's murder. I had found another poetry passage stuffed inside a photo album and written in what seemed to be Carmen's handwriting, also dated March 4th, which stated:

Like a child from the womb,
like a ghost from the tomb,
I arise and unbuild again.
How wonderful is Death.
Mary Wollstonecraft Shelley

The fact that it was written on March 4th made me believe it had some significance, but I couldn't figure out what. I felt a sudden urgency to bring the box to work, make copies of its contents, and then give it to the police. I didn't want it in my apartment a moment longer. I made four trips up and down the back stairs to get the contents into my car and headed to work.

Gypsy Magazine was headquartered on the seventh floor of a twenty-story building on Ontario Street. When I arrived at work, I asked for a security guard's help to get the material up in my office. It was still early and the cubicles stood deserted, like small empty stages waiting for their actors. Immediately, I began making photocopies with the box beside me. I read as much as I could while making the copies and became so engrossed that I didn't hear someone sneak up beside me.

Tony Catania, the photographer, tapped my shoulder. "What's in the box?"

At six-foot-six, he towered over me, grinning in a friendly way. On most days, he had an easy manner and today was no exception. People used to think something would develop between us since our offices had been next to each other for the past three years, but I never liked the idea of dating a coworker.

The few times he invited me to lunch alone, I found an excuse to avoid it, and anyway he always seemed to have a girlfriend. My philosophy was that a love life could get too messy at work.

"Huh?" I realized I wasn't ready to talk about the box yet.

He leaned over me and tried to get a look at what I was doing. "Heard about the story you're on. Does this stuff have anything to do with that?"

"Yeah." News sure traveled fast.

"You interviewed Carmen Dellamorte just before... Well, what happened?"

While trying to decide what to tell Tony, I noticed an unusual camera hanging from his neck. It had extra knobs and doodads. I asked, "Are you going to tell me what that thing is?"

"I get it. You're changing the subject." He gave a look of uneasy puzzlement. "Okay. It takes pictures of ghosts. A phantasmagoric camera."

I was grateful Tony didn't push his questions about the box further, although I knew he'd come back at me in a more subtle fashion later. He couldn't help it; he was a reporter too. "Pictures of ghosts?"

"Edgar found it on one of his trips and passed it along to me."

Edgar Sheldon was the publisher of our magazine, Alyce's boss, and a billionaire tycoon who collected ancient artifacts and high-tech gadgets. He was also my mother's boyfriend. In fact, that particular connection of hers helped me get this job, and of course everyone else on staff knew it too.

"Look, Alex, I know this is none of my business, but...I know how you're always trying to prove yourself around here, and–"

"And what?" My voice rose sharply.

"Nothing, uh...just let me know if I can help, okay?" He headed back into his cubicle with a frown.

"Okay, Tony."

I realized my colleague was right. I *was* trying to prove myself around here. I always felt I had to overcome my mother getting me my job by establishing myself as the best reporter on staff, that Alyce Brownlee had hired me because of my investigative talents, not because her boss was my mother's boyfriend.

I continued to make copies of the box's contents, then shoved the box into my cubicle and opened an e-mail from Alyce. She wanted to meet with me in two minutes. I headed toward Alyce's office, the only one with a door. The only time she closed it was for hirings, firings, and hush-hush meetings. As usual, the door stood open, but my boss wasn't there. I took one of the two empty chairs in front of her desk and looked out her window, which faced Lake Michigan, at the frothy waves licking the shore. She had a collection of crystal animals on her windowsill. I picked up the howling wolf. How much should I tell her?

I heard a rustling sound at the door and turned around to see Beata Szybowski, *Gypsy Magazine's* new reporter. A tall blonde, Beata's chest jutted out like a porch awning.

"So you're doing a murder story, I hear," Beata said. Management respected her English degree from the University of Chicago; however, some of us in the ranks believed journalism degrees were better suited for newshounds.

"Uh-huh." It's not that Beata was a bad reporter, but she'd claimed to have psychic abilities. By my count, she guessed right about half the time, which put her at average in intuitive abilities.

"You're so lucky that way. I'd give up my chakras gem set to get a murder story like that. What a way to advance."

"So what are you doing here?" I asked. "Alyce called me in for a one-on-one."

"Alyce called me in for a meeting, too. Guess we're here for the same reason."

I doubted it.

Alyce stepped in with three gourmet coffees in a cardboard carrier. "Good. I'm glad you're both here." She wore a gray cashmere suit, her brown and gray hair pulled back into a plastic barrette, with the shorter strands straying over her face. She puffed one off her lips as she set the coffee down on her desk. Alyce's entire life revolved around her job, a personality trait our publisher admired since she had single-handedly doubled advertising income in her five years at *Gypsy Magazine.*

"We've got a lot to talk about," she said.

The department secretary stepped in. "Edgar's on line one. Says it's urgent."

"Close the door on the way out," Alyce said to the secretary. Beata and I exchanged glances. I still felt secure in my job, and I doubted Alyce would fire Beata in front of me. This was going to be a hush-hush meeting.

"This won't take long," Alyce said to us, as she pressed a button and picked up the receiver.

"Hello, Edgar. What's it been? Forty-five minutes already?"

Alyce pursed her lips. "As a matter of fact, she just walked in. I've got Beata here too. Yes, she does have a knack for those stories. Yes, I agree. Uh huh. We could double circulation for that issue, sure. Advertisers would love it. Okay. Wonderful idea. Yes, we'll get Tony to shoot pictures. I'll tell them right away. 'Bye." Alyce hung up, smiling broadly and radiating like her aura just doubled in size.

"Well?" I asked. Clearly this was about Carmen's murder and how I would write the story about it.

"Edgar's got big plans for the both of you."

"The *both* of us?" I gripped the arms of my chair. "What do you mean, 'the both of us'?"

"He's on fire about the Tarot story. He thinks if you can solve the murder of the diva, it would boost *Gypsy Magazine's* circulation."

"Really?" I loosened the grip on my chair. This wasn't anything new. In fact, Alyce said as much over the phone minutes after Carmen died onstage. "It's my story. What's Beata got to do with it?"

"Oh, Alex, this story is much too big for you to cover alone. Edgar thinks it could turn into a regular feature where we assign murder stories–related to the occult, of course–and have you, Beata, and Tony solve them in print. With my guidance."

The idea sounded great, except for Beata's role. Of course, I'd try to work with Lt. Joe Burke...I had a decent connection with him. Could raise my profile–help me get more respect around here and prove to everyone once and for all that I wasn't here just because my mother got me the job.

"What do you think?" Alyce asked, looking at both of us.

"It's brilliant," Beata said. She looked like she had just made contact with her guardian angel.

When Alyce looked down for a moment, I squinted my eyes at Beata.

"It works," Alyce said, "since the diva had a passion for the Tarot cards, which you could tie into this story and others like it."

"Okay..." I said.

"Edgar thinks," she continued, "we can launch a series about the Major Arcana of the Tarot cards, set it up with this first story based on the Fool's card."

My mind traveled through a galaxy of possibilities. It coincided perfectly with my ascendancy through the Order of Tarot...I foresaw The Wizard assigning me a test related to each of the murder stories I'd be working on. I saw just one problem...Alyce was determined to have Beata on this story. I'd have to outshine Beata to maintain my position as the top reporter. Perhaps that box would give me an edge. The Wizard's words echoed in my mind: "Entering the Order of Tarot will make life more difficult. Set aside personal ambitions." I could work with Beata if I had to, and it looked like I had no choice.

"Well?" Alyce asked, looking at me. "You knew Carmen the best."

"Sounds great," I finally said.

Alyce folded her hands over the desk. "Of course you'll include the details of your interview with Carmen. This gives you prime positioning for the launch. Because of that, I'm making you the lead reporter. Agreed?" She looked at Beata and me for a confirmation. At least she gave me that much.

We both nodded.

"Is there anything that happened during the interview that was out of the ordinary?" Alyce asked me.

"Well..." I considered mentioning Carmen's strange request, but decided to hold off on that for the moment. I still wanted to go through that box myself. "There's this champagne bottle with a strange note."

"A strange note? What?" Beata asked.

"It was sent from her father, Adriano Capezio. It said, 'To make the poison go down easier.'"

"I've met him," Alyce said. "Quite a character. He's in his mid-eighties, wears a pinky ring, has a full head of hair, a perpetual tan, smooth face, blue eyes."

Beata started taking notes. "What does he do for a living?" she asked.

"Owns a restaurant in Little Italy on Taylor Street," Alyce said. "Called Il Pagliacci. There's a big statue of a clown out in front."

"A clown!" Beata exclaimed. "Wouldn't it be perfect if he were the Fool? The Fool Card usually depicts a court jester, but we could interpret that to also mean a clown."

"That's it!" Alyce said. "Beata, you check out Adriano."

"But he's the prime suspect," I blurted. "I should be checking him out."

"Now, now," Alyce said. "There's plenty of work for the both of you." She swiveled on her chair, opened a file cabinet, reached in, and pulled out a file.

"Here," she said, handing it to Beata.

Beata pulled out a press release and read, "It was common knowledge that Adriano Capezio helped finance the Chicago Lyric Opera and JKL Records, where he bankrolled a fundraiser for the opera that netted $5 million. He runs a coin-operated amusement franchise involving jukeboxes and video poker. He was a known patron of several legendary opera stars, especially his daughter, Carmen."

Beata closed the folder and placed it on her lap. "He's artsy for a hood," she said.

"It does make him stand out, doesn't it? Talk to the opera administrators, see how he's been financing them," Alyce said to Beata. "I can't believe that little restaurant could be everything he's doing. Maybe his daughter found out he was into something, and she threatened to report him."

I sucked in my breath.

"Alex, I know you better than most. You'd probably do anything for a good story."

"Anything?"

"Almost anything."

"Specifically, what does that mean?"

"You need to get to know one of our editorial board members better—someone who was a good friend of Carmen's, someone who has a lot of important connections."

"Bruno?" Beata guessed correctly. "I can talk to him."

My finger started to throb. I peeked at the cut under the band-aid. It wasn't healing right.

"No, no, this is for Alex. I've noticed how he looks at you, and…well…maybe you can use that to your advantage."

"What?" I asked, shocked. Even for Alyce, a hard-core journalist, this was over the top.

A scowl formed on Alyce's face. "It's not like I'm asking you to sleep with him. Just call him for interviews. Ask him for leads. I think he'll say yes to you."

"He should say yes to any of us staff. He's on *Gypsy Magazine's* Board of Editorial Directors," I said. I did not want to be assigned to him.

"From what I hear Bruno is a master at charming women," Beata said. "But it's not like he's a threat to you, right?"

"Absolutely," I said. "He's married."

"With four children," Beata added.

"Good." Alyce's eyes widened. "Hey! He'll be staffing the information booth at the Psychic Fair this Saturday, and I'll arrange for you to join him. You'll be all alone with him."

The pain in my finger intensified.

"Okay," Alyce said. "Carmen's will. Who wants to check that out?"

"I'll do that," Beata said, before I could.

"Good," Alyce said. "Alex, that leaves Parsifal's for you."

"Parsifal's?"

"Carmen owned a spa with an operatic theme. She's had one of the Lyric chorus members managing it. I've been there a few times. It's always loaded with opera patrons."

Alyce stood up, signifying the end of our meeting, and raised her right arm. Beata did the same, and I followed. We were about to utter our magazine's motto. The three of us looked at each other and chanted, "To Pierce the Veil of Death. All for the Story."

Chapter Nine

Parsifal's Spa occupied three city lots on Oak Street Avenue, about five blocks from where I worked. Its motley-colored awning brightened the dull, gray day, its sturdy canvas shielding window-watchers from the pounding, steady rain. When I entered, I noticed the place was full, every waiting chair taken.

I shook off my black umbrella and wiped my feet on the worn welcome mat, then waited several minutes at the counter, listening to luxuriant, mellow opera music, a great wave of sound streaming from two-inch speakers above me. Four women and three men occupied the waiting chairs.

"It'll take a while," said one of the women. "Everyone from the opera is here to get their hair and nails done."

Another woman tittered.

My lips stretched, causing my cheeks to rise, but my heart wasn't into the smile.

Teresita Cuevas entered with a brisk step, gave me a once-over, and *tsked, tsked* as she looked at her appointment book.

"And you are?" she asked. She towered over the counter in a multicolored printed Versace mini-dress that would set me back three weeks of salary.

"Alexandria Vilkas. I don't have an appointment."

Teresita shook her head. "I'm sorry, but you'll have to come another day. We don't accept walk-ins."

I leaned over the counter and motioned for Teresita to do the same. I whispered as amicably as possible. "I was with you in the dressing room, just before Carmen Dellamorte died. Reporter with *Gypsy Magazine*? I'd like to talk to you about the story I'm working on."

Teresita gripped the counter with both hands and whispered back, "This is not a good time, Miss."

I straightened up and said in a normal speaking tone, "I'll

have a manicure, pedicure, and full-body massage. So wonderful of you to talk to the press about Carmen's murder, particularly since you and Jorge were with her just moments before she went onstage."

I turned to glance at the group behind me and watched them lean forward.

"Is that true, Teresita?" one of the men asked.

Teresita threw me a look that would instantly shrivel ripe plums into prunes. "Yes, it's true. I did her nails just before the show."

"Ohhh," gasped the group.

"You'll have to tell us all about it," another man said. "I'll have a haircut with my massage."

"I'll have highlights with my hair tint," said a woman.

I turned to Teresita. "Business certainly is booming."

Before Teresita could answer, a man said, "Nothing like a murder at the Lyric to get Parsifal's hopping." Everyone joined in a quick, nervous laugh.

Teresita sighed at me with a look of ill-natured defeat. "I assume you want to speak with Jorge during your massage, but he's off today. I'll do your nails personally so we can talk, all right?"

"Perfect. I'll catch Jorge another time."

"In the meantime, please take a seat. You can talk to some of the chorus members while you wait." Teresita turned to one of the women. "Michelle? Please follow me."

As Michelle left, I grabbed her chair, trying to make myself comfortable under the gaze of six Lyric chorus members. In about a minute, I knew I was talking to three sopranos, two tenors, and a bass. In the next minute, I learned the sopranos ran an electrolysis business on the side, the tenors waited tables, and the bass deejayed at weddings. They bemoaned the fact that the musicians in the orchestra earned double what they did.

After a solemn moment pervaded by Wagnerian music, a soprano asked, "How is your investigation going, dear? Have you gotten any leads?"

"I'm afraid I've just begun."

"Have you tried Castrato yet?" one of the sopranos asked. "Carmen lived with him."

"I'll be talking to him this afternoon," I said, wondering how much they knew about Castrato. "Is he really...?" I made the scissors gesture.

"Roberto went to great lengths to have the perfect voice with a female tone, incredible vocal virility, and brawn," said a soprano. "The operation has made him famous. He wouldn't be where he is today if not for that nip and tuck."

Everyone laughed.

"I think it was him," said another soprano, looking at her peers. "Well, it's always the one closest to you, isn't it?"

I nodded, smiling. "Statistically, that's true. Most murders are committed by a close family member, often over something that seems trivial to outsiders."

The group launched into an animated discussion about a few recent high profile murder cases–a husband who killed his wife for changing the TV channel, a mother who killed a daughter for eating her last chicken enchilada.

"But what about the diva's murder?" a tenor asked.

The bass spoke up. "It must be something bigger than a triviality. It was so public. Don't you think?" he asked the chorus.

I nodded, encouraging him to continue.

"No, this was a public message of some sort, premeditated. Very carefully plotted out. My God! The final scene! And she dies. How much more methodical can you get?"

"What do you think of it, Alexandria?" the tenor asked. "Come on, don't hold back."

I shook my head. "It's too early to tell. But you can call me Alex."

By this point, the conversation whirled like a dervish dance.

"I think it was the assistant conductor," said the alto soprano. "Felix Vasilakis. He's such an arrogant twit, like he owns the place. Doesn't even know the names of the orchestra or chorus."

The tenor chimed in. "Yes, I can forgive the maestro that transgression since he travels so much. No one can expect him to keep up with the names, but the assistant...well, that's what he's there for, isn't it, to manage things?"

They all looked at me. I asked, "But why do you think he'd kill the diva?"

A tenor had a slight twitch in his left eye when he said, "Are you going to be quoting us in your story–with names?"

"Certainly not. Everything you say here is just for my information. In journalism this is referred to as background," I said.

The tenor, now relaxed, bent forward and the others in the group leaned closer. "The assistant conductor is sexually active, you know. A door whore, a date in and out of your door for one thing only, sort of like Avon calling, but offering skin rather than Skin So Soft."

Everyone laughed.

"Of course, it's just rumors," the tenor hastily added. "But the diva openly threatened him during the last dress rehearsal."

"Threatened him about what?" I asked.

"A lover."

"What did she say? Exactly," I asked.

Now we were in a huddle. "Felix was conducting, taking the diva through *Una macchia*. The orchestra played at a lackluster pace, always does with him. He's hopelessly disorganized and doesn't inspire anyone. No one even looks at him when he conducts!"

"Get on with it," the other tenor interrupted.

"Anyway, during this aria, Carmen had trouble, and somehow Felix noticed, called her attention to it, and they repeated the phrase."

Heads nodded. "Now this can be tricky with divas," the tenor said to me. "You don't want to highlight their weakness in front of a crowd for too long. He probably should have gone over the aria with her in private later, but instead, he kept hammering away, driving her to the breaking point. Until she screamed, 'Felix Vasilakis, if we don't stop now, I will sing at the top of my voice what I saw yesterday!'"

"Oh!" I gasped. "What did she see?"

The tenor leaned back, and so did everyone else. "We don't know, she didn't say. But Felix stopped the aria right then and there, and Carmen walked offstage in a huff. We had to continue the rest of the rehearsal without her."

Romantic German opera music played in the background, a golden stream of tone, while we dwelled on our thoughts. I stretched my legs, walked to a low table with the oversized chalice overflowing with costume jewelry, and grabbed a bottle of designer water. Above the table hung several eight-by-ten color photos of opera scenes. One of the photos featured Teresita as Kundry, the cursed shape shifter, in Wagner's opera Parsifal at the Nacional de Bellas Artes in Paraguay.

"Paraguay. Huh," I said, admiring Teresita's dramatic pose, her arms raised high in a shimmering silver dress, wondering how she landed as a chorus member in Chicago.

"After Carmen finished singing, a man in a black turtleneck and pants stood waiting for her backstage," said the bass. "Did any of you notice that?"

I turned around to join the group again. The others nodded.

"Yes," said a soprano. "I didn't recognize him. Only saw him from the back."

"Really?" I said. "This could be important."

"A black turtleneck and dark pants," another soprano said. "That should narrow it down."

The chorus twittered while I remained silent, the last to understand the implication. Most men who attend the opera wear black, meaning at least a thousand men that Sunday afternoon probably wore a black turtleneck and pants.

Teresita appeared and asked me to follow her down a hallway and into another room, strewn with small round stones along the walls, in the corners, and in little baskets. Fourteen manicurists, beauticians, and masseurs tended to the patrons, everyone buzzing about Carmen's murder. Back here, the nail polish fumes reeked.

"It's been raining for three straight days," Teresita said, as my feet soaked in a mini Jacuzzi. "I wonder when it will stop."

"Can't go on much longer," I said, fingering one of the stones.

Teresita asked me to take my feet out of the swirling water, then methodically scraped the dead skin with her razor, piling the tiny shavings into a small mound. Hunched over, she tossed the shavings with one swift motion into the receptacle, dunked her razor into sterilizing alcohol, clinking the jar as she swirled, and ripped into the ball of my right foot. My last pedicure wasn't this brutal! Was this intentional on Teresita's part since she was unhappy about being interviewed? She peeled the hardened skin intently, neither one of us wanting to ruin her concentration. With her last stroke, she broke the silence.

"You on lunch break?" she asked.

"Yes," I answered. "As I said earlier, I'm a reporter for *Gypsy Magazine*, a few blocks away. Ever hear of it?"

Teresita shrugged her shoulders, then grabbed an Emory board to scrub my sensitive soles. "Ticklish?"

I nodded, gripping the arm rests like a passenger in my mother's car. Next came the foot rub with an apricot-scented scrub.

"Tell me about *Gypsy Magazine*," Teresita said, towel-drying my feet.

"Our motto is 'To pierce the veil of death.'"

Teresita looked up from my feet, scrutinizing my face for a long moment.

"I want to ask you a few questions."

Teresita was now massaging my feet, stretching each toe to its maximum length.

"When I left after interviewing Carmen, you were still with her in the dressing room. How much longer did you stay?"

"I left after she went on stage."

"That would be shortly after I left then, right?"

"Maybe ten minutes later. I cleaned up, then left."

"Where did you go?"

"The police already asked me all these questions. I had to get dressed myself. I'm in the chorus."

"Yes, of course." A life-size brass armor of a knight with a sword at its feet stood in the room's corner. "I noticed your photo in the reception area, as Kundry in Parsifal."

Teresita shrugged her shoulders. "That was a long time ago."

"The opera theme works well here."

"I've always loved opera."

Teresita continued rubbing my legs.

"How did you meet Carmen?"

She seemed to be studying me as much as I was analyzing her.

"At the Lyric. I competed against fifty other women for the chorus position, and Carmen was there that day. She spoke to me kindly, congratulating me, said she had heard of me in Paraguay. It was grand of her to notice me, I suppose. She had a reputation for being melodramatic, having temper tantrums."

"La Tempestua."

Teresita pushed a hair away with the back of her hand. "Yes. I remember the day like yesterday, soon after I arrived eleven years ago. We performed in La Boheme together, and after opening night, she found me backstage and gave me one of her bouquets of flowers, red roses. Said she wanted to help me, that if I needed anything, to just ask."

"Magnanimous."

Teresita fluttered her eyelids and sniffed to hold back tears. "After that, I was drawn to her, like a groupie. She didn't have too many of those. I suppose I worshipped her, practically laid myself at her feet. She listened to me sing, gave me advice, and even recommended me to the right people. But..."

Teresita hung her head, closed her eyes shut, choked back a sob. "I can't believe she's gone. She's always been so good to me."

"Do you have family here?"

Her eyes lit up, and she smiled. "In Asuncion. I have two brothers and my mother."

"Chicago must seem like another planet."

Teresita placed spongy purple toe separators on my feet.

"Adriano Capezio discovered me at the University of Asuncion. I'd heard how he helps singers with potential, so I approached him, eventually auditioned for him. It went well, and he said he had connections in Chicago. At first, I didn't want to leave my family. Finally, he convinced me."

"What was Carmen's father doing in Paraguay?"

"I…I don't know."

The way Teresita stiffened her back gave away her lie.

"So here you are without your family, and you had to get a real job to pay your bills."

"Adriano suggested I work here at his daughter's spa. I started as a manicurist, then Carmen and Castrato asked me to take over. I got the idea of changing it into Parsifal's with an operatic theme, and the rest is history."

Something wasn't adding up with Teresita's story, but I couldn't put my finger on it. "How well do you know Adriano?"

"Like anybody else, I guess. If you mean, did I know how Adriano treated his daughter, well, he argued with Carmen frequently. He managed her entire career. I thought her most ungrateful, taking his help for granted. He gave her everything. Everything! Made her into a diva. His master creation."

Choral music saturated the long pause.

"I know what you're thinking," Teresita said. "That I resent being in the chorus, that I should be the diva."

"Well, I…"

"I only wish I had a father like Carmen's. He made everything revolve around Carmen's voice, like we all had to handle it like a delicate piece of china. Nothing more important. Carmen was very lucky."

"When you left her dressing room, where did you go?"

"Upstairs with the chorus."

"That champagne bottle that her father sent. You

remember. With the note 'To make the poison go down easier.' Was it still corked when you left?"

Teresita nodded. "Yes."

"Jorge left just before you entered. Do you know where he went?"

She shrugged her shoulders in a show of disgust. "He has ten cats. That's all he thinks about. I imagine he rushed home to be with them."

I remembered the pendant of a cat hanging from his neck and how I noticed cat hairs on his clothes. A cat lover.

"Have you heard she may have been poisoned with rubbing alcohol, the kind which Jorge used during his massage?"

"Yes, I read that in the paper. Jorge's no killer. He loved Carmen. We all did."

Teresita rubbed moisturizing cream into my calves. "I know you didn't ask me who I think did it, but I don't like the assistant director. She talked about him when I did her nails."

"Felix Vasilakis?"

"Yes."

"Why didn't she like him?"

"He pushed her hard, maybe too hard."

"But why would he kill her?"

Teresita shrugged. "Just a feeling. He's been spending more time at Carmen's place this past year, and Carmen didn't like that. They argued a lot. What color nail polish do you want? You like this scarlet red?"

A tray of nail polish stood nearby and I reached over to grab a creamy bronze. "Uh, this one looks good."

She shook the bottle vigorously. "I hope you figure out who killed Carmen. She doesn't deserve this."

"No one does."

When my nails were dry, I headed to Castrato's.

But I departed the spa with an uneasy feeling because I sensed Teresita had left a great deal unsaid. How did she really meet Adriano Capezio? Why would she leave Paraguay as a reigning diva and come here to be a chorus member? She practically worshipped Carmen, but I also sensed she resented her. Was the resentment strong enough to kill her?

Chapter Ten

Castrato, the diva's roommate, had an apartment just off Belmont Avenue on Lake Shore Drive, the highway that hugs Lake Michigan. After the valet whisked away my thirteen-year-old Toyota Corolla, I approached the front desk and asked for Roberto Andretti. After the secretary telephoned him to announce my arrival, she pointed me toward the elevators.

Castrato, blond and thin, stood waiting at his apartment door in a pink silk robe, his lacquered red nails gleaming. He had an aristocratic face with a wide forehead and well-defined jaw. He seemed eager to usher me in with an impatient little wave of his hand. Seventeenth century art hung on his white walls. The furniture had a Queen Anne flavor.

Standing near the dining room table, Felix Vasilakis had his coat draped over his arm. His eyelids drooped slightly over a long, hound-dog face with eyebrows that curved like crescent moons.

"Are you going?" Castrato asked with a frown. "I thought you'd stay with me while I speak to Alexandria Vilkas, that reporter I told you about."

I stepped forward and shook Felix's hand. "We met in Carmen's dressing room. Actually, I'd like to talk to you too, if you have an extra moment."

Felix let go of my hand abruptly. "Yes, well..." He put his coat on and buttoned it, avoiding my gaze. "Another time. I must go."

"Can I call you?" I asked.

Ignoring my question, he said good-bye and left in a brusque manner as if he couldn't get out of Castrato's apartment fast enough.

After Castrato closed the door, he explained, "He had another appointment. Don't take it personally."

I couldn't help but wonder why Felix had avoided my gaze

or why he hadn't answered me when I asked if I could call him. "No, of course."

Now I became more determined than ever to find a way to talk to him. But I would have to think about that later.

Castrato led me into his living room. A white grand piano shared the spotlight with the window that overlooked Lake Michigan, now a gray that matched the sky.

"Do you ever get tired of that?" I asked, pointing to his view.

"Eat your heart out, honey," Castrato said, as he nodded toward the full-bodied burgundy sofa. "I'm glad you've come."

Once I sat down, I took out the tape recorder, notebook, and pen, as Castrato fidgeted with his robe. He had a chiseled nose and cupid lips, medium-boned, but his hands were large, like a man's. Up close, the long red nails seemed incongruous on his masculine, hairy hands.

I decided to start the interview delicately. "So Carmen was allergic to cats?"

Castrato's eyes widened. "What gave you that idea? She owns a cat–name's Tango. In fact, I had to find him a new owner. She's coming any minute to pick him up."

"But when I interviewed her on Sunday, she told her understudy she was allergic to cats. Her understudy wanted to give her a kitten as a parting gift, and Carmen reacted as if Donacella were giving her a bomb. I don't understand."

Castrato looked confused, then stroked his chin. I didn't notice any stubble, and wondered if he had to shave. "The only allergy Carmen had was to her understudy, who was fifty pounds lighter and twenty years younger. She must have feared Donacella wanted to steal the show."

Could Carmen's reaction to the kitten have all been an act, just a ruse to disarm her understudy? If she owned a cat herself, there was no other explanation. "Hmm, that's odd. Well, I really came to talk to you about her father."

"Did you get the material on him?"

"Yes, but I still haven't had a chance to go through it."

"Where is it? I thought you were going to bring it with

you."

"Uh…" I didn't want to tell Castrato it was at work. I still didn't trust him, as he seemed too interested in the box. As the diva's roommate, he knew her better than anybody else, and he could be the murderer. "It's still at home."

"You are going to give it back to me, aren't you? Under the circumstances?"

The look on Carmen's face when she gave me the box still haunted me. She wanted to keep it a secret, and if she didn't talk about it with her roommate, she must have had a good reason. I had to think fast. "I…uh…need to give it to the police first, if you must know. It's evidence."

Castrato pursed his lips with an angry determination, then worked at looking calm again. Why did he care about the box this deeply? "Yes, I suppose you're right," he said. "Have you found anything interesting in the box?"

"Paperbacks on the Outfit, her diary, some notebooks and photos."

Castrato clapped his hands. "The Mob! I bet it's true. He has much more money than he could ever own just through his restaurant. And I've seen how her father controlled her– probably just the way he controls anyone working for him. It's been making me sick."

"You think he knew about her plans to write an exposé on him?"

"That's just it! Days before her death, she threatened to write the book and reveal all his secrets. He laughed at her, said she didn't have what it took to write a book, that once she started, she'd be overwhelmed with how much work it takes. He said she'd drink cyanide and kill herself before she'd ever be capable of writing a book."

"In light of what happened, do you think her father had anything to do with her death?"

Castrato's previously suppressed flash of anger returned in full bloom. "That man is a monster! You don't know him. He's capable of murdering his daughter, oh yes. That's why I'm so interested in that box, if you must know. I bet there's something in there that would prove he killed her. He can't get away with it, no matter how many millions of dollars he has, or how powerful he is."

"No, of course." I fingered a pillow nearby, needlepointed with a tree-of-life design. "It probably has no bearing on the case, but I was wondering if you could explain your own background."

"I'm Italian."

"That's not what I meant."

"Oh, you mean my special operation?"

I crossed my legs. "Yes."

He extended his fingers and admired his long, red nails, then clasped his hands together. "I grew up in a crazy Italian household; always felt I should be a girl."

"I see."

"Don't ask me why. I longed to wear frilly dresses, curl my hair into golden locks, paint my fingernails."

"What did your parents say?"

"My parents?" He looked across the room at the dining room table with cabriole legs and drake feet, surrounded by fiddle-backed chairs. "They died when I was in the fifth grade." He grabbed a tissue and blew his nose. "They were in a car wreck, and my uncle raised me."

"I'm sorry."

"Don't be. I do miss my mother, but not my father. He called me a sissy, made fun of me."

"Must have been hard for you."

"Not for long. I think of him every now and then, but I'm glad he's gone." Castrato stared off.

"So when did you decide to…"

"Have my operation?"

"Yes."

"As soon as I could, when I turned eleven. By then I'd been singing in the school chorus for years. A famous conductor told me I had a beautiful voice, a soprano. I played the roles of Arsace, Orlando, Orfeo, Neocle, Rinaldo, and Tancredi."

I nodded. These were known as trouser roles today, where a woman plays a man's role because the voice register is so high. Four hundred years ago these roles were specifically created for the legendary castrati.

Castrato continued. "Castration prevents a boy's larynx from becoming fully transformed, allowing the voice to retain its magnificence."

"If you don't mind my saying, I thought the practice of castrating promising young singers was outlawed."

"You're not wrong. But I got my operation on the sly."

"On the sly?"

"I didn't want to lose my voice. I was a boy wonder. I asked my uncle if I could get castrated. Of course he said no, at first. But I persisted, begged him night and day. He made some phone calls and finally found a doctor who would do it. Said he wanted to write it up for a medical journal."

"Where did you get the money?"

"Trust fund from my parents."

"I see. Do you remember the name of the doctor?"

"Yes, it was… Oh, I'll have to get it to you later."

Why did he stop? Should I press him or let him continue with the story? I made a note to remind him, and one for myself to track down the journal article. "And then what happened?"

"I had the operation."

"Where?"

"Some hospital in Cleveland. I can't seem to remember the name. Does it really matter?"

"I'm just trying to be thorough." I looked at him. "Does it bother you that we're talking about it?"

"Not really. I haven't talked about it like this for years." He grabbed another tissue and started to cry. "Not since my heart-to-heart with Carmen. She was my best friend, like a sister to me." He took a moment to collect himself.

"After the operation, my life continued as before. No one knew what happened, except my uncle. I loved the stage, and the fans adored me right back."

"Go on."

"By the time I turned sixteen, people noticed my voice still hadn't changed."

"What about your fantasy of being a girl? I mean, as long as you were getting an operation, why didn't you go...you know...all the way?"

"Opera is everything to me. I needed my penis to maintain the uniqueness of my voice. Castratos only have their testicles removed. That's how we retain that special quality in our voice. I had to be a male with a soprano voice to stay in opera. That's the only way the roles kept coming. At school, I was a boy. Onstage I played a boy in the trouser roles, but a real boy. And at home, my uncle let me wear dresses, pantyhose, and high-heeled shoes. He'd treat me to make-up and a manicure. It was like being in heaven."

"Where's your uncle today?"

Castrato took a sharp breath and grabbed another tissue. "He died."

"How?"

"I'd reached college by then, so I'm not sure."

My frown betrayed my disbelief.

Castrato covered his eyes and he sobbed again. He looked up, and through a choked voice said, "He killed himself."

"I'm sorry." I waited a moment for Castrato to collect himself. "How did you wind up with Carmen?"

"Like I said, I was a sophomore in college, wearing women's clothes."

I nodded, acting as if I heard about this sort of behavior every day.

"But I still couldn't get any roles on stage. I was like every other actress, just not as beautiful."

I stretched out my hand and patted his...or, er...her hand. "But you are."

"You're just saying that."

"No, really. Your features are very...uh...arresting–the pouty lips, the brooding eyes."

Apparently placated, he twirled the tissue around his

forefinger. "You're very sweet."

"The diva?" I began again.

"So then, after my uncle's death, I transferred to another college in New York, and decided to come out in the open as a cross-dresser. I started out fresh."

"It must have been liberating."

"Oh, it was! It was! Finally, I found success at getting cast in operatic roles on New York stages receiving top billing as Castrato. After the Met, all the opera companies wanted me. I could practically choose my roles."

"And the name of the college?"

He moved right on without answering my question. "I toured so many opera companies across the country. It was incredible. And the Lyric Opera House, they went all out for me. They set up a private dinner between the diva and me, and Carmen told me all about the company. Of course, I didn't give a hoot about the Lyric. They're just as political as any other house. But Carmen! By the end of dinner, she invited me to move in."

"That's incredible."

"It was like we had known each other from another lifetime, like we understood each other completely."

"Twelve years ago?"

"Yes."

"How was it, living with her?"

"I loved it. We shared clothes, make-up, stories, and of course, our love of opera. Do you want to see her bedroom?"

"Yes, I'd love to."

He led me into her bedroom, which was decorated in a baroque style–all in breathtaking shades of peach, pink, gold, and dark violet. On top of her king-size bed lay twenty gowns, most of them unzipped, as if someone had been trying them on recently. I looked at Castrato with new eyes. Would he keep her clothes for himself? Was he already trying them on? I thought that was in bad taste, just days after her death. On the other hand, perhaps it was just his way to get closer to her. I'd heard of people wearing clothes of their recently departed loved ones as a way to maintain their connection to them.

Castrato stood at her dresser, familiar with her accoutrements. "Here it is." He picked up a big fancy silver jar. "She keeps her nails here."

She had a collection of hundreds of carpenter's nails. Most about three inches long, and all bent in that style she'd considered so lucky.

"And here are her Tarot cards." Castrato opened a mahogany armoire filled with various decks of Tarot cards, as well as incense, colorful scarves, and perfumes. Her cards were neatly arranged on one shelf, near a blue velvet piece of rolled-up cloth. Apparently she laid her cards on that cloth when she did a reading.

"She worked with the cards every day. It was her passion. She really believed in them."

"Did she ever do readings for you?"

"Oh yes. She called me her fool. She saw something special in me that no one else could. I really loved Carmen." He grabbed another tissue. "Where are my manners? Oh, dear. Would you like something to drink? Some tea, perhaps? Or something stronger?"

"Tea is fine, thanks."

As Castrato walked toward the kitchen, I remained in her bedroom. Near the armoire, she had a desk with a shelf on top of it filled with books of poetry. I noticed a collection by John Keats as well as other poets–Shelley, Yeats, and Bacon. These four were set apart and placed on a corner of the desk. I opened the book by Keats, looking for the passage that she had inscribed and left in the box of material on her father. I found it highlighted:

"This living hand, now warm and capable of earnest grasping, would, if it were cold.

And in the icy silence of the tomb, So haunt thy days and chill thy dreaming nights."

The word "tomb" was underlined three times in this book. Why did Carmen do that?

The doorbell rang.

"Can you get it?" Castrato yelled from the kitchen.

When I opened the door, I tried to maintain an expression of respect toward the woman standing before me. She wore a psychedelic muumuu that covered her three-hundred-pound frame. She had wild, spiky yellow hair pointed in every direction, accented by a delicate orange bow, with her short bangs gelled to the right side. She looked like a cross between Betty Boop and Mama Cass.

"Hi, I'm Claire Fergusson, here to pick up Tango."

Castrato came back with the tea and set it on the table. He walked into the bathroom and came out with a cage containing a white cat wearing a diamond collar.

"In a cage? You put Carmen's cat in a cage?" Claire screamed.

"Oh, stop being so melodramatic," Castrato said. "He's only been in there an hour or so. Here." He thrust the cage at Claire, then turned to me. "This is Carmen's publicist. Also an animal psychic. She volunteered to adopt Tango. Claire, this is Alexandria Vilkas. She's writing a story about Carmen's murder. Maybe you should talk to her."

"Maybe I should." Claire smiled and nodded, then she closed her eyes and waved her arm over me, caressing my aura. "Oh. Okay."

Castrato closed the door and left us, rolling his eyes, to fiddle with the tea.

She opened her eyes. "May I?" She picked a cat hair off my pink sweater.

"Sure."

"How did you get this cat?"

"From a friend."

"Hmmm." She picked off another cat hair and held it for a moment, closed her eyes, breathed deeply, and went into a momentary trance. Her body stiffened for a few moments, then went limp. "She's a very special cat. Did you know that? She can help you solve cases."

"Cases? What cases?"

"Murder cases. You're on one now, aren't you?"

"Yeah, but…" How did she know I was on a murder case? Of course, she knew Carmen was killed…perhaps she just figured it out.

"It's your calling. You're meant to do it. The universe will send you the murder cases that need to be solved. It's part of the plan."

I felt flustered. It was one thing for Alyce to convince me I'd be writing about murder to increase the magazine's circulation, quite another for an animal psychic to predict my future in murder cases, especially with my cat. Yet maybe this psychic sensed The Wizard's plan for me to enter the Order of the Tarot.

"But you need to pay more attention to your cat. You're ignoring her too much. You're too self-absorbed in your own interests. Cats are people too, you know."

"I…uh…" I stuttered, feeling embarrassed.

Tango meowed. "What did he say?" I asked Claire.

"You're Siddharma's guardian, not her owner."

"Come again?"

"You look at yourself as her owner, like a slave owner, but you need to think of yourself as her guardian. It's your responsibility to make sure she's comfortable. Your cat will bring out the animal in you. In fact, you remind me of a wolf."

"Vilkas means wolf in Lithuanian."

"You miss your father, don't you?"

I was a bit stunned by the truth of her question. "He died when I was young. I barely remember him."

"It's why you're doing this."

"Doing what?"

"Covering the supernatural. You want to connect with your father again."

"I do?"

Then a look of panic crossed Claire's face. "Oh, wait a minute!" She held up my cat hair in both hands above her head and turned it, like an antenna to the southwest side of the city. "She's in trouble."

"Who?"

Claire grimaced. "Your cat. You need to get home right away. Go! Go! Go!"

97

Chapter Eleven

I arrived at home at dusk. A steady rain spat upon Chicago; however, the temperature threatened to plunge and I could feel snow on the way. The streetlights flicked on and off, as if unable to decide whether or not they were needed. I pulled into the garage, an immaculate slab of concrete encased by beige aluminum siding. Gardening tools hung neatly on hooks along the north wall.

I rushed up the back staircase and unlocked the back door, then inhaled sharply as I entered the kitchen. The kitchen table lay on its side, and the cabinet doors hung ajar. I dropped my bags and keys to the floor and covered my mouth with my hands. "Oh, my Goddess!"

I inspected the rest of the apartment, listening for signs of an intruder. It was quiet, but I couldn't find Siddharma. The clothes from my closet had been heaped on the floor, and the paper files in my writing studio scattered like a second carpet. My computer had been turned on; someone had searched through my electronic files. I had never created a password, too afraid I'd forget it, but now I regretted it.

The living room remained relatively unscathed, but there wasn't much to damage–an old sofa, a newer easy chair, a scuffed cocktail table, a medium-sized television set. My father's violin sat in its place on a wall shelf. The place seemed eerily quiet. My Siddharma! Where was Siddharma? I checked the front door. When I opened it and inspected the locks, they had been forced open with something like an axe.

I ran down the front staircase to the entrance. The door to the street was swinging wide open as gusts of cold wind blew in. The small foyer floor had a thin layer of dirt and a few scattered dry leaves, signs that the break-in occurred some time ago. Did the intruder take Siddharma?

"Mr. Mindy! Mr. Mindy!" I shouted, pounding on his

front door.

A muffled voice grunted.

I grabbed the doorknob and rattled it, pounding into the door with my hip, but it wouldn't open.

Another garbled sound came from Mindy.

"Are you all right?" I asked.

He moaned.

"Hold on, Mr. Mindy!"

I ran back up the front staircase, through my apartment, and crossed the kitchen, where I caught sight of a paper in the kitty litter box that didn't belong there. I approached the box slowly. Someone had left a note, steaming hot with fresh hate. On it, scrawled in black marker, was the question, "Did you hug your kitty today?"

Where was Siddharma? Unfortunately, I didn't have the luxury of worrying about her right now…I had to save Mindy.

After running down the rear staircase, I found Mindy's back door open. His enclosed back porch was neatly arranged with a bookcase and an old bed, but the kitchen door had been chopped with an axe along its left edge. The doorknob practically fell off into my hand, and I found Mindy's apartment in total disarray.

Poor Mindy sat in the dining room, his arms and legs duct-taped to a wooden dining room chair. I removed the tape on his mouth with trembling hands.

"Oh, Mindy. You poor thing. I'm so sorry. This is all my fault." I couldn't stop feeling guilty. "What did they do to you? You're supposed to be safe in your retirement, not harassed and tied to a chair."

"Will you just take off this tape? All you talking is worse than the beating from those two goof-balls."

Tears welled up in my eyes. "Oh, Mr. Mindy. I'm so sorry." I stooped down to give him a hug.

"Will you just untape my arms? Jezau! It's bad enough being tied to chair. Now I have to stand your hugs!"

I nodded as I tried to rip the tape off his arms, but it had been wound so tightly that I couldn't remove it.

"Look for scissors in that china cabinet." He looked to the battered hutch with its batwing-shaped drawers.

I opened the top drawer and retrieved a pair of old, nicked scissors. As I cut through the silver tape to free him, I had a million questions and wanted to inspect his apartment for clues.

Of course, this was now an official crime scene begging for a call to the police. "I'm calling my friend, a cop. Okay?"

Mindy nodded and stood up. "I need a shot." He put his hand on his hips and twisted a bit, grimacing, then pointed toward the kitchen. "Look in freezer."

"Coming right up." I headed for the kitchen. Mindy tiptoed over to his gold-colored couch and slowly sank into it, gripping the side arm as he did.

His kitchen had a similar layout to my own, with the same veneer oak cabinets. All the cabinet doors were ajar, although the dishes had been left intact.

"You want ice, Mr. Mindy?" I shouted.

"No, just pour straight, and fill whole glass."

It was a six-inch-tall glass. I filled it with chilled Stolichnaya and brought it to him, hoping it would help calm him down.

He gulped down half of it. "Vodka! The only thing those Commie bastards did right."

As he purred over his liquid, I inspected his apartment to make sure the intruder still wasn't hiding here. I peeked into his bedroom, just off the kitchen, and noticed his mattress was overturned. His clothes hung from opened dresser drawers, and his closet had been emptied onto the floor.

I thought of Siddharma–I had a terrible feeling about where she was. I wanted to talk to Joe without Mindy overhearing me, so after I made sure no one was hiding here, I left Mindy to call Joe from my apartment. First I left a message on his work voice mail, then his home, next his emergency number. For good measure, I e-mailed his home and office.

I made a cup of peppermint tea to calm myself down while I waited for Joe to call me back. The phone rang.

"Joe?"

"Are you stalking me?" He sounded angry.

"Someone broke into my apartment. My landlord's, too."

"I'm sorry to hear that. Did you call 911?"

"I called you, Joe, as a friend. I have a delicate situation here, and you're the only one who can help. I need to avoid a big crime scene."

Joe groaned. "I just got promoted six months ago. I don't want to jeopardize my position."

My heart sank. "Of course, you're right. I shouldn't have called you."

"Do you think this might have anything to do with Carmen's death?"

"I… Yes. I think her father has something to do with the break-in."

Joe's voice softened. "How come?"

"Because I have something of his that I think he was looking for."

There was a long moment of silence. "What could you have that Adriano Capezio would want?"

I thought about the best way to tell Joe what Carmen had given me. It was no use hiding it now; I only hoped I didn't jeopardize Siddharma because of my foolishness. Did the thugs take her as a ransom for the box? "I have his life story, possibly all the details of what he's been involved with over the past fifty years. His daughter gave it all to me just before she died."

Joe whistled. "I'll be right over. I remember where you live."

"Thanks, Joe, and hurry. I'm anxious to question Mindy, but I'll wait for you."

"Alex, be careful. Are you sure the bad guys are gone?"

"Yes, I'm sure, but I wouldn't mind you being here in case they come back."

After Joe hung up, I felt better for a moment until I thought about Siddharma. Save for my mother, Siddharma was the only family I had. Who did this? And why did they have to kidnap my cat?

As I ran downstairs to check up on Mindy, my mind raced

through the possibilities–but it always paused on Adriano Capezio, who must have learned Carmen sent me the material. How did he find out? The only person who knew about it was Castrato, although Teresita noticed the box while she was in Carmen's dressing room. Perhaps she had figured something out.

Mindy was sipping his drink. I doubted it was the same one I poured earlier.

"The police are on their way," I said.

"Good, good."

I wanted to ask him so many questions, but I thought it would be best if I waited for Joe to be here while Mindy talked.

My finger looked swollen and red, the cut made just yesterday. Jeez, who had time for this? I looked around Mindy's place and vowed to clean it up for him tomorrow. As Mindy sipped his vodka, I made some tea for myself in his kitchen. Then the bell rang.

I opened the door for Joe, who was out of uniform, wearing gray sweats and a navy parka, glistening wet from the steady rain.

"Thank Goddess you're here. I was just having some tea. You want some?"

The expression on Joe's face looked like I just offered him piss in a beer bottle. "Let's just go straight to your landlord, do you mind?"

"Sure, sure." Joe followed me. I gently pushed open Mindy's door and saw him swirling his drink.

"Mr. Mindy, this is Lieutenant Joe Burke. He's going to ask you a few questions, okay?"

Joe moved forward to shake his hand, and in return, Mindy said, "You get those sums of bitches, eh?"

Joe threw me a sideways glance before he assessed the damage in the apartment. "Looks like they made quite a mess." His eyes rested on the tattered shreds of tape. "They tied you up, Mindy?"

Mindy waved like he was conducting an orchestra.

"Okay, why don't you start from the beginning and tell me

everything you remember," Joe said, pulling out his notebook.

Mindy cleared his throat. "I was cooking scrambles, just minding my business when I heard '*kraak, kraaak*.'"

"What time was this?" Joe asked.

Mindy looked in the air for a second, then said, "After four o'clock. I was listening to Lithuanian rock star on radio in kitchen. Then newsman say it was four. I show you kitchen."

Mindy tried to stand up, but spilled the drink over himself and flopped back onto the couch. Joe took a step forward. "Here, let me help you, sir."

Mindy wiped his wet shirt with his hand and licked his fingers. "Aach, such a waste!"

We decided to stay in the living room.

"Okay, Mindy, why don't you tell us what happened," Joe began again.

Mindy placed his two hands on his head. "Ay-yai-yai." He pointed at the kitchen door. "There was pounding, pounding. Then I saw axe. They broke my door."

"Who?"

"Two men."

"What did they look like?"

"They were white. Wore blue jeans."

"Did you see their faces?" Joe asked.

"They wear orange ski masks. One always shouting, 'Where is it? Where is it?'"

"'What?' I ask. 'The papers,' he say. 'What papers?' I ask." Mindy looked at me. "But I knew what they look for. That big box trouble. I knew. That's why that Cadillac was in fron' of house."

Joe looked my way with an expression that said he expected a full explanation from me later, then turned back to Mindy.

"They grab me from behind, slap my head, then push me in here. Again they ask about papers. 'I doan know,' I keep say. They put me in that chair and tape me up. Then they go through house. Make such mess. Then they go upstairs and look. They come down, place axe in front door, and leave out back. Before they go, they say, 'We have message for reporter. Tell her get off story.'"

Joe shot me a look that weakened my knees. I took a chair next to Mindy and listened to Joe ask his follow-up questions. They covered the scenario a couple of more times, but essentially the story stayed the same.

"Can you think of any more questions?" Joe asked me.

"Mr. Mindy, what about my cat?"

Mindy furrowed his brow. "When they came back down here, they had black bag and inside I heard cat screaming. 'Tell your renter if we doan get what we want, her cat will go to better life.'"

"Oh no," I groaned. It was my worst fear realized, but instantly I vowed to myself I would get her back.

"I am tired now," Mindy said. "You go to bed and come back tomorrow to help me clean, no?" Mindy reached out his hand, and stroked my cheek. "You good girl, Alex. You good girl. Such shame." His eyes moistened, and he wiped them.

"Get some sleep, Mr. Mindy. I'll see you tomorrow."

We climbed the stairs slowly, Joe following me up the staircase, through my living room, my dining room, and into the kitchen. Once we sat down at the table, I gave him the cat note. After he studied it, he said, "This could be just the start, Alex. I think these guys mean business."

Of course Joe was right. My guilt over not telling him about the box right after Carmen's death consumed me. Poor Mindy! And what did I do to Siddharma? The only relief available to me was to confess everything to Joe.

Chapter Twelve

It took about an hour to recount the interview with Carmen for Joe, and this time I told him about the box. By the time we finished, Joe's notebook brimmed with scrawls, diagrams, arrows, and underlined and circled words. I was too upset to sit still when I talked and spent much of the hour cleaning up the kitchen–closing the cupboards, rearranging my spices, and sweeping the floor, all the while answering Joe's questions.

"Are you sure you've told me everything?" Joe asked.

"I swear I didn't leave anything out." I swept the last bit of crumbs into the dustpan and dumped it all into the receptacle.

Joe sipped a glass of soda. "What about that money from Carmen? Some of my colleagues would ask whether you were trying to bribe her."

"No way! You heard what I said. She wanted me to write the book about her dear old dad, that's all! And besides, I never got any of the money. She never had a chance to give it me."

"But you took the job."

"Look, I'm not particularly happy about how this assignment turned out." How could I tell Joe about The Wizard's test for me to enter the Order of the Tarot? That I thought Carmen's special project was all part of my test? I couldn't. The Wizard had sworn me to secrecy. "I just…I just saw it as a way to advance at *Gypsy Magazine*, a career move."

"But why didn't you tell me about it? That box is evidence in a murder case."

"It was stupid, I know. Okay? God, it was my big break, and for two hours I thought I had my entire life figured out. I'd write the book on her father, get paid, get it published, and then write my ticket to anywhere I wanted to go. When she died, all that vanished. I wasn't thinking straight. And I didn't get that box until the next day. I thought maybe I could still write the book on her father."

"It was very foolish of you."

"I know."

"Look, you're not supposed to know this, but we've been keeping an eye on Adriano Capezio for quite some time. He has a prior arrest record. The CPD organized crime squad guys say he's been involved in specific things around Taylor Street. That's about as much as I can tell you for now, and I'd appreciate it if you would keep this information to yourself. In the meantime, stay off the case. This is not a guy you want to mess around with."

Joe finished his soda as I nursed my second cup of tea.

"Where did you stash the material?"

"It's all at work. I was going to make copies of everything before I called you, and I meant to do that after my afternoon interview. But there was this animal psychic at Castrato's home who told me to rush home. She knew Siddharma was in danger."

Without a look of surprise, Joe asked, "What animal psychic?"

"Her name's Claire Fergusson. She was Carmen's publicist."

Joe wrote her name in his notebook with a serious expression.

At that moment, I decided I'd call Claire the next day and ask her to help me find Siddharma. I told Joe how she'd picked up a piece of cat hair from my sweater and felt danger.

He looked skeptical. "It's funny she knew something was going on here. Anyway, I need to get that box."

"I haven't had a chance to read it all myself."

"It's police evidence, part of a crime investigation. You're going to have to hand it over. I'm sorry."

"What about freedom of the press?"

"Don't pull that First Amendment crap on me. You're going to have to hand over the evidence. I'll come by tomorrow first thing in the morning and pick it up."

I leaned back in my chair. "All right."

"Are you going to be okay tonight?"

"Yeah, I'll be fine."

After we said good-bye, I cleaned up the rest of the mess in my apartment, moving from room to room, putting everything back in place, saving my writing studio for last. It took more than two hours to put all the paper back into the right folders, arrange books back onto their shelves, and dump the excess into two white kitchen garbage bags. The intruders didn't touch my pouch of lock-picking tools on the top shelf of my closet. I fingered them, wondering when I'd have to use them, then put them back.

They had dumped my father's mementos from a wicker box, which was about the size of a sewing kit. I picked up a photo of him playing the violin, another of me sitting on his lap during an intermission at the Lyric Opera House. Soon my vision blurred and I wiped the tears. These were among the few treasured items I had of my father and I shook in rage that they were disturbed. How dare they invade my personal space like this! Whoever did this would have to answer to me. I wasn't going to let the disturbance of my father's items go unnoticed.

Chapter Thirteen

Day Four, Wednesday, March 26

At the top of my to-do-list this morning was speaking to Claire, the animal psychic, even before handing over the box of material to Lt. Joe Burke. He'd be upset, but I was getting used to that.

Driving through rush-hour morning traffic, I flicked on the windshield wipers to clear away the snowflakes. The radio announcer predicted more snow–common weather for early spring in Chicago. I called Joe and left him a message to let him know I'd be late, then grimaced as I imagined his angry reaction.

I knocked on the thirteenth story door of a high rise in Rogers Park, Chicago's most northern neighborhood known for its ethnic diversity and strong gay and lesbian presence. Claire smiled when she recognized me, greeting me like an old friend. She didn't seem surprised to see me. "How's your cat? I felt a terrible vibe about her yesterday."

"She was kidnapped, and I hoped you could lead me to her."

Claire's red hoop earrings were the size of tea saucers, and she had silver and gold rings on every finger, even her thumbs. In each arm, she held a cat.

"Come in," Claire said, inviting me in through her doorway. She looked down the hall both ways before closing the door. Her condo's decor leaned in the voodoo/Caribbean art direction.

"I begged Carmen to stop, but she wouldn't listen," Claire said. I was amazed she had so quickly associated Carmen with the kidnapping of my cat, and I was eager to hear more.

"Stop what?" My back hugged the wall as Claire walked past me. She may be a mind reader, but I wasn't. I watched Claire pace rapidly back and forth, causing all the bric-a-brac to tremble on the large glass table. She squeezed the two cats so tightly they yelped and squirmed out of her arms, then settled onto the white leather couch.

"To stop thinking of ways to die. I knew it would get her killed."

Carmen was thinking of ways to commit suicide? She poured the poison in her own glass? This wasn't possible. Claire jounced her hands like she was shaking off water, then she squeezed them into fists. "I haven't slept all night. Tango's been talking about Adriano Capezio nonstop, and he wouldn't let me rest until I promised to tell you about it. I think this also relates to the danger your cat is in."

I didn't know where to start. "Tango?"

She pointed to the white angora wearing a diamond collar. "Carmen's cat, Tango. He told me you'd be coming today."

I looked at Tango, curious over his ability to sense my arrival, and asked, "Would you mind if we start from the beginning? This is confusing."

Claire took my coat, folded it over the couch, and invited me to sit down, next to the cats.

"I knew that taking on Carmen would be trouble: She's a big star, and for a publicist, she can be a headache. Believe me, I've worked with all kinds. Did you hear about her bathing-suit business in New York?"

As long as I was here, and as long as Claire felt like talking about Carmen, I became a reporter and pulled out my notebook and tape recorder. I had to trust she'd help me find my cat eventually. "No, what happened?"

Claire sank into the easy chair draped in a colorful crocheted blanket, maneuvering herself like an ocean liner into a crowded harbor.

"Early in her career, she was desperate for attention. In this business, honey, if you're not big and outrageous, you're just another blip on the radar screen. Would you mind getting that big red book over there?" She pointed toward a bookshelf. As I took it down, several sheets of paper fell from it, and I scrambled to put them back in place.

Once I brought it over to her, she opened it to a photograph of Carmen taken twenty-seven years ago. She was lying on the ground in front of the Metropolitan Opera House in a bathing suit, with a hunky guy standing on her stomach, flexing his muscles. The caption read, "Never Underestimate the Diaphragm of a Diva."

I let out a whistle. "That must have hurt."

"Not really. Singers' diaphragms are like steel after all the workout they get. But Carmen had a strong case of PRM. Ever hear of that?"

I shook my head. "Please Rescue Me?"

"Public Relations Mania." Claire wrung her hands together. "She's always been like that. She'd do anything for the publicity. And now this! Her death! I'd swear this was just another stunt of hers."

"Come again? A media stunt?"

"I've got it all figured out, with the help of Tango."

I had moved back to the couch, dropped my notebook on my lap, and looked at the cats, especially Tango. I sensed it was important to keep Claire talking, that eventually we'd get to my kidnapped cat. And of course more information about Carmen might lead me to her killer.

"Carmen was looking for a big bang on her way out. For a while, she talked about faking her own suicide, but I told her the whole plan would backfire. The media would turn against her. Am I right, or am I right?"

"You're right."

"I tried to explain this to Carmen. But she told me I didn't have a better way to get her global coverage. So I told her if she went through with this crazy stunt, I'd quit."

"Wait a minute. Are you suggesting she actually tried to commit suicide as a media stunt? I'm confused."

"No, I'm just saying she thought about it. The more you think about something, the more likely it is to happen, you know? She started to lose her voice. Happens at her age. She told everyone she was fifty, but was pushing sixty. Anyway, word got around about her being past her prime, and she had no other bookings after this last Macbeth opera."

I winced at the mention of the play.

"So then she fired me."

"I'm sorry."

"Don't be, honey. She fired me all the time. Then she called back and agreed the suicide idea was bad. But the way things turned out, she still got her global coverage, didn't she?"

She certainly did, although not in the way she had imagined. I picked up my notebook again. Tango rubbed up against my thigh.

"Tango says guns are involved."

"Guns!" I nodded, resolved to take down Tango's every word. First the Wizard predicted guns would be involved, and now this cat. "I've never interviewed a cat before."

"That's because you've never met an animal psychic before."

Of course, that was true. If only my classmates at Northwestern could see me now. They'd probably be mortified over my conversation with a cat. I cleared my throat and asked Tango, "What can you tell me about the diva's death?"

Tango jumped off the couch and into Claire's lap. Claire brushed his neck. "I took Tango to Pagliacci's about four weeks ago. You know that's Adriano's restaurant, right? It was Carmen's brilliant idea. She wanted us to spy on him for that book she wanted to write about him. I ordered a Caesar salad that came with exquisite fresh-baked Italian bread and the most heavenly olive oil, and then I had–"

I did the winding motion with my forefinger. "Uh, can you skip the food and just get to what Tango saw?"

"Let me see. Oh, yes. Well, then I–" she giggled a moment and composed herself. "Let the cat out of the bag. I just love saying that. About half an hour later, Mr. Capezio appeared, holding Tango by his scruff and asked us in the dining room who owned this cat. So I stood up, ever so innocent, and apologized."

I was losing my patience at Claire's telling of the story, but anxious to hear what they discovered about Adriano. "What did Tango see?"

"I'm getting to that. When Mr. Capezio opened his office door, Tango walked in without being noticed–oh, you're such a clever little cat. And inside, Tango saw a desk, a filing cabinet, and a big dresser with statues of clowns on top, right? Right."

This cat business put a new benchmark in the field of journalism.

"Let's see," Claire said. "On the wall, his desk, credenza, and mantelpiece there were numerous photos and certificates. Yup. Tango says there was a photo of Adriano Capezio on the steps of the opera house's lobby with the mayor of Chicago."

"Tango could recognize the opera house?"

"Carmen has taken him there often."

"I see."

Claire continued. "Adriano sat at his desk, opened a drawer, pulled out a CD of his daughter, and listened to her sing. He made a call, talked about shipments to the Great Lakes Naval Station in two weeks."

"A shipment of what?"

"Guns."

"Really? Hmmm." That certainly fit The Wizard's prediction of how guns would be involved in my test, and perhaps it tied into those documents in the box concerning the gun factory in Paraguay. I wrote this all down. "Go on."

"Then Adriano walked over to his dresser, opened one of the drawers with a key, and took out a gun."

I gasped. "While listening to his daughter sing? What's the connection?" Did he know she was planning to write an exposé on him?

Claire looked at Tango. "Adriano has a thing for clowns. He named his restaurant after Pagliacci, Leon Cavello's opera about a clown. He collects guns, and I heard he started to manufacture a new prototype. The gun's name is Ilmato."

"Tango told you he's manufacturing a new type of gun?"

"No, Carmen told me. This was in confidence, but Tango says she would have wanted me to tell you about this. Like I said, she wanted to write a book about him. Last I heard she was looking for a writer to do it."

I cleared my throat. "I believe she found a writer."

Claire's eyes opened wide. "You?" She looked at Tango. "Well, no wonder."

"Yes. She gave me a box of material about her father. She wanted me to write an exposé on him. Before she could tell me exactly what he was doing, she...well..." I wanted to switch gears and explain to Claire how I believed Adriano kidnapped my cat as a ransom for the box, but figured I should help Claire stay on track with this part of the story. "What did Carmen tell you about these guns?"

"She thought Adriano was selling them to the U.S. military, but she also suspected he was selling them illegally to people who shouldn't be getting them."

"Where does he get the guns?"

Claire shook her head. "I don't know. I never thought to ask."

Perhaps he had the guns custom-made by someone at that gun factory. "Ilmato," I said, trying to recall where I'd heard this word before. It was certainly a new name on the market, nothing I'd seen during my lessons at the gun range. Then I remembered the Italian Tarot deck I had and how The Fool was titled Il Matto. "It means the fool in Italian."

"I didn't know that."

Many associated clowns with fools and, in fact, were so depicted on some Tarot decks. Here was another thrilling sign that I was on the right track in tackling my test to enter the Order of the Tarot at the Fool's degree.

I asked, "Can you describe the gun?"

Claire looked at Tango, then back at me. "It was black."

"How big was it?"

Claire and Tango communicated silently before Claire said, "About half Tango's size, and it was flat."

Tango was about eighteen inches long, so the gun had to be about nine. That was a small gun, and I guessed it was a semiautomatic from the description that it was flat.

"And then what happened?"

"That's when Adriano noticed Tango snooping around in his office and flew into a rage. He grabbed Tango by the neck, walked out of his office, and interrogated his staff about the cat. When they couldn't provide any answers for him, he marched into the dining room. That's of course when I acted all flustered and took back Tango."

Tango jumped off Claire's lap and rolled on the carpet, looking very content at the part he played in telling his version of the story.

I said, "I know you think her father killed Carmen, but is there anyone else who would have reason to murder her?"

Claire laughed. "Carmen was a tyrant. Onstage everybody loved her–her voice, her dramatic ability, the way she just knew when to tremble her hand. But offstage, her life was a mess. Anyone with her was there for her money or talent. I don't think anyone truly liked her, except for Castrato."

I felt sad for her. I'd often heard how big stars were taken for granted by the people closest to them. "Do you know if she had a relationship with anyone at the time of her death?"

Claire rubbed her hands. "Maybe Bruno."

I dropped my pen as my finger began to throb. Every time I thought of Bruno, my finger hurt. It was the same one I had cut while grating the potatoes for kugelis when Bruno was on my mind. "Bruno?"

"Yes, he was her agent. The only thing she didn't like about him though was–"

"That he's married," I said, perhaps too quickly.

Claire paused a moment, waved her hand. "Heavens no. That never stopped her. In fact, she often preferred it that way. She loved the added challenge, the extra drama. She was always conflicted about getting married herself. No, the only thing she didn't like about him was that he was friendly with Adriano Capezio."

I picked up my pen again, although it wasn't easy to write with my hurt finger. "What was their relationship?"

"They both adored opera, for one, an immediate bond among men, straight, gay, whatever…and women, come to think of it. Bruno is one of Adriano's partners in his import-export business."

"Really?" Now my finger radiated heat and I put it to my mouth.

"Hey, maybe he's involved in this gun business," Claire suddenly said. "What do you think about that?"

"It's possible. Can you tell me more about the relationship between Carmen and Bruno?"

"He's been her manager for the last five years now. They met in Italy while she was doing Norma at La Scala."

"I adore that opera."

"Me too. Anyway, at the time, Bruno was managing the career of Isabella Cantina, the twenty-two year-old wonder. Bruno was an impresario who knew how to impress his divas. Know what I mean?"

"He does have a certain magnetism," I agreed.

"But then Isabella's voice went wobbly and she began to sing out of her throat too much. Everyone thought her voice coach pushed her too much. Anyway, she needed to take a year off to recuperate, and that left Bruno without a diva to manage."

"I see."

"Carmen saw what Bruno did for Isabella, and she heard about poor Isabella's predicament. That's when she paid a lot of attention to Bruno. Know what I mean?"

"Was it…was it love at first sight?"

Claire laughed, much to my relief. For a brief second, I entertained my infatuation for Bruno, but just as quickly I squelched it. I was not in love with Bruno. He meant nothing to me. I had to keep thinking this way to get into the Order of the Tarot. Like the Wizard said, my feelings for Bruno were a fool's love.

"Maybe," Claire said. "But in the opera world, people usually fall in love with those who can further their career. Know what I mean? Divas are always with conductors, managers, or directors. They rarely marry their accountants."

"So, for the sake of argument, why would Bruno want to

murder the diva?"

"Because she was becoming difficult. She'd say one thing and do another. Getting her onstage became a problem. She had a reputation for canceling often and that was upsetting opera management."

"Did it upset Bruno?"

"Yes."

"Enough to kill her?"

Claire shrugged. "You're the reporter."

I sighed. "About her father, they say he was controlling. Is this what you saw?"

"For the longest time, Adriano managed his daughter's career. You heard of stage mothers?"

I nodded.

"Adriano was the ultimate stage father. He muscled her onto the opera stage. And if you believe the rumors, he paved her road in layers of generous donations to all the opera houses."

"Bribes?"

"Like I said, *donations*. Carmen was good enough to sing on a stage, but her real talent was having a father who could help the opera houses pay their bills. That's what set her apart from the herd."

"It sounds like she was very fortunate." I didn't at all believe it, as I wouldn't want a father like that, but threw the comment out to see how Claire would respond.

"Does it?" Claire asked.

Okay, that netted a big zero for my bank of quotes. "Did she know her father paid off the opera houses?"

"I don't see how she couldn't. But maybe that's what drove her to overcome all that her father gave her. She wanted to manage her own career."

I suddenly identified with Carmen's need to show the world she was talented, despite the help she received from her father. I had the same need at *Gypsy Magazine*, making sure everyone knew I earned my job through my investigative merits, even though my mother was the publisher's girlfriend.

I asked, "So how did Adriano ever let Bruno manage his precious daughter?"

"Carmen was shocked to discover Bruno knew her father, and was even more shocked to learn they were business partners. Toward the end, she suspected her father arranged for Bruno to be her agent. Frankly, I thought that from day one." Claire leaned into her chair. "There, I'm done. I've told you everything."

Tango crawled over to me and pawed at a slip of paper that had fallen out of the red scrapbook earlier. I picked it up and studied it.

"I don't think that's everything." After a long moment, I asked, "Any idea who sent Carmen the belladonna plant?"

Claire grabbed her chest with both hands. "Oh! How did you know?"

I waved the invoice for the belladonna plant. "Tango just told me."

Claire glared at Tango. "Oh, how could you?"

Tango rubbed my leg again.

"Why?" I asked.

"It was just a joke, something we were supposed to laugh about in our old age together."

"A kitten nibbled on that plant and died."

Claire's eyes shut and she looked nauseous. "Oh, the karma! I can't bear it!" She bawled uncontrollably.

Now I knew Claire would help me find Siddharma. "I know of a way for you to balance your karma."

Claire wiped her eyes. "What? I'll do anything? I can't have this hanging over me."

"I need your help to find my cat. I believe the diva's killer kidnapped her."

Claire grabbed at her muumuu, bunching up the material into a ball until it rose to her knees, revealing her knee-highs. "The monster! No boundaries! I'll do anything to save your poor kitty's life."

Claire straightened out her muumuu, and eyed me up and down. "What do you want to know?"

"Can you tell me if she's still alive?"

"Come here."

I approached her so she could pick off a cat hair from my sweater. She concentrated for a minute. "She's alive, but confused. She's been in a dark bag most of the time. Now she's in a trailer."

"What trailer?"

Claire concentrated some more. "I don't know. I'm sorry. I've never worked with a kidnapped cat before."

"You're my only hope. Don't you have *any* ideas?"

Tango sauntered over to Claire and walked between her legs.

"What?" Claire asked Tango. "Really? I'm supposed to ask her about–"

Then she looked to me. "Tarot cards? What do you know of Tarot cards?"

Chapter Fourteen

Tango walked to my big, black bag and pawed at it. I followed him, dug into the bag, and pulled out the Universal Waite deck The Wizard had given me.

"I carry these cards with me all the time. Perhaps I can use these to help find Siddharma." I spread them out on the coffee table.

"Oh, my Goddess!" Claire said with a wide smile. "Yes, it's perfect."

She sat next to me on the white couch, and we faced the Tarot deck on her low glass table, filled with bric-a-brac. She shoved all her porcelain and glass figurines to the side, except for the white bell. Outside, the snow fell in clumps, a white, dreamy haze.

She raised her arms over the deck and closed her eyes. "Let's see what they tell me."

Tango and I observed her. She locked eyes with Tango, then said, "You've been working with the Fool card lately, haven't you?"

I looked at Tango, impressed by her abilities, then at Claire, dumbfounded over her knack at cat-talk. "As a matter of fact, I have been working with the Fool card."

Claire beamed at Tango. "I knew it! Let's start with that."

She pulled the Fool card from the scattered cards.

"The Fool has been described as the most difficult and profound card of the entire Tarot deck, filled with possibility and potential," Claire said. "When you work with the Fool, your process involves spiritual detective work. The Fool is the beginning of all."

I took a deep breath and rubbed my left earlobe. I gazed at the card, noting the brown dog ripping at the Fool's pants leg. I had worked with the cards for so long that I had my own personal connection with the animal at the Fool's side. To me, it signified a wolf because of my surname.

"Have you ever tried scrying?" Claire asked.

"Yes, I'm familiar with the technique." Scrying is the projection of yourself into an inner vision. As the ancient act of divination for the purpose of clairvoyance, it is achieved by concentrating upon an object until a vision appears. As part of my work with the Tarot during the past year, I had scried under The Wizard's supervision with each of the Major Arcana cards.

"You're a natural, I can tell. Let's have you scry through the Fool card to find out more about Siddharma."

I knew the act of scrying helped perceive events beyond the range of physical senses. With The Wizard, I'd used scrying to develop my spirituality. I'd never considered scrying for something so practical as finding my missing cat. "It's worth a shot."

She moved the other cards to the side, and placed the Fool in my direct line of vision. "Close your eyes, and with your imagination step into the card's image, and see what happens." She lifted the porcelain bell sitting on the cocktail table. "When you hear my bell, jump back."

I felt good about how Claire coached me and I said a quick prayer of thanks that Claire was helping me find Siddharma. I shut my eyes, breathed deeply and slowly, and focused on the white light growing between my eyes. When I felt ready to scry, I left Claire's living room with my mind's eye and entered into the landscape of the Fool card, a grassy cliff. I carried a stick with a red knapsack for my journey. Behind me, I heard a low growl. When I turned around, I saw the wolf.

"What are you doing here?" the wolf growled.

"I'm looking for my cat," I said. "Have you seen her?"

"I just chased it off the cliff. Why don't you follow it?"

"You're asking me to jump off the cliff?" Half of me knew it was just a vision, but the other half was convinced I'd hurt myself.

"It's not very high."

I had to see for myself, and I peered over the edge. Six feet below lay ground covered by grass. Ahead lay a valley of grassy knolls. Not very far away flowed a river with a bridge extending over it. I took a step back to prepare for the jump, and inadvertently stepped on the wolf's tail.

"You fool!" growled the wolf. "Get thee gone!" With that, he–pushed me over the cliff and I landed on the soft, spongy grass. I stood. Then I heard a faint meow coming from the direction of the river. I saw a large cross in the distance with gravestones in a cemetery. As I neared the bridge, the meowing grew louder. On the ledge of the bridge crouched a black cat.

"Meow. Here I am," said the black cat.

"But you're not my cat. My Siddharma is white."

"Ah, yes, I saw the white cat previously," purred the black cat. "Just follow the river."

Along the river, daylight quickly faded and gravestones popped up like jack-in-the-boxes from out of nowhere. I found one that read, "Here lies Siddharma. May she rest in peace."

"No! Not my Siddharma!"

I heard a rustling noise behind me. I turned to see the wolf displaying a fanged smile. "It's not your Siddharma. You'll find what you're looking for in there." He pointed to a tower bearing a light at its crown. I reached the tower and rushed up its stony staircase, which rose higher and proved harder to climb. The stairs started out normal in size, but as I climbed, the stairs grew in height. Each stair stretched to my waist. I hoisted myself onto each step and I perspired profusely, but resolved to reach the peak. Down below, the wolf chuckled.

"You certainly have the drive."

I reached the last stair, this one higher than my head. I looked in my knapsack, made of a red scarf, and pulled out a chalice, sword, three coins, and a candle.

"What will you do with those?" taunted the wolf down below.

"I have a plan." I experimented with ways to use the sword and noticed that if I leaned it at a certain angle, I could hoist myself onto the step from the sword's hilt. I placed the candle and coins in my pocket, and wrapped the chalice in the red scarf, which I managed to hang from my neck. I walked up

121

the sword, steadying myself with the stick. The sword's blade dug into my gym shoes, but my soles were thick and the sword never pierced my skin. When I climbed over the stair, I was amazed to see the wolf at the top of the landing.

"Very good, Alex. You've passed your first hurdle. You have more ahead."

At that, a bell rang insistently. "You must leave," the wolf said sadly.

I asked, "How did you get up here so fast, anyway?"

"Didn't you notice the elevator next to the staircase?"

I wanted to cry.

"Next time, find the easy way up. Oh, and…look before you leap, you fool."

The bell rang again, pulling me out of the visualization. I dove outside the card and returned to sitting on Claire's white couch. I felt hot and sweaty, like I'd just jogged through a marathon. At first I was disoriented, but relieved to be away from the wolf.

"Well?" Claire asked, the bell in her hand. "Did you see Siddharma?"

"Yes, Siddharma is in a cemetery."

I couldn't understand why Claire's eyes lit up at this terrible news. "I knew you could do it!" Claire clapped her hands and looked at Tango. "Don't you see? The scrying worked! Now you know where your cat is! Do you know which cemetery?"

My heart sank even further. "No."

"Don't you worry." Claire communed with Tango. "We'll figure out which cemetery we need to explore."

Chapter Fifteen

The drive back to my office took longer than usual because traffic crawled under the heavy snowfall. Time seemed to drag in slow motion, the flakes falling like clusters of thick wool.

Back in my office, I saw Beata sitting in my chair, rummaging through the big cardboard box containing the material on Carmen's father. From the looks of it, with most of the contents scattered across my desk and on the floor, she'd been there for quite some time.

"Well, well, well," she sneered as I approached. "Isn't this box interesting?"

"What the hell are you doing in my office?"

"You've been holding back on us, dear Alexandria. That isn't very nice of you."

"None of this is any of your business."

"Isn't it, now? Weren't we working on this story together?"

It was all I could do to stop myself from lunging at her. She'd clearly figured out the box's contents concerned Carmen Dellamorte. But she couldn't know what sort of project Carmen had given me.

"Let me guess," she said. "Remember, I have psychic abilities." She rubbed her temples, as if channeling information from the Other Side. "I bet Carmen asked you to write a book about her dear old father. You accepted the assignment. Then she died. This is the part that isn't clear to me: You figured you'd hold onto this box of information and keep it all to yourself. Am I right?"

Beata had proven herself as a reporter with her last story on fraudulent psychics in Chicago, but she still hadn't earned my respect as an ethical journalist.

"As I said before, none of this is any of your business. I'd appreciate it if you would leave my office."

She stood up. "I think Alyce should know about this."

"I'm planning to tell her about it, don't you worry."

"Oh now, Alex. This is really something I'd love to tell her myself."

I took a step forward ready to slap her.

"Unless..." She held up a finger.

"Unless what?"

She rubbed her chin, obviously relishing this moment. "Unless you tell Alyce you think I should be the lead reporter for this story. You've suddenly become overwhelmed."

"What? Never!"

"Joe Burke came by about two hours ago. He was *very* upset you weren't here. He said he'd return to pick up the box."

So that's how Beata learned about the box. He must have missed my phone message. I only hoped I had enough time to finish making copies of everything before his return. Then I'd tell Alyce about the box before Beata beat me to the punch. She was not going to become the lead reporter on this story, not if I had anything to do with it.

Through clenched teeth, I said, "I'll be here for him. Now leave my office before I throw you out."

She left with a smug expression. For the next hour, I finished copying every single piece of paper and letter in that box, reading the contents as I worked. I copied the pages of her latest diary, which I had read earlier. Upon closer inspection, I noticed a page torn out, and I couldn't remember noticing that earlier. How odd. Was it possible Beata had ripped it out, or was it removed before she had a chance to go through the contents? A stunt like this wasn't beyond Beata's ethics. On the other hand, maybe I was just paranoid. Blaming Beata was easier than dealing with the sense that I was driving down a blind alley.

By the time Joe arrived, I had finished copying everything.

He had a stern expression when he picked up the box. Part of me wanted to explain how I needed to talk to Claire Fergusson first about Siddharma, but I could tell no explanation would be good enough for Joe.

"I'm sorry I wasn't here earlier. I had to do an interview that came up at the last minute. I tried to call you."

Joe spoke to me like a stern parent to a four-year-old. "We're not working together ever again. This box of information is a key piece of evidence, something a lot of officers have been waiting for. You holding on to it is inexcusable, and you not being here this morning to hand it over is criminal. The only reason I'm not pressing charges is because of our history together and how it led to my promotion in the Violent Crimes Unit. But as of this minute, the slate is even. Do we understand each other?"

"I'm sorry."

Joe sighed. "Did you get that autopsy report?"

"What autopsy report?"

"On Carmen Dellamorte. I gave it to your coworker. She said she'd make sure you got it. She did give it to you, didn't she?"

Beata!

Joe didn't really care if I'd received the autopsy report or not, because he left without waiting for my answer.

Chapter Sixteen

Before I could track down Beata and ask her about the autopsy report, my phone rang. Donacella Dimitriano was waiting for me in the reception area, and she had only a few minutes to talk to me before she had to leave. Right now? All I wanted to do was grab the autopsy report out of Beata's hands and dash to Alyce's office to tell her about the box. If Beata got to Alyce first, she'd no doubt paint me in a bad light. But Carmen's understudy was here. My mad dash to Alyce's office would have to wait.

"Tell her I'll be right there," I said to the receptionist. I counted to ten with several deep breaths to calm myself, then left the cubicle to greet Donacella, who I found looking at a lithograph of the Chicago skyline.

"Donacella Dimitriano?"

She turned to face me. "Mizz Vilkas, it's a pleasure to meet you." She stepped forward, her black overcoat draped on her arm. She wore a long chocolate brown dress with a modest V-neck.

"I appreciate your seeing me on such short notice," she began.

"Glad you came."

I escorted her to a conference room so that she could speak freely with the door closed behind us. She seemed agitated and kept looking over her shoulder, as if she were scared she might be overheard. I sensed she was conflicted about being here and was on the verge of changing her mind and leaving. After declining coffee, she settled into a chair.

This was the smaller room with an elliptical polished oak table surrounded by eight chairs. On the walls hung award-winning cover stories of *Gypsy Magazine*. I grabbed a pen and yellow pad, and turned on the tape recorder.

"I...I haven't been able to sleep since the diva's death. I

keep tossing and turning. I know I'm a suspect based on the testimony you've given to the police. And everyone has heard about that damned curse. I'm being blamed for Carmen's death."

I had my hands folded while the tape recorder whirred.

She continued. "I heard you're doing your own investigation for *Gypsy Magazine*, and I was just wondering how much detail you were going to provide in your story about that…incident." She sent me a piercing look.

"Frankly, I haven't decided." I eyed her suspiciously. "Why?"

Donacella pushed a strand of dark curly hair behind her ear. "Of course I feel terrible about what I said to her, but…I didn't kill her. The media is bludgeoning my career. They're making it out like I did it on purpose, like I meant for her to die. I thought perhaps you…you'd get to the bottom of what really happened. You were there. You saw how it happened. And now with the Lyric Opera House threatening to close its doors because of the curse…"

I frowned, weighing my words. "I don't believe it was the curse that killed Carmen Dellamorte. And honestly, I don't think anybody else does either. It just makes good copy. Do you have any new information?"

"Yes, but what I'm about to tell you needs to stay confidential."

I settled back into my chair to listen. "All right."

Donacella's tongue darted out and curled upward, grazing her taut upper lip quickly. "Carmen was horrible. Everyone hated her. Everyone I know at the Lyric had something against her, some grudge."

"Grudge?"

"If Carmen didn't get her way, then no one else did either. We all revolved around her. If we didn't, she had a tantrum."

"Like what?"

"She'd throw props and say cruel things. In some ways, this murder was a long time coming. The entire cast, orchestra, extras, designers could have banded together to kill her. I know it's terrible of me to say, but it's the truth."

I shook my head. For the most part, I wasn't surprised to hear this. After all, Carmen was known as La Tempestua, and I now knew it was because of her temperament on and off the stage.

"But...but...you won't quote me on that, right?"

"Don't worry. What would you like to say about Carmen for the record?" I poised pen to paper.

Donacella looked up at the ceiling to form words. "Carmen Dellamorte was an example for all sopranos. Her voice rang gorgeously, a full-bodied sound. I loved the weight and volume of it when she sang Wagner, as well as its brilliance and flexibility in lyric roles. La Tempestua had a dazzling career as a great heroine. She filled the role of Diva magnificently." She smiled. "How's that?"

"Very nice," I said. "So who do you think killed her?"

With no hesitation, as if waiting for this question all along, she answered, "Adriano Capezio, her father. He's always complaining about Carmen, that he's done so much for her, that she's so ungrateful."

I met her gaze. "How would you happen to know this?"

"He...he's my sponsor, you see. And...we talk."

"Sponsor?"

"He got me into the Lyric...his connections."

"Let's back up a minute. How did he decide to sponsor you?"

She looked down at her hands. "He has a reputation for giving new artists a lift. I heard about him through a friend, so I visited him at his restaurant."

"When?"

"Maybe two years ago." Then as an afterthought she added, "As it turns out, I live near his restaurant."

"Okay."

"And he liked my...voice."

I wondered what else he liked. Perhaps it was no accident she lived so close to his restaurant. "So he decided to sponsor you?"

"Yes."

I formed my mouth into the shape of an O. "So now you're willing to implicate your sponsor?"

"My career means everything. With the Lyric about to go under because of the curse, I have to let someone know. I haven't even told the police yet."

"Why not?"

"I know they wouldn't keep my relationship with Adriano confidential. Plus I was so distraught over the curse, on Sunday, even I believed it might have had something to do with Carmen's death. But for the past three days, I've had a chance to think about everything. I've recalled a conversation I had with Adriano last week, and…"

"Have you spoken to him since Sunday?"

"No, I haven't been returning his phone calls."

I looked out the window, twenty floors up. The people looked like tiny wind-up toys below.

Donacella sucked in her breath. "You see, Adriano and I have been lovers for two years."

I nodded, having already figured this out from her earlier statements.

"It was the only way I'd get noticed at the Lyric. I'm not exactly proud of it, but…I'm not a murderess."

Just a mistress who wanted to turn her lover in. But if she really believed Adriano Capezio killed Carmen, perhaps she felt justified with her accusation. "What makes you think he killed his own daughter?"

"Last week, he visited me at my apartment, and we talked. He was upset about a project his daughter was going to start, something about writing a book on her relationship with him. He knew he hadn't been a good father to her, but he felt he had nurtured her career."

So he did know about Carmen's plan to write a book about him.

"He said if he ever found out who was going to help his daughter write the book, he'd kill that person."

She glanced uneasily at me, and I felt the hairs prickle on

my neck. Did she know it was me? I suddenly felt very cold.

I asked, "Do you think he found out?"

"I'm almost sure of it. You see, Teresita talked about you to the rest of the chorus, about that box of material that Carmen left for you. She suspected Carmen had asked you to write the book about her father."

So Adriano had known since Sunday that Carmen asked me to write the book. He *must* be the one who had Carmen killed, who threatened me, and who kidnapped Siddharma.

She said, "You need to be very careful with Adriano. I'm telling you this because I don't think you realize how powerful he is. He's used to getting his way."

"I've heard a lot of rumors about him. Do you know anything about his involvement in…"

Donacella raised her hand in a stop-sign gesture. "Don't even say the word. I have no idea. I never ask him about it. I don't want to know. But if he did kill his daughter, he's gone too far."

"I appreciate you talking to me. Is there anything else?"

"I couldn't bear it if the Lyric closed. I want to do everything I can to find Carmen's killer, to help prove that it wasn't the curse that did it."

"Then you and I are on the same side," I said. "You'll recall that you spoke with Carmen just before the opera began. Where did you go after you left Carmen's dressing room?"

"Up to the fourth floor, the chorus dressing room. I told them how Carmen tried to kick the kitten, how she upset me so, and how…how I did the unthinkable. I don't know what possessed me."

In my mind, I replayed how she screamed, "Macbeth, Macbeth, Macbeth."

"I compounded my error when I told the chorus about it. I saw how they worried it would affect their own performance. Such a silly superstition. Saying the production's name shouldn't mean anything. I just wanted to rattle Carmen."

Donacella fidgeted with her hair, then dropped her hands to her lap. "Opera people can be so irrational. One chorus member went hysterical, screaming, 'We're doomed! We're doomed!' Within minutes, everyone heard about the curse. I couldn't stand it anymore. I was beside myself."

"During that last act, did you notice anyone give the diva something to drink?"

"After her last aria, everyone surrounded her, congratulating her. She walked past me toward her dressing room. That's when I noticed my kitten was dead. That consumed all of my attention. Later, I found out Kitty had nibbled on a poisonous plant left for Carmen. I just..."

"I understand. If there's nothing else, then you know where to find me."

"Yes, thanks."

Before Donacella left, she asked one more question, "You won't tell anyone about my relationship with Adriano, will you?"

I considered her request. Most relationships were more public than a furtive couple realized. Yet, for now, there was no reason to upset Donacella any further. "I'll do the best I can."

Silvia Foti

Chapter Seventeen

Once Donacella left, I dashed to Alyce's office. I wasn't surprised to see Beata engrossed in a conversation with our boss. How much had Beata told Alyce already?

Alyce clapped her hands with force. "Oh good, Alex. You're here. I want to have another meeting to get this organized–Carmen, suspects, motives, and our plan. Alex, what have you got?"

"I...I still need a minute to collect my thoughts," I said. I still couldn't believe Beata hadn't blurted everything out to Alyce. I figured if Alyce wasn't exploding over it by now, I still had a chance to bring it up first.

"Beata, you've got the autopsy report, right?"

Although I knew Beata already had it, I was interested in hearing her explanation of how she received it. "The autopsy report?" I sat up straight.

Beata smiled and spoke to Alyce. "Alex's friend, Joe Burke came. He was looking for Alex, but she wasn't around." Then she turned to me. "We are a team, aren't we? All for the story?"

I pursed my lips and told myself it didn't matter who got the autopsy report first.

"Okay," Alyce said with impatience. "Let's begin."

Alyce had a pile of Universal Waite Tarot cards on her desk. She pulled out the Queen of Cups, pushing the other cards to the side. Then she pulled a photograph of Carmen Dellamorte from her file and placed it next to the Tarot card.

"Carmen is the Queen of Cups. A mature woman, emotional, poisoned after drinking rubbing alcohol poured in a cup."

Beata pulled out the autopsy report and scanned the document. "I'll just read the most pertinent parts, which I've highlighted in yellow. This is Case Number Two-One-Seven-

132

blah-blah-blah, Carmen Dellamorte. Okay, here we go. The body is that of a well-developed, well-nourished fifty-nine-year-old Caucasian female with black hair and brown eyes. The body is sixty-nine inches long and weighs 230 pounds. The skin is of normal texture. There is a single scar in the center of the lower abdomen from a previous Cesarean section."

"She had a baby?" I sat up straighter.

"Looks like it," Beata said. "I wonder where the child is now."

"We'll have to check into that," Alyce said. "What else does the autopsy report say?"

Beata ruffled through more pages.

"She was poisoned with isopropanol rubbing alcohol."

"Exactly as the papers stated," I said.

"I did some research on rubbing alcohol," Beata said, digging out another file. "It's one of the most perfect poisons because of its availability. Just pour into a drink, and the victim never notices. Reaction time is ten minutes to half-hour. Tastes like booze, just more bitter."

"Wouldn't she have smelled it though?" I asked.

"Not if it's covered up by…say, champagne," Beata said. "Even at her weight, she'd only need to swallow about two teaspoons to kill her."

Beata pulled out a bottle of cheap champagne from her bag along with another bottle of rubbing alcohol.

"After reading the autopsy report, I ran to the convenience store down the street and picked up these items. I thought we could try a little experiment ourselves."

"That's brilliant!" Alyce said. "Isn't that just brilliant, Alex?"

Wasn't Alyce turned off by Beata's underhanded and bald-faced ambition? Didn't she care how Beata was stepping all over me? Obviously not. I only saw a gleam of admiration in Alyce's eyes as she helped Beata prepare everything for the re-enactment.

Alyce produced a coffee mug and teaspoon in lieu of a champagne glass, while Beata popped the cork off the champagne. Beata filled half the coffee mug with champagne while Alyce poured in two teaspoons of the rubbing alcohol, and stirred. Alyce sniffed it first, then passed the cup to Beata, who after taking a big whiff, passed it to me. I breathed in deeply. It definitely smelled like champagne, and all three of us agreed the rubbing alcohol wasn't noticeable if one wasn't suspecting it.

"Who would have thought of using rubbing alcohol like this?" Alyce said, shaking her head.

Beata ruffled through more pages of the autopsy report. "The mechanism of death was hemorrhage. The manner of death homicide."

"Homicide. It's official," Alyce said. She pushed the Queen of Cups and photo of Carmen to the side, next to the bottle of champagne, rubbing alcohol, and coffee mug. "Was the murder planned out? Or a last-minute opportunity taken? Either way, the chaos of a public death gave the killer a chance to run from the scene of the crime. So who wanted the diva gone?"

Beata cleared her throat. "If I may?" She set aside the champagne bottle and rubbing alcohol and reached across Alyce's desk to grab her Tarot cards. She sifted through the cards and pulled out the Hierophant, a priest in a red robe on a throne, preaching before two acolytes. "I'd have the Hierophant stand in for the Lyric Opera House's administrator Denise Johnson. This is somebody in authority who wanted Carmen to follow the house rules."

"What have you learned about her?" Alyce asked.

"I had a lengthy conversation with Ms. Johnson," Beata answered. "She was very helpful. The Lyric Opera house wanted Carmen out. She had been badmouthing its administration for years, especially in the past six months." Beata pulled out a *Chicago Tribune* article. "This article quoted Carmen as saying, 'They have forgotten all I have done for them! They devour their artists shamelessly, paying poorly on contract and overworking us with a grueling schedule.' In short, the article depicted Carmen as a diva on the wane, screaming sour grapes on her way out."

"I remember that article," Alyce said. "But I can't believe the Lyric would kill Carmen for that. Have you gotten a copy of her will?"

"Not yet," Beata said. "I'm still working on it."

It was time to share some of the knowledge I had gleaned during my interviews. I sifted through Alyce's Tarot cards and pulled out The Emperor.

I offered, "Adriano Capezio, her father, played a huge role in shaping his daughter's career and paving her way with generous donations, especially to the Lyric. According to the information I'm finding, people wondered how he could afford it. He only owns a restaurant on Taylor Street and there is talk that he may be involved in something else, perhaps even something illegal, something that Carmen wanted to uncover. So far my sources think he's the murderer. His champagne bottle with the note is most incriminating. In fact–"

"How'd you come up with all that?" Alyce asked.

"I'm piecing it together through the interviews I've conducted with Castrato, Teresita, and Donacella. I also–" I was about to mention the box; I realized the contents of the box could explain my reasoning.

"Before Carmen died, she left me a box of information about her father."

"Yes, Alexandria has been holding back on us," Beata oozed in an oily voice. "She's had that box since Monday. Lieutenant Burke just picked it up because it's considered evidence in the murder investigation."

Alyce looked at me with questioning eyes.

"Yes, it's true," I said. I slumped in my chair. I deserved no sympathy from Alyce or anyone else for waiting so long to bring up the contents of that damn box. As I regarded Beata with a dark respect for her astonishing initiative, the Wizard's words came to me from one of our previous lessons: "All confrontations are a mirror of your inner turmoil. Look inside to understand the deeper meaning and to discern the root cause." I inhaled slowly and quietly so that I could figure out the root cause. I brought this situation on myself by failing to be forthright with Alyce, for trying to hoard information from my team to give myself the upper hand in this story. My pride caused me to be miserly with the box. To move forward, I had to share whatever information I had with the team. Inwardly, I saluted Beata for underscoring this lesson.

Alyce stared at me, her hands folded.

"It's about my cat," I finally answered.

"Your cat?" Alyce asked.

"When I interviewed Carmen last Sunday, she gave me a box of information about her father. She instructed me not to tell anyone about it, which I now realize I shouldn't have heeded, especially after her death. But you must understand that at first I was trying to keep my promise to her. Then someone broke into my apartment yesterday, as well as my landlord's, looking for this box. They took my cat as ransom. I don't want them to kill Siddharma. I'm afraid that if they don't get the box, they'll kill her."

"Has anyone called you to get the box?" Alyce asked.

"No."

"Then how do you know they kidnapped your cat because of it?"

"They told my landlord they were looking for it. Plus there was a black Cadillac parked in front of my apartment the day after Carmen died. I suspected they were watching for the box's arrival."

"Who knew about this box?" Alyce asked.

"Teresita was in the room when Carmen gave it to me. And Castrato knows about it. Apparently her understudy mentioned it to the chorus during the performance. Last night, I finally told Lieutenant Joe about it. I wanted to make copies of everything before he arrived."

"I see," Alyce said. "Were you able to make copies of the contents?"

"Yes."

"That's one smart thing you did. So what's going on with your cat?"

"This morning I interviewed an animal psychic. She believes...I believe Siddharma is alive."

"An animal psychic?" Alyce asked.

"Claire Fergusson is also Carmen's publicist. It's all linked together. She gave me valuable information on Carmen's murder. She was the one who told me about Adriano's illegitimate business."

Beata looked at Alyce, then at the cards on her desk. "Gee, we don't have a card for this...uh...Claire Fergusson. Why is that?"

"Not everybody we interview is a suspect for murder," I said, searching Alyce's face for a hint of sympathy and not finding it. "Discovering my cat's kidnapper might lead to Carmen's murderer. If someone is so interested in retrieving the contents of that box that they will kidnap my cat to get it, maybe that's the same person who killed Carmen."

"Is there anything in that box we should know about?" Alyce asked.

"Yes, I believe Carmen left us a clue, that she may have suspected she was about to be killed. I've gone through most of the contents, which includes Carmen's diaries, newspaper clippings, and books on the Outfit."

"The Mob?" Beata said. "You didn't think that was important?"

I ignored Beata's comment. I wanted to speak to Alyce alone. We had a history together, and I didn't want it to unravel. She had to trust me.

Alyce looked upset. "Why did you hold back on me about the box?" She continued without waiting for an answer. "I hope you realize the murder of Carmen is more important than the kidnapping of your cat, although I do grieve for your loss. Your judgment so far has been questionable. We have a deadline, and the story comes first. If it doesn't for you, I may have to make Beata the lead reporter on this article until you get your priorities straightened out. Do you understand me?"

From the corner of my eye, I could tell Beata savored this moment. She looked like she was sucking on a sweet piece of candy.

I felt tears punching my ducts and it took all I had to keep the dam from breaking. "I do," I said.

"I expect copies of the clues from the contents of that box in this office immediately, along with your analysis of what they mean."

I stood up to leave.

Chapter Eighteen

Back at my desk, I squeezed my eyes shut, covered my face, and rocked back and forth in my chair. It wasn't supposed to be this way, Beata having the upper hand and Alyce worried about my integrity. For now, I had to keep my mind on Carmen's murder.

I pulled out the folders of photocopies I'd compiled on the diva's material about her father, and zeroed in on the message she had written on March 4th. As I combed through the material, I found four bookmarks, each with a line of poetry dated March 4th in her handwriting:

The living hand, now warm and capable
of earnest grasping, would, if it were cold
And in the icy silence of the tomb,
So haunt thy days and chill thy dreaming nights.

> John Keats

Like a child from the womb,
like a ghost from the tomb,
I arise and unbuild again.
How wonderful is Death.

> Mary Wollstonecraft Shelley

Now know that what disturbs our blood
Is but a longing for the tomb.

> William Butler Yeats

Whence we see spiders, flies, or ants,
entombed and preserved for ever in amber,
a more than royal tomb.

> Francis Bacon

I typed into my report Carmen's four notes, written the day I called her to schedule the interview. Were the two events connected? Carmen must have sensed danger and wanted a way to leave a clue. She had known I would interview her and planned accordingly. Perhaps she already suspected somebody close wanted to kill her and she didn't trust anybody she knew. Since I was an unknown, I would be safe to confide in.

I continued to work on my report about the contents of the box. Those four poetry passages in Carmen's hands were key. I remembered how Carmen had underlined the word tomb in one of her personal books of poetry and decided the word "tomb" was significant. What tomb was Carmen referring to? The only tombs I knew about lay in cemeteries. Perhaps Carmen knew somebody was trying to kill her and she wanted to leave a clue in her own tomb.

I'd already heard Carmen's burial was scheduled at Resurrection Cemetery. With no other tomb to investigate, I'd operate under the assumption Carmen hid a clue in her family's crypt. Tomorrow, after attending her wake, I'd go to Resurrection Cemetery, and look for something she had left. All of this I included in my report for Alyce.

Next came Carmen's diary, a jumble of impressions, offering little with which to work, but it went into the report nonetheless. I was still perturbed about the missing page, but continued with my analysis. Where the diary lacked concrete detail about her father, with nothing fingering him as a mobster, it overflowed with raw emotion. The pages revealed how she thought about killing her own father, not the other way around. In one telling passage, she wrote, "I hate my father. I wish he was dead. How he looks right through me with no emotion, like I don't exist. I hate how he controls me with his money. Yet I know his dark secrets, and I intend to expose him. He just laughs at me. I'll show him!"

After I left my report in Alyce's inbox, the phone rang. It was Bruno. I had called him earlier for an interview, and now he returned my call. Suddenly the pain in my finger became unbearable, and I wondered why my cut wasn't healing faster.

Chapter Nineteen

How could I have built such a big castle for Bruno Scavoro on so few grains of sand? I first felt the sexual tension between us a few months ago when he flew from New York to Chicago for an editorial board meeting. I sat next to him, noticing his glances in my direction, how the air around us seemed to glow. He seemed to be telling me with his eyes that he wanted to know more about me. My first grain of sand.

The next day he stood at my desk, sharing stories on opera and ghosts and inquiring about the particulars of an article. He smiled often and touched my arm. Another grain of sand. That night, Alyce invited me to dinner with the magazine's editorial directors, which included Bruno. He sat next to me, and we shared dessert. More than once we locked eyes and I found it difficult to turn away. Another grain of sand. That was the first night I lost sleep over him, wondering if I dared go on a date alone with him. I talked myself out of it because it would be wrong, yet I admitted that I enjoyed thinking about it. During the last few months, we spoke frequently, always about a story for *Gypsy*. Sometimes we talked about our mutual love of the opera. At one point, he complimented my writing, comparing it to the singing of Maria Callas. Oh, that floored me!

I never thought I could feel this way about a married man. Every time I saw the golden ring on a man's hand, the entryways to my heart would seal shut like a prison lockdown. Cling. Clang. Clong. How had Bruno managed to invade my security system? Yet I knew I had to resist him.

Now came the phone interview. My first "hi" followed by his first "hi" clinched it. I knew by the way we spoke that we were both attracted to each other.

"How are things going?" he asked.

I rubbed my finger as we spoke. "Things aren't going as well as they could be."

"If there's anything I can do…"

My mind raced to another topic we could talk about. Perhaps he could put in a bad word about Beata. If he did want to help me… No, I shouldn't impose on him. This was between Beata and me. Yet before I could stop myself, I asked, "Do you know Beata Szybowski?"

"Yes, why?"

"What do you think about her?"

"In what way?"

"Just in general."

"Ambitious. Dedicated. Decent writer."

No! I wanted him to hate her, disrespect her. I wanted to tell him about how Beata was trying to take over my story, stealing my ideas and turning Alyce against me. But of course, I couldn't. It wouldn't be professional.

"You can talk to me anytime. About anything."

I needed to be more careful, be all business. The competent journalist in me took a big step forward and shoved aside the dithering woman who needed more time to reassess her misguided feelings for Bruno. "Tell me about Carmen's line of thinking just before her performance. What was she worried about?"

"You are a dedicated reporter, aren't you? Very well. Lady Macbeth is a demanding role, but one that suited her temperament perfectly. Carmen kept saying she wanted to be spectacular so that other companies would still ask for her."

"And?"

"Highly unlikely. As it was, I had to strong-arm her in for this season over two years ago. Opera companies plan way in advance."

"Strong-arm?"

"I promised the Lyric she would sing five shows for the price of four."

"What did Carmen say to that?"

"She never knew. She let me handle all the finances and contracts so she could concentrate on her art."

"She certainly put an enormous amount of trust in you."

Bruno sighed. "It's a responsibility that perhaps I shouldn't have been given."

I stayed silent a moment, taking notes as I assessed Bruno's character. He was an agent who wanted his twenty percent, and he pushed Carmen as far as possible. But would he kill her because she couldn't produce anymore? On the face of it, it didn't add up. Killing her wouldn't bring him any more income.

"Go on."

"And that turned into the last deal I could swing for her. Eventually I had to tell her it was her last show because no one else signed her on."

"She must have felt terrible."

"A writer's career can blossom at the age of fifty," Bruno explained, "whereas a singer's usually goes downhill. Two different ballgames."

"So, for the record, she was not happy about her singing career coming to an end?"

"She stopped trying. She just didn't have the energy and drive like she used to."

"Can you give me an example?"

"Well, before, she wanted to be alone. She'd vocalize at the piano, continue studying the score in her dressing room. But lately she wanted to fill the dressing room with people as if…as if she wanted company."

That accounted for all the people in her dressing room on Sunday, including me.

I asked, "Remember during the first act, when we were talking?"

"Etched in my mind forever."

What a flirt! How could he be so brazen about it? But I didn't acknowledge it. I stayed all business.

"Where did you go after that?"

"Denise Johnson wanted me to visit Carmen backstage."

I remembered how determined the Lyric's administrator looked when she approached Bruno. "Why?"

"It was about Carmen's will. She was going to change it,

and Denise wanted me to stop her."

"Change her will?"

"Yes. She...I suppose there's no hiding it now. Carmen had a daughter in Florence."

"She did?" That explained the Cesarean section found in her autopsy.

"Her father convinced her to give up the baby for adoption. This daughter wrote to Carmen last year, asking for a reunion. At first, Carmen put it off. With her career ending, she felt she could devote herself to being a mother. It gave her a new purpose. Apparently, she wanted to change her will and leave everything to her daughter, Katarina Mendoza."

This was a new direction to pursue. I asked, "Do you know about Carmen's will, who she left her estate to?"

"I have a copy of it, at least the one she put together three years ago. She left her entire estate to the opera house and her roommate, Roberto Andretti."

"Really?"

"They were the two loves of her life," Bruno said. "The opera house stood for the child Carmen had never raised. She launched her career there. The other half goes to Castrato, apparently the only man she could count on."

"I interviewed Castrato and he never mentioned this. Do you know how much her estate is worth?"

"Last I heard, it's worth about twenty-two million dollars, available in stocks."

I whistled. That certainly put Denise Johnson and Castrato in an interesting position. I'd have to talk to Castrato again.

"You're saying Carmen wanted to change her will, leave everything to her daughter?"

"Yes."

"And this upset Denise because originally Carmen's will left half her estate to the Lyric Opera House."

"Yes, I just said that, didn't I?"

"I'm sorry about being so repetitive. I just need to have it straight in my mind. How did Denise hear about Carmen wanting to change her will?"

144

Bruno paused. "She said Castrato told her."

"I wonder how he got that information."

"Maybe Carmen told him."

"Maybe. You say you have a copy of the previous will?"

"I do, as does Denise Johnson. I can send you a copy if it would be of any help."

"That would be great. Did you and Denise talk to Carmen about her wanting to change the will after all?"

"No, we didn't have a chance. The second act had already begun by the time we arrived backstage, and we couldn't get a moment alone with Carmen."

"So you both hung around backstage?"

"Yes, Denise was distraught. If I didn't know better, I believe she would have given Carmen another role at the Lyric if Carmen would have promised to keep the company in her will."

"But I thought you said her father was financing her career at the Lyric, that even his money wasn't enough to make up for the loss in her voice."

Bruno sighed. "Yes, that's true. It's just the impression I had at the moment with Denise. I couldn't prove it. And you're right, it doesn't make much sense."

"Were you and Denise together the entire time throughout the second act?"

Bruno considered for a moment. "Yes, neither one of us left each other's side."

Of course, I'd have to check this with other people backstage, especially since Bruno had worn a black turtleneck and dark slacks. Now Denise Johnson had a strong motive to kill Carmen, as did Castrato. Did Bruno have a stake in Carmen's will? If he helped kill Carmen, would Castrato or Denise Johnson share any of the wealth with him? In three days, I'd be manning the information booth with him at our magazine's Psychic Fair, and maybe I'd learn more then. The beat of my heart had calmed considerably, and I found myself talking to Bruno as if he were just a source for this story. He had given me new information about Carmen, perhaps the key to solving her murder. For that I was grateful.

"Will I see you at Carmen's wake tomorrow?" I asked.

"Most likely."

After we said good-bye, I rubbed my hands together, and moaned from the pain emanating from my right index finger. It had transformed into a pink sausage, impossible to bend at the joint from the swelling, blotched white and red.

Chapter Twenty

Day Five: Thursday, March 27

Carmen's wake dominated the news, on a snow-filled spring day, at a funeral home on Burlington Avenue in Riverside, a serene village west of Chicago with curvilinear streets and quaint gas-lit street lanterns. It was bad enough attending the wake of a loved one, let alone that of a client to gather more material for a story. Plus I hated funeral homes, probably as much as most. The embalmed dead body, the fake-looking makeup reminded me of the time Mom forced me to kiss my dead Lithuanian aunt on her cold forehead when I was eight.

My plan was to come early to beat the crowd, but I had miscalculated the devotion to Carmen. By 1:00 p.m., quite a throng had gathered, most red-eyed with lacy handkerchiefs wrapped around their fingers. The funeral parlor, an opulent sprawling ranch home in the shape of an H, had four separate wings, each capable of hosting a separate proceeding. On this day, two other showings had been scheduled, yet all the attention swayed to Carmen. Carmen had a flamboyant funeral, typical of a Chicago gangland send-off that included politicians, priests, policemen, artists, and enough cousins to populate a small town. Opera stars flew in from far parts of the world to watch the diva in her last public appearance. Even in death, she created high drama.

An older blond man approached me. "Oh, Alex, thank God you're here."

It took a moment to recognize who was speaking to me. "Castrato! I barely recognized you in that dashing suit."

His wrist swayed back and forth, covering more territory than the North Wind. "I do prefer the silk gowns, I admit, but I can wear one of these when I need to be a man."

"And with style." I wondered if he dated men or women. I

couldn't figure out if he was gay or a castrato who happened to be straight and love women. He wasn't flirting with me, but that wouldn't rule out his heterosexuality in a court of law. However, Castrato had an obvious predilection for women's clothing, so at this point I tended to think of him as a gay cross-dresser without testicles until proven otherwise.

He grabbed my elbow and ushered me toward a secluded striped loveseat, past the growing crowd. "I'm glad you're here."

I looked more closely into his red and swollen eyes. "I'm so sorry for your loss, but I have to ask you something."

"Anything," he choked. "Anything to help Carmen."

"Somebody ransacked my place while I was visiting you, and kidnapped my cat."

"What? Are you okay?"

"Yes, I'm fine. Did you tell anybody about that box?"

"I…I guess I mentioned it to Adriano when he came to visit Monday afternoon."

"Why would you do that?"

"I had no idea he'd do something like that. I am so sorry about your cat. He just…I just…We started talking, and he knew Carmen was thinking about writing a book on him. She threatened him more than once with it. He asked about the material she collected. He'd seen it, or knew about it."

"So you just said, 'It's sitting at Alexandria Vilkas's house? Here's her address?'"

"He's so powerful. I knew that box would be trouble. Besides, now that I think about it, he brought it up first. He said somebody from the chorus told him about it."

Castrato couldn't have known what Donacella told me about her visit to the chorus during Carmen's performance, so it must be true. I wondered if Castrato was afraid of Adriano. "I understand that he made donations to the Lyric Opera, that some believe they were connected to Carmen's success at the opera house. I have to ask. Does he have that sort of a relationship with you?"

Castrato stiffened his back. "No, absolutely not."

"Then what are you so afraid of?"

"I never said I was afraid of him."

I wasn't sure I believed Castrato at that moment. But I had another question to ask.

"What happened to Carmen's baby?"

Castrato couldn't hide his surprise as his eyebrows arched sharply. "Her baby? How did you know about that?"

"Her autopsy revealed she had a Cesarean."

Castrato sighed. "Yes, she had a daughter. Adriano bought off the baby's father and forced Carmen to give her up for adoption. Adriano convinced Carmen the baby would ruin her career, that she had to choose between them."

"And she chose her career."

More people crowded around us as the room filled with visitors intent on seeing Carmen. I feared we wouldn't have much more time to talk privately.

"I understand Carmen intended to change her will. You were about to lose half her estate."

Castrato squeezed his eyes shut. When he opened them, he spoke calmly. "We're all so devastated. Carmen was one of a kind. Her death is a shock to everyone."

He was evading me. "Did you hear what I just told you? We found out about her will."

He pulled out a linen square from a side pocket and blew his nose.

"That doesn't mean anything," he said, after he put away his handkerchief. "You know, I'm singing next Tuesday at the Lyric's fundraiser. I'll be playing Hecate–laughing in the face of death. If I killed Carmen, do you think I could perform so soon?"

I didn't see how one action had anything to do with the other, but before I could respond a lady with blue hair approached us. "Oh, Roberto! I just can't believe she's gone!"

Castrato stood up, took a step toward her, and wrapped his arms around her. They both trembled in melancholy. Ushers constantly carried in wreaths of flowers to place near the diva's coffin. I wasn't going to be able to talk to Castrato anymore, so

149

I moved along.

Waiting my turn in a long line to pay respects, I noticed Carmen's family near the front–Adriano, the father, mother and two sisters, accompanied by three rows of close relatives– aunts, uncles, cousins, grandparents–at least I assumed they were Carmen's family. They wore black, sat stiffly, and looked uncomfortable. Adriano Capezio crowned the head of the receiving line, which was swamped with visitors. I decided to pay my respects to Carmen first.

I approached her coffin, white, gilded with gold. What lay in the coffin resembled Carmen, but this body was an empty vessel and nothing to fear. Only the living could make me tremble. Carmen lay with a rosary wrapped around her fingers, a gold cross on her white frilly blouse. Her face looked more relaxed than I'd ever seen it. Her high forehead and wide face with full lips were shining because of the parlor's bright lights. Through thick makeup, she resembled a porcelain doll. She wore a pink silk blazer that matched her nails, and her raven hair was in a bouffant with tiny silk pink flowers placed to one side.

If an artist strove to depict a temperamental soul in physical features, the artist would do well to model Carmen. Her volatile nature still emanated, even from her corpse...residue of a life charged with excitement, thrills, agony, and drama.

Seeing Carmen in front of me, I imagined what the medical examiner found inside her. Her murder remained practically invisible on the exterior, all the damage by the rubbing alcohol performed internally. With the autopsy, her organs were removed and shifted. During the embalming, her body fluids drained. Externally, her face, her body, the structure of her bones could make one think she hadn't died by a hand of horror.

I shook hands with Carmen's relatives in the receiving line, briefly murmuring condolences, then locked eyes with Adriano Capezio. He looked as distraught as everyone else and showed his eighty-five years in a haggard face, wrinkled and gray, yet his back stood stiff.

"We finally meet in person," he said, clutching my hand with a grip that surprised me by its strength. Before me stood a man still filled with an ageless energy and an ability to command acquiescence. "I understand you were one of the last people to have a conversation with my daughter. She gave you something of significance."

"Yes, she gave me a box of material and asked me to write a book."

"Are you still planning to do that?" He had a suspicious tone, like he thought I would sensationalize Carmen's life in the retelling. Or perhaps that tone meant he wanted the material back and would stop at nothing to make sure I wouldn't write that book.

"I still haven't decided."

"If you're a decent individual, you'll return all that to me. Carmen doesn't need to have that book published anymore."

I remembered how nervous Carmen seemed about my taking her box, how she relaxed only after the messenger had come to take it, the same messenger that brought the champagne bottle.

"She seemed terrified," I said. "I think she knew she was going to be murdered."

"And everything in that box points to me, doesn't it?"

I swallowed hard and nodded. "There was a lot of information in there about you. But, outside of the box, you left that note on that champagne bottle."

With a grimace, he grabbed my right arm and guided me away from the crowd near the coffin. It was all I could do to keep myself from stumbling. He drew me to the chorus section, walked me a bit further. He noticed my pleading glance at Castrato, and said, "Don't..." but he stopped short of finishing his sentence. He looked like he'd changed his mind on what he was going to say about Castrato.

"I want that box back," he said, squeezing my arm harder.

"Let go of my arm, please."

"I will when you tell me what's in that box."

His face looked desperate. Perhaps he was tormented by Carmen's death. I debated over how much to tell him. I gambled on being frank with him.

"In that box, Carmen left some notes that led me to believe she left a clue to her killer in her tomb."

He released my arm. "No, she wouldn't do that. It makes no sense. How could she know?"

At that instant, with him standing before me, I couldn't be sure he killed his daughter. I wondered if he kidnapped my cat. I decided to assume he did, and see if he would deny it.

"Why have you kidnapped my cat?"

He bit his lower lip, looked around the room, and wiped his brow. A renewed resolve returned to his demeanor, and he stiffened his back.

"I want all the material about me returned. There's no reason for you to have it anymore. I realize my relationship with my daughter wasn't ideal, but I don't need you to write a book about it. As soon as I get it, you'll have your kitty."

"So you do have my cat! Is she all right?"

"For now she's fine. But I want that box."

"That material is part of a murder investigation. It's sitting at the police station. I can't get it back for you now."

Adriano laughed hollowly. "I might not get my daughter back, but I won't have you disintegrating the rest of my family."

He pulled out a cell phone, punched in a number, and barked, "Angel? Do it…. Now!" Hanging up, he inched closer. "Find Angel at Resurrection Cemetery in the mausoleum. He's got a message for you."

Chapter Twenty-One

At Resurrection Cemetery, in Justice, just southwest of
Chicago off Route 171, I drove through the bronze gates,
parked near the mausoleum next to a green Jeep, got out, and
looked for Angel. How would I recognize him? The wind
picked up and snow swirled. I entered the mausoleum. A stroll
through the cool mausoleum felt macabre. I barely noticed the
soft classical music, the stained glass windows, the life-size
statues of saints placed every ten feet or so. I found the life-size
wooden statue of St. Casimir. My father prayed to St. Casimir
and died twenty years ago on the Feast of St. Casimir. Ever
since then, I'd kept a special place in my heart for St. Casimir
as well.

As I looked around, I noticed a gruff looking man with a
bristly gray beard and stocky figure approach. The caretaker
had his name embroidered on gray overalls: my messenger.

"Angel?" I asked.

He nodded.

"I heard you had a message for me."

He grunted, then motioned for me to follow him back into
the parking lot. Back in my Corolla, I followed his Jeep past
the pond with a fountain, the Pope John Paul II shrine, and
down a short, hardscrabble road. Was he taking me to
Siddharma? I envisioned hugging her, promising to pay more
attention to her. My wipers swiped the snow rhythmically,
leaving wet streaks on the windshield. My vision blurred as
tears filled my eyes, which I wiped away. A single yellow
bulldozer crawled around on the grounds, stopping to dig a
hole for another grave. Before I knew it, Angel and I were at a
secluded section of the cemetery in front of a tall elm tree. We
got out of our cars and walked across the snow, past countless
Polish and Lithuanian gravestones, until we reached a tall,
aging sycamore.

153

Angel showed his gapped teeth, grayish green, as he pointed to a small, freshly dug hole in the dirt. When I looked inside, I shrieked at the small, bloody carcass that lay rotting. The head of a skinned cat lay to one side, severed from the body. Once Angel saw the emotion register on my face, he pulled me toward the other side of the tree. Hanging there on the trunk was a white, longhaired fur pelt, pierced by a big hunting knife with a nine-inch blade, still flecked with fresh blood.

I staggered as my vision blurred. Cold flakes matted my hair and face. No, God no! Why? Why did Siddharma have to die so brutally? She was in the prime of her life. I couldn't stop imagining the scene of a knife cutting her open while she was still alive, how her blood slowly drained away until mercifully her heart finally stopped.

"Did you do this, Angel?" I finally asked.

He stared back.

I pointed at the pelt and back at Angel, repeating myself. "Angel, did you do this?"

Angel clapped his hands, stained with nicotine, smiled, and nodded excitedly. He tried to tell me something, but it came out in grunts and groans. He dug into his pocket and pulled out a $100 bill, presumably the payment for his deed.

"Did Adriano Capezio give you that money to mutilate my cat?"

Angel shrugged. I think he understood my question, but wouldn't answer. Still, I didn't need him to. I knew it was Adriano, and I was back to believing he killed Carmen because she knew something about him that she planned to expose.

"That bastard," I muttered. I dug into my purse and pulled out a twenty. "Angel, can you give your friend a message from me?"

Angel grabbed my twenty, nodded, and clapped.

"Tell him there's more than one way to skin a cat. Now, they're going to see *my* method. Show me Carmen's tomb."

Angel looked pleased to help, content to receive the money. I almost felt sorry for him, a mute caretaker whose life was given meaning only by attending to the dead. I even forgave him for what he did to Siddharma, recognizing he was just an instrument of Adriano. Adriano, however, would pay for killing my cat.

Angel stepped in front of me, leading the way. We walked for what seemed like an eternity, the snow reaching my ankles in some spots on the road. I had worn my dressy black ankle boots, which provided a thin layer of leather between my feet and the snow. For the most part the cemetery was deserted. Fresh flowers sprinkled with snow dotted some of the gravestones.

Suddenly Angel stopped and stood before an aboveground tomb, ten feet high, with CAPEZIO FAMILY engraved above the doorway. The crypt's two bronze doors were so old they'd turned green. They were unlocked, and I pushed through them. A slab of marble had been removed from one of the shelves, leaving a gaping hole ready for Carmen's coffin to be slid in next to the others. Angel stood behind me, watching, and I told him he could leave. He stood for several moments, and I waited because I wanted to be alone. Finally, I heard his steps crunching in the snow.

I looked around, recalling a phrase that I uttered softly. "Like a child from the womb, like a ghost from the tomb, I arise and unburied again."

Teddy bears, cards, and old red balloons filled the space, large enough to hold thirty-two coffins in its walls, but nothing seemed left by Carmen. I looked through the cards and fingered a black-beaded rosary draped around a porcelain doll, mementoes left earlier for other members of the family. I knew that while Carmen was still lying in state at her wake, this would be a good opportunity to see if she left anything while still alive in her tomb. Tomorrow, when she was brought here to her eternal rest, it would be too late. I read the names engraved on the walls of those who lay here, but nothing seemed significant. Nothing looked out-of-the-ordinary.

I spoke aloud to myself. "'Nor know that what disturbs our blood is but a longing for the tomb.' What did you mean by that, Carmen? Where's your message in this tomb?"

The cold air had its effect, and my toes and fingers became numb. I sucked in my breath, looked outside the doors, noticed the snow had stopped, and that it sparkled under a late afternoon sun. Then I heard footsteps, and in the next moment saw Tony appear. I was never so happy to see him, his friendly face looking so assured. He wore a green parka, knit hat, gloves, sturdy brown boots, and had two cameras slung around his neck, with a large black bag on his shoulder.

"Tony! What are you doing here?"

"I came here to take ghost pictures of Carmen. Alyce sent me to the wake after she read your report. She said if you weren't there, to find out where Carmen was going to be buried. She assumed you'd be looking for something in her tomb, and she wanted me to take pictures of it."

Thank God for Alyce's thoroughness. "You're the first good thing that's happened to me today." I smiled. "I'm glad you're here."

He looked around the crypt and shuddered. "How long have you been here?"

"I don't know…a while."

Tony lifted his camera and started shooting, flashing into the darkness like a strobe light.

"Did you find anything?"

"Nothing," I said. "Carmen didn't leave anything. I can't believe I've been so wrong."

"Are you sure?"

"I'll go over everything one more time."

Tony stood by, watching me reread the cards and letters, check the stuffed animals, scrutinize medallions of saints, rosaries, and crosses. I was so sure I'd find a clue in her tomb. All four passages she had written in her hand pointed to something in a tomb, but I'd searched every nook and cranny of that tomb and was sure Carmen had left nothing for me.

"Let's get out of here," I said.

Moments later we stood outside the crypt. I looked up. It had stopped snowing. The late afternoon sun blazed through a hole in the clouds. Two angels over the crypt's bronze entranceway blew trumpets with long banners. A silent white blanket covered the grounds, and the shadows extended even further.

"Alex, are you okay?" Tony asked, his face hovering close to mine.

"My...my...cat...was here...and...and she...." I covered my eyes and sobbed uncontrollably, the frustration and fear overwhelming me. Tony put his arm around me.

"What happened?"

I couldn't put it into words. The very thought of describing it, giving a name to the heinous act, would make it even more real. I pointed in the direction Angel and I came from, our footsteps marking the trail.

"Wait here. I won't be long."

Tony jogged down the path of footsteps we had left. About ten minutes later, he returned, out of breath, looking fearfully concerned.

"Why don't I take you home?"

157

Silvia Foti

Chapter Twenty-Two

Tony drove separately in his own car, his cell phone connected to mine the entire way back home.

"Are you sure you're all right driving home alone?"

Despite Tony's misgivings, I'd convinced him it would be more sensible we each drive our own cars so I wouldn't have to worry about picking up my car at the cemetery the next morning.

"Yes, I'm fine. You're right behind me, and I'm grateful for that." I'd eaten little that day and realized I was hungry. "As long as you're coming over, do you want some dinner?"

Tony hesitated. "I don't expect you to do any cooking. Why don't I stop somewhere and pick up something? What do you like?"

It had been a long time since a man prepared a meal for me. "An omelet would hit the spot. No meat though."

"I remember. You're a vegetarian. Can you make it home alone now? I'm pulling into Dominick's."

"Yes, I'll be fine. See you soon."

From my rear view mirror I saw him drive into the store's parking lot, and I continued home. After I parked my car in the garage, I climbed the back stairs to my apartment, my body slowly beginning to relax. I dropped my purse on a kitchen chair, walked into the bathroom to look in the mirror, and barely recognized myself. My face seemed rubbery, the skin a plastic mask that pinched together until a small trickle of fluid glided down my cheek. As soon as I wiped away the teardrop, another followed. Siddharma! The grief for her loss rolled through my body in a strong wave. I splashed some cold water on my forehead and eyes. I felt a stab of pain in my right index finger, the one I'd slashed when my mind was on Bruno while making kugelis. Why couldn't I fall for someone nice like Tony?

The doorbell rang. When I ran downstairs and opened the main entrance door for Tony, Mindy peeked out his front door.

"Hi, Mr. Mindy," I said.

He swung his door wide open. "Is this man going upstairs with you?"

"Yes, Mr. Mindy. Is that all right with you?"

"You never bring anybody over. Does your mother know about this?"

"It's about that story I'm working on, you know."

"Aach! That story. You be careful." He shook his head as he shut the door.

"Landlord?" Tony asked.

"Yep." I led Tony in. He had two bags of groceries as well as his camera equipment.

"Nice place," he said, barely looking around.

"Thanks."

Tony pulled out a two-pound T-bone steak. "The steak's for me. I hope you don't mind." He continued grabbing food items from the bags, spreading them out on the kitchen table.

"No, that's fine. I wouldn't expect you to switch your eating habits because of me." I helped him unpack the groceries, enjoying this domestic moment with someone else in my apartment.

"Uh, look Alex. Why don't you take a bath and I'll whip up the eggs."

"Well…"

"Go on, relax. In the meantime, I'll make myself useful." He looked around the kitchen, analyzing the place, keeping his thoughts to himself. A few minutes later, I had slipped into a warm tub full of bubbles. I slid underwater, squeezing my eyes shut.

My thirtieth birthday had passed without fanfare a few months ago, and I reviewed my life as a single woman with my cat. She had outlasted the few men I dated, and I considered her the child I never had. I already missed how she waited for me when I returned, how she nuzzled my legs and sat on my lap, played with a string of yarn. I came up for a gulp of air, and plunged underwater again.

I sank deeper into the tub, bubbles blowing out of my mouth. My seven years as a reporter hadn't prepared me for getting involved in a murder. I was supposed to interview sources, stay at a safe distance from the killer, and sift through facts and clues at a desk. I wasn't supposed to lose my cat. If only there was a way to bring back Siddharma.

Again I came up for air, then slid back underneath the water. So this is what it's like to go through the Order of the Tarot. Did I want to continue? Flashes of my life stretched before me, and all I could imagine was passing through the twenty-two degrees of this secret society, how I'd have a predestined purpose to my life, how I'd connect with my father in some mysterious way as I passed my tests. Of course I'd continue–I couldn't turn back.

Slowly, I eased out of the tub, feeling as if I were stumbling underwater with blocks of cement on my feet and arms. My poor Siddharma! My finger still hurt. I opened the medicine cabinet, found a bottle of ibuprofen, and popped two in my mouth.

"You need some help, Alex?" Tony inquired through the door.

"I'll be right out." I pulled a towel tighter around my body and quickly stepped to the bedroom, off to the side from the kitchen. Tony politely faced the stove to tend to a sizzling steak in one pan and a vegetable omelet in the other.

Minutes later, sitting in a pink terrycloth robe and fuzzy slippers, I sat swirling fresh bread in a plate of olive oil and sipping red wine. Tony was already on his second glass.

I studied Tony as I rubbed my earlobe. He had never told me much about himself, keeping his past a mystery. He lived in a one-bedroom condo on the north side of Chicago in Rogers Park, read science fiction, and loved red meat.

"Why do you do that?" Tony asked, mimicking my gesture as he rubbed his earlobe.

As I dropped my left hand heat rose through my face. "It's something my father taught me when I was a kid."

"What does it mean?"

Tony asked the question like an anthropologist studying a new breed. I liked having him as a friend; but I had a sense that he'd be hell as a boyfriend. During our three years together at *Gypsy Magazine*, he'd already gone through four girlfriends. I'd heard enough details about them to convince me Tony was not for me. Even so, this was the first time he sat in my apartment having a conversation like this. It felt natural, and I was glad he was here.

"Well?" Tony asked.

"Sorry, I was thinking about something else."

"Why do you rub your earlobe?"

"One of my best memories was sitting next to my father at the opera. We always talked during intermission. We were watching Hansel and Gretel, and I was scared of the witch throwing me in the oven. He whispered, 'Just rub your ear like this, and I'll be right next to you.' I felt so safe. Every time I watch an opera, I see him."

Tony took a long sip of his wine. "All women compare other men to their father. It's easier for a guy when the girl's father is an asshole. By comparison, I'm the knight in shining armor."

"What if the father's gone?"

"Oh, that's even worse. It's tough for a man to compete against a ghost."

I smiled, liking Tony's response. He probably couldn't compete against my father, but he was good company. Tony stood up, added paprika to my omelet and pepper to his steak, then set the plates on the table. We sat in silence for several moments, each of us lost in our thoughts and absorbed in dinner. Every clink on a plate seemed louder than usual, and I thought about turning on some music. I wondered if Tony liked classical music.

"Do you mind if I turn on the radio?" I asked.

"Go ahead."

I turned it on and adjusted the volume. The classical station was playing music of Carmen Dellamorte as a tribute.

"That's perfect," Tony said. "Are you ready to talk about your cat?"

The image of Siddharma's fur stabbed onto the tree was still seared in my mind. I shook my head. "Not now, not yet."

"But it's important. When I went back there, I–"

I recoiled at the subject. I wanted to avoid it. Talking about her wouldn't bring her back. I had to emotionally process what happened to her alone before I could talk about it. "Not now, all right? Just wait."

A bubble of silence grew between us. While we listened to Carmen's singing, Tony stared at me and the moment stretched a beat too long. Then he dropped his gaze. I knew then he liked me, but what did I feel for him? What would I say if he asked me out this minute? I'd still say no. My analytical side told me he would certainly be better for me than Bruno, yet I didn't feel overwhelmed by any chemistry between us. Why did I always go for a Mr. Wrong when there was a Mr. Right in front of me? My finger renewed its throbbing pain, sending spasms of agony through the central nervous system.

I pulled off the band-aid and stared at my finger.

Tony's eyes widened. "Wow, I think you have an infection. You're going to have to see a doctor about that. I bet it really hurts."

"It does." Tony was right–my finger would have to be drained. I was grateful for his company, and it was so nice of him to escort me home. It was a side of him I hadn't seen before. Yet I didn't want to lead him on. He had to know we were just coworkers.

Tony trimmed some fat off his steak and set it to the side.

"Hey, can I see your ghost-picture machine?" I asked.

Tony looked relieved we had something new to talk about. "Yeah, sure." He left the table and walked into the living room. When he returned, he handed me the contraption. It resembled a camera with incomprehensible doodads.

"Do you believe in ghosts?" I asked.

He sat down and looked at the photos of my mother, father, and Siddharma on my refrigerator. "No, I... You want to know a secret?"

"Sure."

"I think I'm an atheist."

"It's funny that Alyce has you hunting for a ghost with that contraption, isn't it?"

"Yeah. If she wants to pay me for that, it's her dime."

"So what about the soul? What's your take on that?"

"Just a human feeling of being connected to the universe. We're here and we want to understand why, so we make up gods and religion and creation stories."

"How long have you been thinking about this?"

He shrugged. "I don't know. Probably always. I'm beginning to feel like a fraud. Here I am writing about the supernatural, about the spirit–whatever that means–but I don't feel anything exists beyond this life. Have you ever felt that way?"

"Yeah," I said, rubbing my left earlobe. In my three years of writing for *Gypsy Magazine*, I'd never witnessed a supernatural event. Of course, I'd interviewed hundreds of people who said they witnessed something special. Even with my year of studying the Tarot cards with The Wizard, I'd never seen anything that resembled a ghost or looked like it came from the beyond, yet I was convinced there was a God, or a Goddess. "So what happens if you do get a picture of a ghost, Mr. Atheist?"

"It's not gonna happen. I'm just going through the motions to make Alyce and Edgar happy."

I pushed away my plate and grabbed my wine. "But just for kicks, let's say you take a picture of a ghost. What then?"

"It's not gonna happen."

"Let's pretend, Tony."

Tony shrugged. "And we prove it's not a shadow, a light, a blip, a speck of dust? A bit of undigested beef?"

"Dickens. A Christmas Carol."

Tony smiled.

"Yeah, conclusively proven, airtight."

"Well, maybe then I'll believe in a god."

"Why?"

I stood up to slice the pecorino cheese lying on the wooden board near the sink, and lifted the wet green grapes from the colander, shaking off a few drops. I sat back down across from him at the table and offered him the plate of cheese and grapes. He took a slice of the pungent cheese and snapped off some grapes.

"A ghost would be a manifestation of a spirit. It would prove there's something permanent in us that survives when our corporeal body dies. Ergo, a soul."

I smiled and popped a grape in my mouth. "That's probably why you're working for this magazine."

A shock of hair fell over Tony's brow and he jerked his head in a way that reminded me of my father. He looked like he was struggling to say something. Finally he asked, "Now can you talk about your cat?"

I didn't like how he pushed the subject with me, that he didn't get my none-too-subtle hint that I didn't want to talk about it. I noticed the kitty litter box, and blinked a few times. Would talking about her bring her back?

He said, "Tell me what you saw at the cemetery."

I took a deep breath, visualizing the act, feeling a guilty despair. She was gone because of me. I had put her in harm's way. "This mute hired by Carmen's father...name's Angel. He ripped her open, skinned her, and left her pelt on a tree. It was horrible. But you saw her yourself, didn't you? That's why you left me at the cemetery to see for yourself."

"That's what I've been wanting to talk to you about ever since I arrived here." He smiled wide, as if he were about to burst with some good news. "How do you know it's your cat?"

Was there a chance it wasn't her? "I guess I don't. I just assumed it. The fur was white."

"I have proof it's not your cat."

"What? Why did you wait more than two hours to tell me this?"

"I tried to tell you before, but you wouldn't listen. Remember?"

That was true, and I was jubilant over the news.

Tony stood up, and I followed him into the living room where he rummaged through his big black bag and pulled out a plastic grocery bag holding the fur piece. The blood on the pelt had dried, but Tony held the underside through the plastic bag, showing only the white fur. I approached and studied it, stroked it with my finger. Up close like this, it didn't look like Siddharma's fur.

"This belonged to a rabbit, not a cat."

It's not Siddharma! She's still alive? There's a chance I can get her back!

"How do you know for a fact this is rabbit fur?"

"My father used to take me hunting, and I must have shot a hundred rabbits if I shot one. Nothing I'd want to brag about to a vegetarian, though."

He had a big grin and I almost hugged him. I couldn't believe how happy I felt at that moment, relieved to know that Siddharma wasn't dead, that she was still alive. I don't know why Adriano and Angel went to so much trouble to try to fool me, but I let that go for the moment. A warm feeling of joy spread through me, and I could barely contain it.

"Oh!" I laughed.

Tony couldn't stop smiling either.

We stood inches apart, and I didn't know what I wanted with Tony, not yet. The elation I suddenly felt near Tony must have been a response to the news that Siddharma was still alive.

Tony cleared his throat. "I should go, then. It's getting late."

We heard an insistent rapping on the door.

"Alex, are you there?" yelled Mindy.

When I opened the door, Mindy stepped through the doorway, holding the kugelis pan and inspecting the living room. He nodded at Tony, then looked back at me and thrust the pan forward. "Here. That kugelis was good."

"Thanks," I said.

Tony looked at his watch. "It's time for you to hit the sack.

We can talk more at the office tomorrow."

"Good idea," Mindy said.

I sighed, about to tell Mindy how I didn't appreciate his barging in like this, but I was tired and I wanted Tony to go. It had been a day of new revelations, and I had many impressions to sort through.

After Mindy said goodbye, Tony asked before leaving, "You sure you'll be fine?"

I nodded. "Goodbye, and thanks for everything."

"You're welcome."

After Tony left, I shut off the light and flopped onto the bed. Was it possible that thoughts of Tony could replace thoughts of Bruno? At least he wasn't married. Maybe I was finally getting over Bruno. A sense of satisfaction took over. Just before I fell asleep, I thought of Siddharma, still alive!

Chapter Twenty-Three

Day Six: Friday, March 28

When I awoke, the finger was beyond recognition–
unbendable, pulsating like a cartoon, a true emergency. My
brain's five-bell alarm howled, "Doctor! Doctor! You need a
doctor!"

Within an hour, I sat at the clinic on Archer Avenue, my
mind whirling over what had happened yesterday, but
powerless to do anything because of my finger. The doctor, a
young woman, tsked *tsked*.

"It's infected; we're going to have to drain it. You really let
it go too long," she droned. "It's at the point where the infection
could affect the bone, and if it gets there we're in big trouble."
She grabbed a surgical blade from a drawer, tugged the finger,
and told me to brace myself.

"No painkiller?" I gulped.

"Won't help." She proceeded to slice a one-inch gash near
the knuckle and squeezed with determination. White and green
pus, with blood, spurted out like a volcano. "Wow, there's a lot
in there," the doctor declared with enthusiasm. It was all I
could do to keep from fainting.

With the finger wrapped in bandages and a ten-day
prescription of antibiotics, I drove down the Stevenson
Expressway, feeling like I should crawl into a hole. I had to
admit, though, that with my finger drained I could think clearly
about what to do next. To find Siddharma, I needed Claire
Fergusson's help. When I called her from my cell phone, it
didn't take long for her to agree to accompany me to
Resurrection Cemetery.

"I had a vision of an angel," she said on the other end of
the phone. "It was the ugliest angel I ever saw–old, white hair,
and with green teeth. He said, 'Follow me. I'll lead you to the
lost cat.'"

"Really?" I said, impressed with her vision and knowing exactly what she described.

"Do you have any idea what this means? Tango said you'd know."

"Bless Tango," I said, flipping down the sun visor to avoid the glare as I drove east toward the lake. I held the phone between my ear and shoulder as I gripped the wheel. "There's a man named Angel who works at Resurrection Cemetery. I met him yesterday and he led me to believe that he killed Siddharma. In the end, he was just trying to trick me for some reason. Anyway, he might know the whereabouts of Siddharma, and I want you to meet him."

Claire squealed in delight. "Well, am I fairy godmother to animals, or what? Oh, Tango, you were so right." She cooed to her cat another moment before telling me, "Of course I'll go with you."

I smiled, thinking maybe my psychic abilities were blossoming. "I knew you would. I'm on my way."

As I drove to meet her at her apartment, I thought of the vision I had with the Fool card, how the wolf led me to a gravestone in the cemetery that made me think it was Siddharma's, but it wasn't. Yesterday at the cemetery, Angel led me to a carcass that I thought was Siddharma, but again, it wasn't. The cards spoke to me.

Half an hour later, Claire sat in the passenger seat of my car, a floppy straw purse on her lap with Tango's head peeking out. Her makeup was strong and loud, like her purple muumuu and the paisley silk scarf wrapped around her head. We drove back down the Stevenson, through Summit into Justice, until we arrived at Resurrection. On the way I filled Claire in about the wake, seeing Castrato, Adriano, and what happened at the cemetery. I described to her the bloody carcass and the white fur pelt stabbed on the tree.

"When I first saw it, I was convinced it was Siddharma," I said.

Claire nodded. "Angel wanted you to believe that."

I guessed Angel was under orders to kill Siddharma and it

was important I assumed so, but I couldn't figure out why he skinned a rabbit instead. He didn't seem like the type to have a soft spot for cats.

"But last night… Well, my coworker told me the white fur pelt came from a rabbit, not a cat."

"Oh, your precious kitty is alive," Claire said. "Tango is sure of that, and so am I. But what I still don't get is why. Why take your cat?"

"Before Carmen died, she gave me a box of information about her father. She wanted me to write a book on him. I believe Adriano kidnapped my cat as a ransom for that box. I'd give anything to return the box, but the police have it."

"What's so special about the box?"

"I've gone through most of it, and I believe there's incriminating evidence against Adriano. There have been persistent rumors that he's with The Outfit, into vending machines and maybe gunrunning. I saw some receipts that might prove that. I also think she left a special message for me that would tell me who she thought would kill her."

"You mean she knew she was going to get killed?"

"Maybe. She wrote poetry passages dated March 4th that made me think they were clues she left for me to find. I thought she left something in her family's tomb, like a note that explained who she thought would kill her. But I didn't find anything."

"What did the poetry say?"

"One is by Francis Bacon. 'Whence we see spiders, flies, or ants, entombed and preserved forever in amber, a more than royal tomb.'"

"Hmmm," Claire said. She scratched Tango's neck. "Are you listening to this?" She lifted Tango and rubbed her cheek next to his face. She put him back in her bag. "He has no idea."

"I don't know. Maybe I was just reading something into nothing."

"Oh, now, take heart. I wouldn't totally dismiss your idea about the clues. You may be right. Keep an open mind."

I pulled into the parking lot of the cemetery's office. Claire and I stepped inside and approached the middle-aged blonde in front of a computer. "I'm looking for a guy named Angel," I said.

She sized us up. "You guys cops?"

I suppressed a giggle, as I couldn't imagine anyone mistaking Claire for a cop. Her ten silver and gold bangles on each arm clinked as she rebalanced her purse with Tango inside.

"No," I said. "Just friends. Angel has something of mine."

She turned to a gray-haired man in a suit behind her. "Looks like Angel's got company again."

The man now approached. "Angel is extremely popular lately. Is he in trouble?"

"Who else came to see him?"

"Somebody with a big wad of money, that's for sure. He never gave me his name. What's going on with Angel?"

It did sound like Adriano was here. "I just need to need talk to him."

The man laughed. "Talk? Angel's a mute. No tongue."

"No tongue!" Claire gasped.

"Oral cancer. And he still smokes, if you can believe it. He's also illiterate. Despite his handicaps, though, he's one of my best workers."

"I won't take much of his time."

"Just get on the road and look for him."

"Thanks."

We found Angel running a yellow bulldozer, digging a fresh hole. When he noticed us, he stopped the machine, though stayed seated inside. He looked surprised, almost happy.

"Must not get a lot of attention," Claire muttered to me as we approached.

"Hey, Angel, remember me?"

He nodded.

"You didn't really kill my cat yesterday, did you?"

Angel shrugged, faced the windshield, and turned on the ignition to show he didn't want to talk to us. Claire stepped in front of the bulldozer. Luckily Angel didn't drive the bulldozer forward. We both suspected he was hiding my cat in his home.

"Take me to your home, Angel," I said, walking next to him. I pulled out a $20 bill. Then a second one, followed by a third. Angel still didn't move. Claire moved close to the bulldozer and pulled out a pack of cigarettes from her purse. Angel grabbed the $60 and cigarettes and hopped off his bulldozer. He opened his wallet to stuff the bills inside and pulled out an ID to show me his address, then grunted and gestured.

"He wants us to drive," Claire said with Tango at her ear. "He'll go with us."

In ten minutes we pulled into Sterling Estates in Justice.

"You knew Siddharma was in a trailer park," Claire gushed to Tango. "Didn't you?"

Tango amazed me more with each passing minute.

Angel's trailer stood on the back of the lot, its aluminum frame the color of corrosion. Empty milk cartons, cans, and paper littered the front yard. An old box spring stood upright, leaning against his trailer, damp and moldy. We followed Angel inside.

Claire huffed and looked like she needed to catch her breath. Gray underwear and towels covered every possible seating surface. Angel shoved a layer of clothes to the end of the couch, and Claire plopped into it.

"I know, honey," Claire purred to Tango. Then she looked at me. "Your cat was here. Definitely."

I faced Angel. "*Was* here? Where is she now?"

He grunted and groaned. I stepped into every possible nook and cranny of the trailer, taking all of ten seconds. There was no sign of Siddharma.

"A man came yesterday, and took her," Claire explained.

My heart sank. "What man?"

Angel grunted.

"His name!"

A groan.

I pulled out a paper and pen. "Write down his name,

please."

He shrugged with another grunt.

"He can't read or write," Claire said. "Remember?"

"Illiterate. Just my luck. Now what?"

Tango jumped out of Claire's arms and clawed at my purse.

"What, Tango?"

I thought for a moment, and pulled out my deck of Tarot cards. This would be a first in suspect identification.

"Maybe you can point me in the right direction with these pictures," I said to Angel, fanning my deck. I stepped to the little Formica table, each corner severely nicked. I wiped off the rags from one chair; Angel did the same with the other. Then I cleaned the table's surface, moving the garbage onto the pile settling in the sink.

"Tarot cards!" Claire said. "This is interesting." Tango jumped back onto her lap.

The three of us huddled around the kitchen table. I pulled out all the court cards from the Rider Waite deck, lining them up in four rows of four cards.

"I don't have a photo of all my suspects, but with these court cards, Angel might be able to narrow it down with a rough description."

"Good idea," Claire said. Tango purred.

I pointed to the row of Queens. "Was it a woman?"

Angel shook his head, and I removed the Queens. Angel smiled and clapped his hands, thoroughly enjoying this game.

"Was it a younger man, like a teen-ager?"

Angel shook his head no, and I removed the Pages. That left eight cards, four Kings and four Knights.

"Who took my cat? If you had to answer with one of these eight cards, which one would it be? A Knight is a young adult male, say in his twenties. A King is an older, mature male."

Angel cracked his lips apart, revealing yellow-green teeth, then pointed to his heart.

"Yes, Angel. You're a king. A mature man."

Angel smiled and nodded. He took his time studying each card, picking up each Knight, then putting it down. Finally he pulled out a King of Wands and a King of Cups. This confused me.

"Was it two men who took my cat, Angel?"

He shook his head no.

"Just one?"

He nodded.

"Can you pick just one card?"

I removed the others so that Angel could focus on just the two, the King of Wands and the King of Cups.

Angel finally chose the King of Wands.

My memorizing the meaning of each card paid off. "This man has wit, charm, fondness for excitement, and is a skilled communicator. Like an agent?"

Angel clapped his hands.

"Bruno Scavoro?"

Angel nodded.

What was he doing with my cat?

As my anger mounted over Bruno's betrayal, my mind spun. It was possible, I thought. Bruno was in Chicago this week not just for the diva's funeral, but also for the Psychic Fair. He was also Adriano's friend, but why would he be a party to this?

I looked at Claire. "What does Tango say?"

Claire scratched Tango's neck.

"He doesn't know," Claire said.

I turned to Angel. "Where's Siddharma now?"

Angel shrugged.

After a moment, Claire declared, "She's in a fancy hotel, eating fresh salmon and drinking heavy cream from a silver bowl."

"Oh, just like home," I said, and even Tango smiled.

"I have a lot of clients who travel with their pets," Claire said. "It sounds like the Ritz Carlton or the Four Seasons, if you ask me."

I knew Bruno stayed at one of those hotels when visiting Chicago. I'd see him tomorrow at the magazine's Information Booth in Navy Pier. The challenge now was to penetrate his hotel room to find Siddharma. Should I break in or have Bruno invite me?

Chapter Twenty-four

Much as I wanted to go straight to Bruno's hotel room, I knew I wouldn't get in without an invitation. That meant I had to go to work and brainstorm ways with Alyce and wait until tomorrow when I'd see Bruno at the Psychic Fair. Besides, I hadn't been in the office for a day and a half, and I had plenty of work waiting for me.

By the time I arrived at the office, it was 2:35 p.m. I tried entering incognito…with any luck, I'd be spared the question-and-answer session I'd be bound to get from anyone who saw me. What happened at Carmen's wake? Why did you go to the cemetery? Is your cat all right? I still had much to do to prepare for the Psychic Fair tomorrow, and to figure out how to get into Bruno's hotel room.

As I stepped off the elevator into the office, Alyce sauntered by. "Where have you been? Are you all right? Tony told us what happened at the cemetery yesterday."

"I…" I wanted to tell her about my conversation with Adriano and how I didn't find anything in Carmen's tomb.

"Look, I want a meeting in my office in one hour with you and Beata."

"Alyce, I–" I also wanted to tell her how I discovered that Bruno had my cat.

"We're still planning the Psychic Fair, and I've got no time now. One hour, okay?" She threw me a withering stare.

"Okay," I mumbled. I supposed I could wait an hour to explain everything.

Alyce stormed away, heading for the conference room, shaking her head.

Then Beata Szybowski appeared around the corner from the offices and strolled down the hall, heading my way. "Alex! What happened yesterday?"

"I went to the wake and…"

She raised her right arm like she was stopping traffic. "Tony told me all about that incident at Resurrection. Why didn't you tell me what you were up to? I think I could have helped."

She looked so angelic with her wide-eyed innocence, but she didn't fool me, not one bit. "Help, my foot! You just want to take over the story."

"Normally I'd feel sorry for someone like you, but you know what, Alex? You are evil. Evil, evil, evil, and I'm watching out for you." She stood in a warrior pose, her arms crossed and legs spread out, and she pointed her right finger at me, waving it like a little Polish flag. "You may be fooling everyone else around here, but I'm on to you."

"What are you–"

"Oh, don't play Miss Innocent with me. You knew exactly what you were doing when you went to Resurrection Cemetery. You were looking for clues in Carmen's tomb. Tony told me everything. As usual, you've been holding back on the rest of your team, and I for one do not appreciate it."

"If you must know, I didn't find anything. There was nothing you could have done to help." I tried walking past her, but she blocked my way.

"If you had told me about the box sooner, I could have helped you go through the material. Maybe together we could have figured out where she left her clues. Obviously you misread them."

With her know-it-all attitude, she was trying to bully me, and my anger mounted. Again I tried to walk around her, but she wouldn't let me pass.

"I was only trying to help. We're working on this story as a team, remember?"

We stood inches apart, and I smelled her pungent coffee breath. Her blue eyes bored into me with righteous indignation, but all I saw were two dark wells of treachery and deceit. I exploded, spewing my words out like a professional knife thrower.

"Help, right! Like grabbing the autopsy report from Joe

Burke and failing to give it to me. Like going through that box of information and then telling Alyce about it. And possibly ripping out a page from Carmen's diary! You are trying to steal my story and you are a conniving, devious, underhanded bitch."

She pretended to look puzzled. "Are you all right? I think you've lost your mind."

"You're not here six months and you're taking over my story," I huffed. "How long have you been planning this? I bet you've been stalking me for just this sort of opportunity! Well, I'll tell you one thing. You're not going to get away with it."

The look of confusion on Beata's face could have won her an Academy award. "I have no idea what you're talking about."

"Oh, don't you?" I raised my hand and swung it back, ready to slap her, but I stopped, realizing what a bad idea that would be. She'd run to Alyce immediately, and my boss might be forced to fire me.

Beata took a step forward with a taunting gleam in her eye. "I was with Bruno last night. At the Four Seasons. All alone. I just wanted you to know."

I walloped her hard on her face and she staggered back against the wall. Instantly, I regretted it.

"How dare you!" she screamed, holding her left cheek.

The receptionist came around from her desk and rushed to Beata's side. "Are you all right?"

Beata nodded. But when she looked at me, she had a slight curl to her lips.

My right hand still stung from the harsh contact, and I looked at it like a foreign appendage. I'd never slapped anyone in my life, and here I hit this woman without a second thought. What had gotten into me?

Beata straightened up. "Alyce is going to hear about this. Start gathering your things because you're going to take them home by the end of the day." She turned away from me, thanked the receptionist for her attention, and headed for her office.

The receptionist *tsked, tsked*, and returned to her station.

What had I done? I made a beeline for Alyce's office to tell her about the fight before Beata did. I willed Alyce to materialize, but of course, she had just told me she was going to a meeting. My anger and fear mounted as I stepped to my own cubicle. Alyce could fire me for this.

Tony bopped into the office holding a stack of photos. He noticed my scowl. "You want to talk about it?"

I shook my head, not knowing where to begin. "It's Beata. She's sabotaging me because she wants to take over my position. And I just slapped her."

Tony sat in the chair before my desk. He looked concerned, but had a hint of a smile. "You're kidding. You slapped her?"

"It's not funny. She could get me fired."

Stress lines appeared on his brow. "She probably could. But you've been here for three years and Alyce knows you wouldn't do something like that unless you were provoked. It's completely out of character."

"Thanks for your vote of confidence. But, God! I fell right into her trap. If only I could take the slap back."

"You're under a lot of stress. Even Alyce has to see that. I'm sure she'll give you another chance."

I rubbed my eyes and replayed the slap in my mind, the look on Beata's face, and her determination to make sure Alyce knew every single detail of that scene. "I hope you're right."

Tony's face grew haggard with worry. "There's something else about Beata that you should know about."

"What?"

"She's having an affair with Bruno Scavoro."

I had the sensation of a trapdoor opening in my belly and me falling through a big, black hole. Did everybody know about this, except me? I imagined Bruno flirting with Beata and she not having any regrets about kissing him or even spending the night with him. When I pictured them together, I saw compatibility.

"Did you hear me?"

"Yes, sorry. How'd you find out?"

"It's been going around the office, but I wouldn't print it in the employee newsletter."

"Well, I would because I just heard it from the horse's mouth."

Tony gave me a long searching look. Did he suspect any of my former feelings for Bruno? I hoped not. Besides, I was over Bruno. Now that I'd heard of Bruno's involvement in the kidnapping of my cat, I knew I had to forget about him. Only a mean person could use an innocent animal for his own ends. I looked at the bandage on my finger, realizing it already felt better. Removing Bruno from my mind was as easy as squeezing out the infection from my finger.

"They deserve each other," I said.

Tony smiled broadly. The same smile he'd given me yesterday when he revealed that Angel couldn't have skinned Siddharma. He was turning into a good friend.

That's when I noticed the stack of photographs Tony held in his lap. I figured they were the ones Tony had shot at the cemetery in his search for Carmen's ghost. I nodded toward them.

"Well?"

"Well nothing." He shrugged. He even looked disappointed, which I thought odd since he didn't believe in ghosts.

"Does this mean you were hoping to have proof of a ghost so you could convert from atheism?"

"Nah. Hey, it's a living, right?" His unconcerned act didn't convince me...he *wanted* to see a ghost. The phone rang in his office, and he walked back to his cubicle without comment, leaving me to my thoughts. So Beata was dating Bruno now. How could I convince Alyce that Beata was trouble...and save myself from getting fired?

Chapter Twenty-five

My mind, running in a continuous loop of figure eights, needed a diversion from Beata and Bruno, so I pulled out my Tarot cards from my purse, laid them out on my desk, and worked with their energies. Hoping nobody would interrupt me at my desk, I worked quickly. Eventually, I found my way to the Fool card, the zero card. It had conflicting meanings, from a buffoon who knows nothing to a divine God who is ready for anything. In its most positive aspect, the Fool is a person with a clean slate–a *tabula rasa*–ready to be filled with creative potential.

I stared at The Fool card, recognizing Castrato as the fool in this cast, wild and unpredictable. A memory gnawed at me from my first interview with him. I remembered the quivering misgivings I felt in the front of my torso when Castrato told me about his operation. Where did Castrato have his testicles surgically removed? He wouldn't answer me directly, saying he didn't remember since he was only eleven years old. He had been crying and holding on to his paper tissue, dabbing his eyes…and his sense of grief over the loss of Carmen, palpable in the room, distracted me at the time from pursuing the question further. Now, looking back on the moment, I wondered if he had told me the truth.

I breathed deeply, closed my eyes, and focused on the point in the middle of my forehead that grew white hot, pulsating steadily for several minutes, radiating an inner warmth and sureness that connected me to the best in the Universe. Finally, the image faded. I sat still another few minutes, welcoming all thoughts, yet gently pushed away the ones that didn't concern my question. How could I find out where Castrato had his operation?

When I opened my eyes, I looked at the computer before me and searched through the Internet for that article about

Castrato's operation in a medical journal. The article would have to be at least thirty years old. Castrato had said his doctor agreed to perform the operation if he could write about it, but what doctor would agree to such a devilish deal? I looked through several medical databases but, as expected, couldn't find the article. It was a long shot, but I thought a medical journal might archive its studies and make them available to the public for a fee. Although that was a logical reason why I couldn't find the article, I also sensed Castrato had lied about his operation. From what I had just read about castrated men, they all became endomorphic after their operation because of the decrease in male hormones. Castrato, on the other hand, was thin and angular, not an ounce of fat on him. If he lied about his operation, what else would he lie about? How could the operation be proved, short of asking Castrato to drop his trousers?

For the moment, I stopped my search for proof of Castrato's operation, and returned to reliving how I'd slapped Beata. At the time, the impact of my palm on Beata's cheek felt so satisfying, but with each passing minute the satisfaction ebbed until I only felt regret. The Fool card lay in the middle of my desk. A silly buffoon, careless about his steps ahead, would fall off the cliff. I couldn't help but identify myself as the fool in a journey.

When I approached Alyce's office, I saw she had already arrived. We were alone, and I wanted to use the next few minutes to tell Alyce how Beata used Carmen's box to put me in a bad light and how she made me slap her. My ultimate goal was to write the story without Beata's "help."

"Well, well, well," Alyce said, her hands clasped before her on her desk. "Where should we start?"

"As long as we're alone, I want to tell you something about Beata."

"About Beata? Funny, she's been talking about you a lot too. She gave me an earful a few minutes ago. What's going on between you?"

From the tone in Alyce's voice, I could tell Beata had told

her about my slap. I was about to respond, but then Beata stepped in. "Did we start the meeting without me?"

I could have slapped Beata's other cheek.

"No, we didn't," Alyce said. "Alex was just going to tell me what happened yesterday." She threw me a you-better-fess-up look.

Beata took the seat next to me and rubbed her cheek, sending me a sly glance.

Alyce cleared her throat. "I've got another meeting soon and want to focus on the murder case. The deadline is looming. Alex, are you ready to explain what you found out yesterday?"

For some reason, Alyce didn't talk about the slap. Wasn't she going to demand an explanation? Should I bring it up first? Maybe Alyce just wanted to move along, without dwelling on the slap. Or she would talk about it alone with me when she had more time. Either way, I experienced a small sense of relief, because I knew that if Alyce meant to fire me, she wouldn't be conducting this meeting about the story. Surely I'd get a warning.

"Yes." I recounted to Alyce and Beata everything that had happened at the cemetery yesterday, how Angel led me to a decapitated cat that looked like Siddharma, how I searched through Carmen's tomb and found nothing, how Tony proved to me that Angel had skinned a rabbit, not my cat, and how I decided to visit Angel's trailer this morning.

"Why would Adriano go to all that trouble?" Alyce asked.

"He doesn't want me to write about him. He also wants that box of material back, even though I told him the police have it. The fact that he wants it so badly makes me believe there's something in the material that would prove he's in the Outfit and that he killed his daughter."

Alyce considered this. "We'll need to go through that material very carefully. I'm going to ask Beata to help."

"Beata?" Although as soon as I said her name, I realized it sounded like I was questioning Alyce's judgment, and I regretted it. In light of my recent episode with Beata, I should be grateful I'm still sitting in Alyce's office working on a story for *Gypsy Magazine*. Nobody said those words, but they hung in the air as if they came booming out of a megaphone.

"Yes, your co-reporter," Alyce said with an edge in her voice. "You've had the material since Monday and you still haven't figured out who killed Carmen or why Adriano wants that box back. You need help."

Beata smiled demurely. "I'd be happy to go through that material."

I bet she would, but I smiled back at her just as demurely.

"We still have to sort our suspects," Alyce said. She pulled out her deck of Tarot cards and sifted through them until she found the Emperor. She shoved it in the center.

"Let's talk about our number one suspect, Adriano Capezio. No matter who did the actual killing, let's assume Adriano had a hand in it. It was his champagne that Carmen drank. And from what Alex just explained, he kidnapped her cat to scare her away from writing the book on him. Is there anything else?"

"There is one more thing on Adriano," I offered.

"Go on," Alyce said.

"In Carmen's diaries, she said he was covering up an illicit scheme and she threatened to expose him."

"An illicit scheme? Like what?" Beata asked. "Drugs?"

"I don't think so," I answered.

"Racketeering?" Alyce asked. "Loan sharking? Gambling? Money laundering? Securities fraud?"

I shook my head to all of them.

"How about political corruption?" Beata asked.

I looked at both of them, wondering where they got their material. "I think it's smuggling."

"Smuggling what?" Alyce asked.

"Guns. An unusual type. It's called an Ilmato."

Alyce and Beata both looked puzzled.

"Il *matto* means the fool in Italian. I'm guessing Adriano had something to do with creating the name. His restaurant Il Pagliacci means the clown."

Alyce's eyes blinked with incredulity. "He does have a

thing for clowns…and fools. This *really* fits into our fool theme." Her face beamed with good cheer, for now the story was taking shape. If a prominent man like Adriano were found to be Carmen's killer, it would be exciting news and she wanted to be the first to come out with it. So did I.

"But where does he get the guns?" Beata asked.

I answered, "I'm still not sure. I found receipts from a gun factory in Paraguay. I believe he imports them and stores them, possibly at the military base. I also believe he funnels the profits from the guns to his passion–opera, and that's why everyone in this town is looking in the other direction. Too many people are benefiting from Adriano's generosity."

Then Alyce's face twisted into a dubious expression, like this was all too good to be true. "How did you come by all this information?" she asked.

I scratched my neck, not wanting to talk about my interview with Tango just yet. It was the sort of thing that would only play well if I could find some concrete proof. Even though Tango had seen an Ilmato, I hadn't. Even for *Gypsy Magazine*, basing the entire story on a psychic conversation with a cat would be too much. "Uh…information on the streets."

Alyce held her thumb and forefinger about an inch apart.

"Do you realize I'm this close to yanking you off the story?"

The corners of Beata's lips lifted slightly.

She must be upset Alyce hadn't fired me for slapping her. I felt good about that. Even so, I was not going to tell Alyce about Tango yet. Plus The Wizard said my test would take ten days. It wouldn't be much longer until we found our killer. At that point, Tango's role wouldn't matter. In the meantime, I'd keep my source a secret.

"It's a reliable source," I said. "Trust me."

Alyce raised an eyebrow in a questioning slant, then must have decided to drop it.

"Okay," she said. "How does Bruno fit in with the catnapping?"

I breathed deeply, recovering from my close call in revealing Tango as a source, then braced myself for thinking about Bruno's role. It was something I'd been wondering myself. "Bruno must be involved in Adriano's gun scheme. It's the only explanation for his sudden involvement in kidnapping my cat."

Beata asked, "You're going to be spending tomorrow morning with him at the Psychic Fair, aren't you? That would be a perfect opportunity to find out more."

I wondered if she was going to be spending the night with him. A picture flashed in my mind of the two of them kissing. "As a matter of fact, I am. But I don't know how that's going to get me into his hotel room where I could snoop around for my cat and find evidence about his involvement in the gun scheme. It's not like he'll just admit to all this."

"You've got a point," Beata said.

We sat in silence, thinking. Alyce drummed her fingers on the desk.

I snapped my fingers. "I've got it! I'll talk about my ball gown with Bruno tomorrow. Complain how I don't have a place to change."

From Alyce's glance at me, I gathered she seemed to appreciate the craftiness of this strategy.

"I think that will work," Alyce said. "Staff is required to wear formal gowns for tomorrow evening's extravagant *Gypsy Magazine* Psychic Awards ball to honor readers who furthered the legitimacy of the supernatural. Bruno will pick up on the hint of your wanting to get into his hotel room, and will invite you in an instant."

Of course, I realized he'd invite just about any woman into his room, but I let that go. Of course, I hated Bruno for kidnapping my cat, but I knew I had to manipulate my way into his hotel room to find proof of Siddharma and possibly Bruno's involvement with the Ilmatos.

Alyce threw me her conspiratorial look, the one I'd missed for the past few days, the one that said she regarded me highly. Maybe she had forgiven me for slapping Beata.

Beata stroked her chin. "It could work."

"Okay, we all like the idea," I said. "Now let's talk about Bruno as a murder suspect."

I pulled out a King of Wands from the Tarot deck. "He wore a black turtle neck and black pants at the opera. I spoke with him during the first act. At intermission, Denise Johnson interrupted us and walked away with him. He has since told me that he went backstage with her to talk about Carmen's will."

"Yes, he told me that too," Beata beamed.

I glared at her, wondering how many other things he told her, then continued. "Apparently Carmen was about to change her will and leave everything to her daughter."

Alyce said, "Of course that would upset Denise Johnson and Castrato. But how would it upset Bruno?"

I slumped back in my chair. "I don't know."

Beata shook her head. "Me neither. Bruno and Denise Johnson are each other's alibis. They both swear they didn't leave each other's side while they were backstage."

Alyce said, "Let's keep working on Bruno. In the meantime, what about Castrato? How does he fit in?"

Beata looked at me and jumped in. "This all started with Carmen's interest in the Tarot, especially in the Fool, which was her favorite card. Like Alex said, Carmen always referred to Castrato as her fool."

"And he's not the murderer?" Alyce asked, looking at me.

"I don't know."

"Pity," Alyce said. "It would wrap up the story so nicely. Are you sure?"

"There is something odd about him."

Beata and Alyce exchanged glances and snickered.

I smiled and made a snip-snip gesture with my fingers to show I understood their laughter. "It concerns his castration, yes. I searched for proof of his operation. He said the doctor who performed it wrote a medical study on it, but I couldn't find it. I'm beginning to think he may not be castrated."

"Really?" Alyce said. "That is fascinating. But how does that make him a murderer?"

"I don't know. We do know, however, he was in Carmen's will, ready to inherit half of her estate. Perhaps he wanted to stop her from changing her will and leaving everything to her daughter."

"His motive is very strong," Alyce said. She looked at her watch. "Sorry. I've got another meeting. We're going to have to continue this some other time."

Beata pouted. "But we haven't even talked about Donacella Dimitriano, her understudy; Felix Vasilakis, the assistant conductor; or Teresita Cuevas at Parsifal's Spa."

It was true. I was just beginning to enjoy this process and especially appreciated how Alyce seemed to act as if everything was okay between us. Maybe she would even listen to me about Beata. I had to find a way to talk to her alone.

Alyce waved her arms as if she were erasing a blackboard. "You certainly have a lot of loose ends to tie up."

She stood to end the meeting.

"Alyce, I need to talk to you. Alone."

"Alright, kiddo, but make it fast. I've got five minutes left before I go to another meeting, and for four of them, I'm going to the john."

Beata said good-bye, and I followed my boss into the bathroom. I looked under the stalls to make sure we were alone.

"It's about Beata."

"What about her?"

I tried to form my words carefully, but Alyce's lack of patience made me nervous. "I think you should fire her."

Alyce looked ready to explode. "Alex, you're just jealous. Beata graduated valedictorian of her class, volunteered in a leper colony in Argentina, and did an internship at *Time Magazine*. You're here because Edgar's girlfriend is your mother. Why should I fire Beata?"

The receptionist walked in and smiled at both of us as she headed into a stall.

"Never mind," I mumbled, crestfallen.

"And furthermore, Beata told me how you slapped her in

the hallway. Now, I'm not saying she didn't provoke you. She told me how she became overenthusiastic about that box and admitted she may have overstepped her bounds. But you know what? It doesn't justify your slapping her. I've had just about enough pettiness from you. This is your last warning. Get it together, or get out. And I don't care who your mother is dating."

After Alyce left, I stepped into a stall and flushed the toilet ten times, equivalent to the amount of tears I held back. Nothing I did would ever be enough around here. It was always going to be about my mother. I had to prove I could get somewhere without her influence. And the only way was to find Carmen's killer first.

Chapter Twenty-Six

Day Seven: Saturday, March 29

Saturday morning felt spring-like with the warmer air, sunny sky, and snowless streets. Fresh dew clung to the grass, and I welcomed the clean smell as I walked through the backyard into the garage. After sliding into the car and turning on the classical music station, I sampled my black coffee and thought about Bruno. For days, I'd been looking forward to spending time with him in the information booth, but now felt frightened about what would happen. Everything was mixed up and needed sorting—my feelings for Bruno, my yearning to see Siddharma, and my desire to determine who killed Carmen. I wanted so much resolved today, and it all hinged on my obtaining the key to his hotel room. The Wizard's words echoed in my mind: "Harness the power of your 50,000 thoughts within a day and lead them all in the same direction."

Behavior is the result of your goals, The Wizard had instructed me on several occasions. If your goals are clear, your feelings and actions will follow. Align your thoughts so that they match your goals. First I examined my feelings for Bruno…a ping of desire shot through my bosom at the thought of seeing him. I commanded myself to stop desiring Bruno because he was married, but I struggled with this because my objective was to get his hotel key. And to do so, I'd have to flirt, which would involve placing myself in the heat of temptation.

Once I got the key and entered his hotel room, I'd have the opportunity to look for Siddharma. Imagining my reunion with Siddharma, I saw myself cleansed of my desire for Bruno. I couldn't love a man involved in the kidnapping of my cat—it was as simple as that.

Then I'd question Bruno on his entanglement with Adriano's gun-smuggling operation. I needed proof of his connection to the Ilmatos.

My plan came to me in a flash, like a meteor of insight bursting through my consciousness. I sipped more coffee and felt confident, more sure than I've felt since beginning this assignment.

I turned my head to look at the full-length gown I'd hung on a hook in the back seat. This two-piece, turquoise, shimmering acetate dress was my ticket into Bruno's hotel room. I pictured myself telling Bruno I needed a place to change, and envisioned him giving me his key. Then I shifted into drive and pressed the gas pedal.

I headed to Navy Pier where *Gypsy Magazine* was hosting its weekend Annual Psychic Fair that attracted subscribers from around the world. In its third year, the Fair had already increased in size from 500 to 3,000 attendees who came to browse nearly 100 exhibitors showing seers, channelers, chakra healers, meridian unblockers, witches, Reiki rattlers, and feng-shui fortunetellers.

During the two days, we also hosted several workshops on contacting your guardian angel and basic Tarot. Attendees could learn about meditation, crystal healing, drumming and visioning, past-life recollections, communing with angels, and soul purpose.

The theme this year was Tarot cards, and Alyce wanted me to connect this aspect of the fair with Carmen's murder. No easy feat.

As I neared Navy Pier, my stomach lurched into a swirl of jitters thinking about Bruno. I just want the key, I just want the key, I told myself. I parked my car and walked to my station at the Information Booth. Navy Pier was the size of three football fields jutting out into Lake Michigan. The Information Booth was already crowded with registrants; Bruno, wearing a colorful Fool's cap, stood waiting for me.

His smile sent a jolt of electricity through me. "Nice hat," I said.

"Want one?" he asked.

"Staff isn't allowed to have one," I responded, sure I was

glowing.

"I can get you one. I have connections."

"You can?" Our eyes locked, and he took a step toward me, then stopped. We were surrounded by passersby. I cleared my throat and looked down, feeling the heat blooming on my cheeks. This was not supposed to be happening, and I needed to get a grip. I'd only been here a minute and already Bruno had wrangled his way into my heart, controlling it like putty in his hands. A woman stopped at the counter to ask a question, and Bruno turned to answer her.

In the meantime, I took several deep breaths to calm myself over my longing to feel Bruno's skin against my own, and decided to use this time as I originally planned–talk to Bruno about opera, Carmen, and cats until I could muster up the nerve to speak of my gown and the need for a place to change.

A crowd of people surrounded the booth, impatiently waiting to ask their questions.

"We've got our work cut out for us," Bruno said, ready to begin giving out information to the attendees.

"Don't I know."

Behind the counter stood a table with piles of brochures, pamphlets, bookmarks, leaflets, and premiums. We proceeded to stuff one of each into a bag, which we handed to anyone who walked by. For the most part, I think we both welcomed the distraction, and I directed our conversation to opera. As he spoke, I took mental notes, gathering much more information on opera imbroglios than I thought possible.

"Do you like cats?"

Bruno pushed back a thick lock of hair that had fallen on his forehead. "I could have done without Carmen's cat."

"What do you mean?"

"Carmen insisted on bringing Tango everywhere. When she could, she'd rent out an entire floor for her and Tango, and we'd instruct the hotel to bring fresh finely chopped salmon for him. Since Carmen always wanted children, she treated Tango like the child she never had. She lavished so much attention on him, it became embarrassing."

"So you traveled often with Carmen?"

"She couldn't stand to be alone."

"And the cat wasn't enough company?"

"Not enough for her and too much for my pocketbook. Some opera houses drew the line with paying expenses for Tango. In Venice, we almost lost the contract when Carmen demanded Tango be the good luck token."

I smiled because I knew of the practice in Venice of letting a cat walk down the center aisle just before the beginning of each performance. I had always wanted to attend a Venice opera to see this.

"I've met Tango. I heard he's psychic."

Bruno laughed as he stuffed a brochure into a bag. "Don't tell me you talked to Claire! Oh my dear Alex, Tango is not psychic. It's just a big act."

"You don't believe Claire's an animal psychic?"

"No more than you or I."

Feeling more confident, I pressed forward, perhaps recklessly. "But…what about the guns?" I asked.

Suddenly Bruno's mood shifted. "What guns?"

"Tango spied on Adriano Capezio in his restaurant."

Bruno put down the bag and faced me. "What did Tango say?"

"Oh, all of a sudden he's psychic now?"

"C'mon, Alex, don't mess around with this."

Until now, my information had come from a cat, and I needed to corroborate it. If Bruno would at least give me a hint that Adriano was involved in shipping guns, I would know I'm on the right track.

"He heard a conversation about a shipment of guns this week. Tango believes Adriano is selling guns."

"All this you heard from Claire, correct?"

I nodded.

"Claire is a dangerous woman, Alex. Be careful around her." He picked up the bag again and continued to stuff it. I noted he didn't deny the information, and that was significant.

"Why would you say that?"

"How well do you know her?"

"I've interviewed her a couple of times since Carmen's murder. The rapport between her and cats is amazing." I hesitated, debating whether to tell Bruno about our visit to Angel's trailer yesterday, but decided to confront him with the information after I'd had a chance to look over his hotel room.

"It's just an act," Bruno said.

"I don't know about that. Adriano has a fascination for clowns, right?"

Bruno gave me a look that said, "So?"

"So he named the guns that he smuggles Ilmato, which means The Fool in Italian."

"I'm impressed, Alex. How do you know about this Ilmato?"

"I just told you. Tango saw them in Adriano's office at his restaurant. And you're not denying their existence."

"What do you think Adriano does with these guns?"

"Assuming they exist?" I asked.

"Yes."

"They're special in some way. He sells them and uses profits to fund the Lyric Opera House. He's like a Robin Hood to the arts."

Bruno studied me intently.

"So is it true?"

He brushed my cheek with his finger. I felt split by his touch, half of me longing for him to caress me, the other half wanting to break his finger.

"Don't ruin a good thing, Alex."

I couldn't respond because three women and two men approached the counter at the same time with questions. But I couldn't let go of my last question. It had to be true, if Bruno didn't deny it. We spent the next few minutes explaining the courses available to the attendants and sent them on their way with bags in hand.

Alone with Bruno again, I tugged my hair. "I have this evening gown for tonight," I said.

"Where is it?" Bruno asked.

"It's still in my car. I…I'm not sure where I should change."

Bruno bit his lower lip, then smiled. "I think I can help you with that." He pulled out a key card to his hotel room and handed it to me.

Even though I predicted this, I was surprised at how easily Bruno handed me his card.

Still holding the card, he said, "I'm at the Four Seasons."

I hesitated, my breathing becoming shallow. I was only taking it to find out whether Siddharma was in his room. "Okay." I grabbed the key and placed it into my wallet.

He seemed happy. "You don't have to worry about a thing. As long as you're there…I'm having a little reception before the ball with the trustees. You're welcome to stay."

"Thank you. I'll see how much time I have."

"So when will you be there?"

"About six." If Siddharma's in the room, Bruno will have time to remove the cat, and I worried about this. But I thought it was important I get in that room and have a chance to investigate on my own. Even if he removed her, maybe I'd find proof she was there. In any case, I hoped I could get there before six so I would have time alone.

"Perfect. I'll make sure you have the place to yourself. My intentions are entirely honorable."

Yeah, but mine weren't. I massaged my left earlobe.

A new crew arrived at eleven o'clock, and we both had our own things to do. Before Bruno left, he leaned toward me and I felt his breath on my left ear. "You will dance with me tonight, won't you Alex?"

"Of course."

Hours later, I returned to the exhibition hall, disappointed I couldn't break away from my duties earlier. Now it would be six o'clock by the time I arrived at Bruno's hotel room. As I approached the information booth, I saw Bruno talking to Beata. They smiled at one another, and she looked at him like her knight in shining armor. I felt sick to my stomach. How could I have ever fallen for him? Bruno patted Beata on her shoulder, and never even saw me.

Beata passed me in a trance. I stopped her. "Isn't Bruno great?"

She looked at me. "He said my writing reminded him of the way Maria Callas sang."

"Really? He said that once to me too."

"Julie in Finance warned me."

"About what?"

"That he always comes around her office to flirt, but she's sure he's having an affair with Sue in advertising," said Beata.

"The nerve!" Even Beata wouldn't make this up: Bruno was more of a dog than I realized.

"You know he's married, with four children."

"I've heard." I fingered his hotel room key in my pocket. I would just look for my cat, find evidence about the Ilmatos, and get the hell out of there.

Chapter Twenty-Seven

Minutes later, I gathered my garment bag and gown from my car and grabbed a cab, which took me to the front door of the Four Seasons Hotel.

I pulled my garment bag over my left shoulder and greeted the doorman.

"Hello, Miss. Welcome to the Four Seasons."

I smiled and moseyed past the lounge, elegant with rich woods, loomed textiles, and custom marble, and headed toward the elevator. Once on the seventeenth floor and standing in front of Bruno's secluded Executive Suite, I slipped the key card into the door and entered his hotel room. The parlor, furnished with overstuffed chairs, gleaming coffee tables, and a bar, had an executive view of Lake Michigan.

On top of the polished bar sat a bowl of fruit. Next to it lay a fool's cap with a note from Bruno. "Here's your hat for your journey–The Fool."

He had gotten me the hat after all. I probably shouldn't have stuffed it into my garment bag, but it looked so cute. Plus, I thought The Wizard would have wanted me to have it, like some cosmic hand placed it before me. After all, he foretold how a married man would give me a gift as part of my test. In a few days, it would be the perfect trophy to remind me of how I passed my fool's test to enter the Order of the Tarot.

I draped my garment bag on a cushioned chair and searched everywhere for Siddharma, but there was no sign of her, not even a cat hair. Where was she? Was Angel wrong? Had I misread the clues again? When Angel had chosen the King of Wands, I had assumed it meant Bruno, but now I wondered if I had jumped to the wrong conclusion. I had told Alyce and Beata I was so sure Siddharma would be in Bruno's hotel room. They'd never let me live this down, but even worse was that I had no idea where Siddharma was.

I opened the French doors to the bedroom and found a writing desk facing the window. To its side was the king-size bed–I threw my garment bag on it and sat on the bed to think. I still had a good reason to be here...if Siddharma wasn't here, I could still look for evidence of Bruno's involvement with the Ilmatos.

The closet next to the bathroom was stocked with Bulgari toiletries, two white terrycloth robes, and Bruno's navy blue suitcase. With no remorse or guilt, I opened it and rummaged through his clothes. I needed to find Carmen's killer, and if it meant sneaking through a man's suitcase, then so be it. Eureka! I found a steel case about the size of a cigar box with a picture of an Ilmato on it. Oh! I *was* right about this. Bruno was involved with these guns. But the case was locked. Where was the key?

Suddenly, I heard a door open. I quickly placed the case back in the suitcase, ran to the bathroom, flushed the toilet, then came out into the parlor.

"Hi," I said.

"Hi," Bruno said. He was staring at me with hard eyes that drew me to him like a strong current. I still wasn't over him. What I was feeling was precisely what I should not have been feeling. He took a step toward me.

"I didn't expect you to be here," I said.

"Didn't you?" He took another step closer.

My brain screamed, "Stop!" But my will weakened and I couldn't stop. Not yet. My heart flip-flopped and grew feverish with desire. He stood inches from me. I stroked his cheek with my right hand. He raised his left hand to caress me. "I'm so glad you're here," he whispered.

"I am too." I closed my eyes and allowed myself to step into his arms. Our lips met gingerly, then more boldly. The passion within me mounted, then near its peak my ardor fizzled, surprising me with sudden clarity. *I don't love Bruno!*

I released my grip. "Do you mind if we slow down a second?"

Bruno looked frustrated and nodded. Suddenly, I saw him

as another married, middle-aged New Yorker who needed female attention to make himself feel important. Love had nothing to do with it. I was finally over him. Bruno removed his suit jacket and hung it on a barstool.

I looked at him. "Thanks for the hat."

"You're welcome." Bruno looked back at me provocatively, shooting flitting glances up and down my body. "The reception will start in about half an hour." He left unsaid that we had only half an hour to be together, and from the way he looked, he planned to have a roll in the hay with me. Goddess, what had I gotten myself into?

I needed to stall for time. If I could just hold things off for half an hour, I'd avoid his advances, plus I still needed to use this time to find the key to the gun case. How I'd get into the locked case with him there was another matter. "Uh, how about a glass of red wine?"

Bruno met my gaze and held it for an uncomfortable moment. "I see you haven't had a chance to change yet."

"I...I...just got here." I sat down on the stool where he'd hung the jacket.

As he poured the wine, from the other side of the bar, I tried to feel the pockets for his wallet to see if he kept the key there. If I found the key, how would I get into the case while Bruno was still in the hotel room?

"Carl Russo. Do you know him?" Bruno asked.

"Do I know who?" I was totally lost in my thoughts.

"Carl, one of our trustees."

"No," I said softly.

He set down his wine glass and stepped into the bedroom, saying, "He has a booth in our exhibit hall, says he can read past lives. Excuse me for a moment, will you?"

"Uh, sure," I said, using the time to check his wallet. I felt the lump of his wallet in his pocket and pulled it out. I opened it to photographs of his wife and four children, and as I suspected, the key to his gun case. I slipped the key into my purse. When Bruno returned, my palms grew clammy and I felt sweat trickling down from my armpits.

"Are you hot?" He pulled out a handkerchief and wiped my brow. "No need to be nervous around me," he crooned. "I'll be gentle."

"I…uh…have to go to the bathroom. Excuse me."

"Take your time."

I swiveled the chair and stepped toward the bedroom, shutting the door behind me. Oh, why did I just shut the bedroom door? Maybe he'll think I'm getting ready for him, changing into something sexy and coming out regaled in a flamboyant come-and-get-me outfit. Or maybe he wouldn't think my closing the bedroom door odd at all. After a deep breath, I strode three paces, and kneeled in front of his suitcase.

I heard hotel staff come into the room to set up for Bruno's reception. "Where should we put the cheese tray?" a waiter asked, while I felt like a sneak.

"Next to those flowers," I heard Bruno say.

I inserted the key to open the steel case.

That's when Bruno said, "What happened to the cat?"

"Ah, yes sir, your friend did come. I had quite forgotten. He came two hours ago."

"Great."

He had a cat here! What friend? Where was Siddharma now?

Then trembling, I lifted the gun with ILMATO .45 inscribed on the barrel. It was a semiautomatic .45 caliber, a subcompact that weighed no more than a pound. The carry magazine had six rounds. I noticed the gun came with a second longer magazine, but couldn't tell how many more rounds that had. Why did Bruno have one? And how could this be connected to Siddharma?

When I heard Bruno open the bedroom door and say, "What's taking you so long?" I slid the gun back into the case, but didn't have time to lock it. A half-wall shielded the closet area from the entrance into the bedroom, so Bruno didn't see me run into the bathroom and close the door. I flushed the toilet, counted to twenty while I composed myself. Now he's probably wondering why I just closed the bathroom door. Did I give myself away?

I opened the bathroom door and walked out as nonchalantly as I could. My plan was to ask him about Siddharma and get out as fast as I could.

"Still dressed?" he asked. He walked toward me and began to unbutton my jacket.

"Bruno, I…" I grabbed his hand, but he kissed my neck. He wasn't stopping, even though I was clearly letting him know I didn't want to be with him. He wouldn't do this against my will, would he?

I pushed him.

"Oh, you like it a little rough, do you?"

"No, I…" How dare he? He wouldn't try to rape me. He was a scoundrel, but he wouldn't go that far. On the other hand, considering he kidnapped my cat and was involved in some shady gun activity, I wouldn't put it past him.

He ripped the buttons off the jacket of my two-piece suit in one motion, slipped it off, and hooked a finger on my bra strap, ready to pull it down. "Sure you do."

"Please, no." Goddess, he actually meant to do it! As his fingers caressed my spine, I had the sensation of a spider crawling up my back. A sickening wave of terror welled up from my belly, and I screamed.

He clamped his hand over my mouth. "Nobody can hear us."

Would I be able to hold him off until somebody arrived for the reception and could hear my scream?

He unsnapped my bra and kissed my shoulder.

Things were moving too fast.

I caught my breath. "I'm sorry. I can't do this." I took a step back, crossing my arms over my bare breasts.

He removed his tie. "Don't play hard to get, Alex. I really want you."

"I…I can't. I don't want to." God, help me! I don't want to be raped!

He pushed me onto the bed. "Oh yes you can, and oh yes, you want to," he said, falling down next to me. He unzipped my skirt and I struggled against him removing it, but he grabbed the hem with two hands and yanked. I still had my pantyhose. He was not going to do this, I'd fight! He groped my breasts, but I pushed him away, this time as forcefully as I could. If I had to, I'd run for his gun.

"Stop. I don't want to do this." I rolled onto my stomach, but he flipped me over onto my back, grabbed both my wrists, and yanked me up into a sitting position on the bed. "No woman accepts a key for a man's hotel room unless she means business."

"Let me go," I said, panting. "That's not why I'm here."

Something must have snapped in him, and to my relief he stopped struggling and asked, "Then why did you come here?"

I caught my breath and locked eyes with him, waiting for myself to calm down. He still held my wrists tightly. Finally, he let go, though he remained tense, as if ready to pounce on me again.

"You're married, Bruno." I scrambled for my buttonless jacket.

"You were sending me some strong signals, you know."

"I know. For a while I thought I could, but I can't. If you were…it doesn't matter. Besides, now that I know you kidnapped my cat…. Where is she?"

Bruno looked resigned and not at all surprised. "How did you find out?"

"Let's just say my Tarot cards told me. Where is she?"

Bruno's face grew drawn and pinched. "Adriano called me, asked me to take care of that cat."

"Why?"

"I didn't ask, but I owe him."

"You owe him what?"

Bruno breathed heavily, refusing to answer. I suspected it had to do with the Ilmatos, but I wanted to find out about my cat first.

"Where is she?"

Bruno shrugged, like his answer wouldn't matter anyway. "A guy named Jorge came by to pick it up. I still don't know what the big deal is."

"Jorge, the masseur at Parsifal's Spa?"

"Yeah."

I still wanted that gun for evidence, and made the mistake of glancing at his suitcase. Bruno noticed. I had my buttonless jacket covering me, and Bruno stared at it intently, then yanked it from me and felt the pockets.

"Where is it?"

"Where's what?"

His eyes landed on my purse. He opened it, overturned it, and his key tumbled out. He glared at me with incredulity.

My instincts told me to run as Bruno reached for the case that held his gun. Before he could turn around, I rushed past him into the bathroom, and tried to lock the door, but he was too fast. He was already inside the bathroom holding his gun against my temple. I screamed and clawed at his chest.

Someone had entered the parlor. A staff person who was ready to help serve during the pre-reception party must have opened the door to the parlor. "Is everything okay?"

Finally! Bruno couldn't hurt me now.

"Yes, everything is fine," Bruno shouted with his hand over my mouth, as I struggled.

"I'm just changing," he said. "Help yourself to some wine."

"Thanks," said another man. It sounded like Edgar Sheldon, *Gypsy Magazine's* publisher.

I stopped struggling, feeling safer now that someone I knew was in the next room, and Bruno let go.

I wanted that gun, for evidence. I didn't know how Bruno was involved in all this, but I planned to find out.

"Look, I'm going to forget what just happened," said Bruno. "Be a good girl, change into your gown, and go on with your life. Stop digging for trouble."

"Is that a threat?"

"Take it any way you want."

More guests arrived. Bruno changed, and before entering the parlor, he turned and placed his gun back in the case. Then he locked it and placed the key in his pocket.

"Why don't you slip into your dress now? Don't let it to go to waste."

He left me alone, during which time I steeled myself to finish the job of finding that gun. I picked up the lost buttons from my jacket, scattered around the bed, then changed into my gown. I checked his suitcase. I could just take the entire gun case and figure out how to open it later. I needed that gun for evidence of Adriano's illegal trade, to incriminate him for the murder of Carmen, and to enter the Order of the Tarot.

I reached for it, but then chickened out, suddenly feeling it was too dangerous. I could just tell Lt. Joe Burke what I saw, and he could chase the bad guy. When I entered the full parlor, I headed straight for Alyce. By this time, the place was jammed with nearly forty people: trustees and their wives, the publisher, and other staff.

"What happened?" Alyce asked, noticing the look of panic on my face.

"He was going to rape me."

"He what?"

"You heard me. Remind me never to flirt with a married man again."

Alyce shook her head. "I'm so sorry! I didn't mean for that to happen to you."

"I know."

I watched as Bruno greeted Beata. He whispered something in her ear. She brushed his cheek. They kissed each other lightly on the lips. How could he do that? This man had to be stopped! It suddenly dawned on me that I could take his gun case after all. With all these people around, he wouldn't dare make a scene. I walked straight to his suitcase and pulled out his gun case. As I went to leave, Bruno stopped me.

"Where do you think you're going?"

Heads turned our way. "Leave me alone!" I lowered my voice. "I could tell the crowd how you just tried to rape me."

"Give me back my gun."

I gripped the gun case tighter and on my way out, said,

"Why don't you report your stolen gun to the police?"

Bruno's nostrils flared and a vein at his temple swelled dangerously. He took another step toward me and stopped. He saw his wife and four teenage daughters, suitcases in tow, walking down the hallway toward their daddy's room.

"Did the party already start, honey? Ooh, I just love the Four Seasons."

His daughters, all with long, straight, blonde hair, strode up to their daddy to give him a hug. Bruno looked stunned. I think I could have knocked him over with a Tarot card. I turned to have a good look at his wife. She looked like a woman who had four children and was too busy to get regular exercise. I wasn't surprised to see her face look tired, overburdened–but then again it couldn't be easy managing her husband's many appetites.

I introduced myself, and she said, "Oh, my husband is always raving about the wonderful staff at *Gypsy Magazine*. You're a writer? How wonderful."

If she only knew. I immediately identified with her and, in turn, despised myself for betraying her.

Chapter Twenty-Eight

Day Eight: Sunday, March 30

The number of tears I shed on my living room couch the next day could have filled a teapot. Twirling a tissue around my finger, I dabbed my stinging eyes, swollen from repeated rubbing and wiping. For the past nine hours, I'd been staring at the fool's cap Bruno had given me in his hotel room, listening to Verdi's Macbeth, and sipping my lotus tea. My hands cupped my tea mug as I drank slowly, feeling the heat of the liquid glide down my throat. Stunned into a stupor, I couldn't take my eyes off the fool's cap. Laying on the low cocktail table, its rainbow of colors with bells along the fringe and red pom-pom at its point screamed as a poignant symbol of the farce I'd just experienced. Balls of crumpled tissue littered the floor near my feet as I stood up to pour another cup of tea. I moved stiffly in my pink terry robe to the kitchen, my soul black and blue from the severe emotional wrenching I'd just endured.

After heating up the water again, I poured myself more tea and headed back to the living room. More than anything, I felt foolish for falling so hard for Bruno. I'd reluctantly fallen in love with him, knowing all along that it was the sort of love that wouldn't go anywhere because he was dangerous, the ultimate Mr. Wrong; hell to date, and hell to leave.

The Wizard had told me we live a thousand lives and, in the evolution of our soul, we experience everything we need to learn and grow. First-hand knowledge is the best teacher, he had said, and our soul retains this wisdom at a deep level so that we can carry it over into the next life. I prayed that I would forever steer clear of men who were bad for me.

That look on Bruno's face when his wife appeared with their four daughters! I shook my head, wondering how I'd ever move forward. I knew this much–for the rest of this lifetime, I'd be immunized from falling for a married man. This also taught me to desire only a noble love, one that would be open and pure. The Wizard had told me that what we feel is human and beyond our control, but what we do with our feelings, how we act upon them, is what makes us divine.

The Macbeth music ended. It was six o'clock in the evening, and I still hadn't done my yoga stretches. Now I craved the movement. Standing in my cotton jammies in my living room, I started with several deep-cleansing breaths, then moved into the triangle pose, my feet apart, my right arm on my shin, and my left raised toward the ceiling. I am balanced and secure, open to new possibilities, I affirmed. I wasn't exactly proud of letting him kiss me, but I respected myself for the outcome. I left with new information about my cat and Bruno's involvement with the Ilmatos.

I moved into the yoga mudra pose, clasping my palms behind me by interlacing my fingers, then letting my arms fall forward as far as possible, holding the pose. I release all obstacles to full and free expression, I affirmed. I had learned Jorge took Siddharma, most likely to Parsifal's Spa. I had also learned Bruno owned an Ilmato. This wasn't going to be the last of Bruno, not with me stealing his gun. I needed to decide what to do about the possibility of Bruno going after me.

For the next half hour, I moved through my yoga poses, then my apartment became silent. I closed my eyes and calmed myself, taking several minutes to breathe deeply, focusing only on inhales and exhales. For a long moment, my mind became a blank, then filled with a burst of white light, which eventually faded. More blackness as I concentrated to keep my mind open and blank, available for insight. Images of Tarot cards flashed in my mind–the Emperor as Adriano, the Fool as Castrato, the Knight of Cups as Teresita, and the Knight of Pentacles as Jorge. The Page of Swords, as myself, stood on a red-carpeted staircase leading to a balcony and brandishing a sword. The Emperor commanded the Fool and two Knights to toss me over the high balcony. The Knights grabbed each of my arms, and together we fell hundreds of feet. A giant-size deck of Tarot cards cushioned my fall; the two Knights, however, *thump-*

thumped on the marble floor and lay breathless at my sides.

I opened my eyes and sat still, reviewing events. Adriano met Teresita in Paraguay, and now she owned his daughter's spa. Was it just a coincidence? Could Teresita be connected to that gun factory in Paraguay? I retrieved the gun case I'd taken from Bruno yesterday, moved to my studio with the case, and found the pouch of lock picks. I worked through several of them until I opened the gun case. The Ilmato was still there. I let it lay in the palm of my hand.

Where did this gun come from?

I moved to my computer, still holding the Ilmato. Once online, I put down the gun and began to type, pulling up a CIA report on Paraguay. Situated among Argentina, Bolivia, and Brazil, it had a population of six million. Corrupt politicians created poor economic conditions; Paraguay was a major producer of cannabis. I looked at the Ilmato on my desk. Yes, the Ilmato was manufactured in Paraguay.

At that moment I decided to call Lieutenant Joe Burke. I gripped the receiver tightly as I waited for Joe to answer. Please be there, please be there. He answered.

"Oh, Joe. I have so much to tell you."

"You don't sound so good. Is something wrong?"

"Siddharma is still missing." I did some more explaining, telling him about my visit to Angel's trailer with Claire, how he told me Bruno took Siddharma, how I followed the trail to Bruno's hotel room, how Bruno told me Jorge, from Parsifal's Spa, picked up my cat, and how I now had Bruno's Ilmato.

Joe listened without saying anything for the ten minutes it took me to explain all the events. He waited another moment before saying, "It would be good for you to get your own gun, you know."

"Can't I just keep this one?"

"No way. I'll have to take a look at it. I'd come tonight, but I need to be home with my wife and kids. It's my daughter's birthday. Can you wait until tomorrow?"

Joe never talked about his family to me. I sensed a strain in his voice, like it was important to his wife he choose to stay home tonight rather than go out to work like he always does. I was done trying to break up any more marriages. "Yes, of course."

"In the meantime, hide it somewhere."

"Where?"

"I don't know. Tomorrow, go to a gun shop and buy your own gun. Try the one on 103rd in Chicago Ridge."

Maybe he was right. "Okay Joe, I will. There's another reason I called. Do you still have a few more minutes before the birthday party begins?"

"Yeah."

"I think Adriano is manufacturing Ilmatos in Paraguay."

Joe remained silent for three seconds, then said, "Why do you think that?"

I sensed he knew more. "You're not denying it."

"Just tell me what you know."

"Jorge and Teresita are cousins, both from Paraguay. Adriano met her there, and now she owns his daughter's spa. I believe Adriano manufacturers these guns in Paraguay, sells them to people he shouldn't sell them to, and funnels the profits to the Lyric Opera House. His daughter found out about it and threatened to write a book on all that. Adriano didn't like being pushed around, even by his daughter, so he killed her."

"Shit," Joe said.

"Well, what do you think?"

Joe exhaled so strongly, he could have blown out his daughter's birthday candles. But he wouldn't verbalize his reaction.

I said, "You can't talk to me about this. Is that it?"

"I'm amazed you figured this much out."

"Look, I don't want to get you in trouble, Joe. If you can't talk to me about it, I understand."

Joe remained silent, perhaps weighing his options.

"There's another angle to this," I continued. "Behind the scenes, Carmen had been threatening to expose the Lyric's connection to the arms industry. Closer scrutiny of this connection would topple the public's opinion of the virtues of classical music–an industry that parades lofty ideals. If the real story got out, the Lyric's pristine image would be shattered. They wouldn't–couldn't–stand exposure."

"What are you saying?"

"The Lyric needs this money to survive. If patrons find out huge donations come from the sale of arms, they may question the opera company's motives. Nobody from the Lyric would want this information to come out."

"Okay, Alex. You figured a lot out already. We've been keeping an eye on Adriano. He's definitely into something. The CPD organized crime squad guys have confirmed Adriano is behind the gunrunning. But none of this conversation goes in your story until we have Carmen's murderer in our custody. Is that a deal?"

"Yes, of course. What do you know about the Ilmato?"

Joe waited a long moment. I could hear his children laughing in the background.

"It's a new prototype…the lightest .45 ever created. The barrel is thinned out and lined with a ceramic coating, which accounts for the light weight. The slide is titanium steel, another factor to make it so light. On the scale, the gun weighs eighteen ounces. And, yes, they're manufactured in Paraguay. Adriano and some partners own the factory."

I picked up the gun and held it in my hand, now better appreciating its light weight. "Are the guns legal?"

"Oh, yeah. They're being sold to our Navy. What's illegal is that some of them are getting into the wrong hands, and that's where we think Adriano comes in."

"For a lot of money."

"Of course."

"How do they bring the guns here?"

"Once a month, there's a Hercules C-130 flying from Paraguay to the naval base on the lake."

"So somebody takes a few guns to sell on the side. An inside man."

"That's what it looks like." I heard the children ask for him.

"So who's the inside man?"

"That's what we're still trying to figure out. Either way, it's time for you to stay away from Adriano, if I haven't told you that yet. Listen, the birthday party's starting. Gotta run. I'll come over tomorrow to get that gun from you."

"Thanks Joe. Stay in touch."

Now where to hide the gun? The best I could come up with was between the mattresses, so I did. In the bathroom I carefully removed the bandage on my finger and ran warm water over the lance until the soft scab peeled off. I set to work squeezing out the white and green pus, slowly kneading the knuckle from all angles until no more oozed out, then slathered it with antibiotic cream, my new best friend.

Chapter Twenty-Nine

Day Nine: Monday, March 31

On Monday morning, I emptied the Ilmato, tossed it in my purse, and drove to the gun range at 103rd and Southwest Highway in the small southern suburb of Chicago Ridge. I felt refreshed, having spent the rest of my Sunday working with the Tarot cards. I was starting to connect with my new deck. The cards were right about Bruno, about Siddharma; and now I wanted to see if they were right about guns.

The cards gave me equivocal advice on getting a gun–I pulled an Ace of Swords and a Reversed Eight of Wands. They told me that although I should own a gun, I wouldn't get one soon enough to protect myself from danger. I decided I should try to obtain a gun anyway.

I parked in front of a low white shack with a sign that read, "No Admittance without Firearm Owner Identification– unless applying inside." I had not considered this detail. I remembered from my lessons on the gun range that The Wizard mentioned I would need an F.O.I.D. to purchase a gun, but at the time I didn't worry about getting one.

"Those who are on the path to protect the spiritual world from evil must be prepared to defend themselves on the physical plane," The Wizard had said shortly before firing off a round and hitting the target every time. "Shooting a gun is a skill you must use sparingly."

I had taken The Wizard at his word and waited for him to recommend the time I should get a gun. He had continued to tell me to wait, that my time hadn't come. Now that The Wizard had finally given me permission, I worried that the F.O.I.D. would block me from my goal of purchasing a gun today. Still in my car, I called Joe on my cell phone and left him a message, asking him to stop by, as I suspected I might need help getting the F.O.I.D. I also reminded him that I had the Ilmato with me and could hand it over here.

I strolled inside, intent on getting a new gun. Behind the counter stood a tall, burly white man wearing a black short sleeve T-shirt, ponytail to his waist, and large arms covered with tattoos of green dragons and devils.

"Can I help you?" He had a friendly voice.

"I'm here to get an F.O.I.D.," I said.

He gave me a form, about the size of an oversized index card. In about a minute, I filled it out, adding my driver's license number. He directed me to stand next to the counter for a Polaroid. Maybe this wouldn't be so complicated after all.

While the photo developed, I looked around at the faded paneling and mounted deer head. Guns of all shapes and sizes lay like dead soldiers in locked cabinets, their price tags clearly visible. Bersa, Walther, Smith & Wesson 500, Ruger, Browning, Glock .45 Auto. I just wanted small and light.

"Is this your first gun?" the man asked.

"Yes." I had never owned one.

He assumed a posture of superiority, leaning over the counter and spreading his hands before the guns in the case.

"I'd go with a revolver then. Just aim and fire, and you're all set. With the semiautomatics, once you unlock the safety–say in a home invasion–you'd be fumbling all over for it and probably get killed."

I looked at the revolvers. They looked clunky compared to the sleek semiautomatics. I wanted something like the Ilmato. I spotted a Junior Colt, although I knew it had little power. "That's cute."

"If you plan to shoot a rat," he said, his nose wrinkling up in disgust. "Against a man, all you're gonna do is piss him off."

I agreed, and asked about my first choice, if money were no object. "I like how the semiautomatics look. How about that Glock?"

"The Glock is our most popular because it's easy to use."

He pulled it out of the case, checked the safety, set it on the counter for me to look at, and walked away for a few seconds to check on my photo. In the meantime, I held the Glock in my hand, at first gingerly, and then more surely. This was the gun I wanted.

"Shit. We're going to have to take it again. Photo's blurry."

I put the gun back down on the display case and walked over to the camera station, smiled for the camera, and waited. I still assumed the only delay in my getting an F.O.I.D. would be the development of my photo.

"You know, unless you're a cop, you can only have a gun in your home. You can't walk around with it concealed in your purse or glove compartment. If the police find out, it's a felony."

"Yes, I've heard that." I gripped my purse, making sure it was well fastened. I was counting on meeting Joe soon so I could hand the Ilmato over to him. It wouldn't look good if anybody else saw the Ilmato first.

"If you transport a gun, it needs to be empty and locked in a box."

After studying the prices, I realized, not for the first time, that the purchase of a Glock, ammo, and a lockbox would cost me more than a week's salary, but I was anxious to get one. I had waited months for The Wizard's sanction.

"How long does it take for the F.O.I.D. to be approved?"

"After the state checks out your history and makes sure you haven't committed any felonies, five weeks."

"Five weeks? I need a gun today."

"Everyone does. We don't make the rules though."

Maybe I could just rent one. "Do you rent guns?"

"No."

"Know of any place that does?"

"Not nearby. Been too many lawsuits against that."

"Why?"

He lifted his right index finger, pointed it at his right temple, and said, "Ka-Pow! People come to a gun range and rent a gun to kill themselves. Heck, they do it with their own gun."

"How terrible!" An image of a poor, desperate man

shooting himself on the gun range overtook me; as I took a step back to lean against the counter, my purse hit the glass case with a metallic *thunk*.

He regarded my purse curiously. "Whatcha got in there, Missy?"

I felt the toes curl in my shoes as I looked down and saw my purse open and at just the perfect angle to reveal that I had a gun in it.

"I...uh..."

"Take it out and show it to me. Now. I thought you just told me you never owned a gun before."

When would Joe show up? How much trouble was I really in? I regarded Tattoo Man, feeling the blood pound in my throat. No matter how many yoga stretches I'd done this morning, I couldn't take him. I tried to look confident as I pulled it out of my purse.

I slid it over to him. He opened it to make sure it was empty.

"They call them Ilmatos," I explained. "I'm supposed to give it to a friend, a cop. He's supposed to meet me here."

Tattoo Guy frowned. "You need an F.O.I.D. for this. I could call the cops."

"No, don't do that. My friend should be here any minute."

"Yeah, right." He called some old guy out of the back room to inspect the gun. He had a dour mouth and ill-fitting dentures, which he swished back and forth in his mouth as he looked over the Ilmato. "Looks like a built-to-order," he finally said. "Can I take it on the range?"

How could I say no? Joe was going to kill me. When would he get here? I nodded and followed the old man to the gun range. He loaded the Ilmato, set up the target, and shot the entire magazine, hitting the bulls-eye every time. When the old guy finished the round, he gaped at the gun pop-eyed. If I didn't know better, he looked like he was in love. "The trigger mechanism is butter smooth and ultralight. It's a small gun with a short barrel, but with high precision. A .45 auto that fits the hand, made for close-quarters battle. The look is all business.

Where the hell did you get this gun?"

"Uh, a friend gave it to me. But, like I said, I'm waiting for my cop friend to show up so I can give it to him."

"This is off the charts. A new prototype. Are you a cop?"

I laughed self-consciously. "No. So how long will this F.O.I.D. take, you say?"

"If you're not a cop, then–" But he stopped himself and led me back into the gun store.

He stood behind the counter, next to Tattoo Guy. They both exchanged a glance. When the old guy raised his eyebrows and cocked his head in my direction, I had a feeling I was in trouble. When he looked at me with squinty eyes, I was sure.

The old man's mouth quirked in annoyance, as his dentures click-clicked. "We don't need trouble." He reached for the phone. "Undercover investigators are checking on gun shops, pretending to buy illegally, just to test how far the owners would go." He punched numbers into the phone. "Every week, we've got some undercover cop testing us," he muttered to Tattoo Guy. "It's just not worth it anymore."

Tattoo Guy grunted.

"It's not what you're thinking. My cop friend should be here any minute."

"Sorry, Miss." He was waiting on the phone, holding the Ilmato.

In desperation, I said, "Look, my mother works for the mayor. All of this is not what it looks like."

Before I knew it, a Chicago police car pulled into the parking lot and, to my relief, Detective Joe Burke stepped out of the car. I was never happier to see him. "Joe! Thank goodness it's you."

Once inside, Joe's face grew pinched. "Alex, what's going on?"

"You know him?" Tattoo Man asked me.

"Yes, he's a friend of mine. The one I was supposed to meet here."

The older guy hung up the phone and squinted at Joe.

"She's got an unregistered gun. Not only that, it's something completely new. I don't want any trouble over this, understand?"

"Can I see it?" Joe asked.

"Sure," the old guy said, handing Joe the gun. "Like I said, if you say she's a friend of yours, no problem. But I want the record to show that I called the cops when I suspected something funny."

"Thank you for your fine work, gentlemen. I'll pass the word around about how conscientious you two are. In the meantime, I'm going to take this woman in."

The shopkeepers looked pleased with themselves. Joe shook their hands, then turned to me, and bellowed ferociously, "Go on outside."

He followed me to his car. Before he said anything he swiftly removed an evidence bag to toss in the gun.

"What the hell are you doing here?" he snapped. "With this gun?"

"I wanted to give it to you."

"How many people touched this gun today? How many more fingerprints do we have to check on it, huh? I don't have time to babysit."

"Joe, I–"

"Look, with a lot of luck, I'll overlook the felony charges and explain you were about to give me the gun anyway. Jesus, I told you to keep it hidden in your apartment. Why do you think I said that? You could get us both in deep trouble."

I realized how lucky I was he had arrived, because if a cop from Chicago Ridge had come first, I'd probably be in jail.

"I'm sorry, Joe. Once I get the F.O.I.D., I'll do it all by the book, I promise."

The muscles around his neck tensed, and he regarded me with a cold speculation. No amount of explanation would soften him.

"I said I'm sorry."

"I've heard that before." He slammed his car door and drove off in a fury. I hated to see him like that. I'd give him a few hours to cool off, then I'd call and try to explain. In the meantime, I still had a chance to get a gun today with my mother's help. If I asked her, she could pull a few strings in the mayor's office to get me my F.O.I.D. Okay, if I begged her. I wanted a gun in my hands before I went to rescue Siddharma from Parsifal's.

Chapter Thirty

I stood in Mom's sunny office adjacent to Mayor Robin Dryad's. She sat behind a desk between a stack of files and phone messages.

She hung up the phone and scanned me from top to bottom.

"Oh, Alex, just look at you. A ponytail? Please! You look like a horse groomer, not a…a…"

"Mom, I don't have time for this."

"And your clothes! My God! They look like they were on sale at the Floor-Mart. Please let me take you shopping."

"Mom, please listen."

But it was as if she couldn't hear me.

"Everybody's wondering about me."

"About you?" I said. My objective to have my mother help me obtain an F.O.I.D. card shattered with her last statement. I knew exactly what she had in mind, and it was a conversation that was long overdue.

"What a terrible mother I am. How you grew up without a father and now can't form a lasting relationship with a man…and…" She stopped talking and zeroed in on my right cheek. "Come here."

Dutifully, I stepped closer.

"Right here." She extended her right hand. "Let me see."

I leaned in closer and she examined my face.

"Have you switched to a new foundation? Because I'm not sure about this one, honey."

"No, I…"

"And what happened here?" she asked, referring to the bandage on my right index finger.

"I cut my finger cooking and have a little infection. I'm fine."

Mom wrinkled her nose. "Alex, for me, go get your hair

done." She opened her purse and pulled out a $100 bill.

I sat down. "I need a gun, Mom, not a haircut."

Mom's face twisted with incomprehension. "A gun?"

"I need an F.O.I.D. to pick out a gun today. I don't have time to wait five weeks."

She moved the money closer to me. "Take it already, will you? It makes me nervous to have it lying around like this."

"Can you get me the F.O.I.D.?"

She looked at me hard. "Why would I help my daughter get a gun?"

"I need it for protection. It's the story I'm working on...I just..."

"Since when do you need a gun for a story? I'll talk to Edgar."

"No!" I unclenched my fists. What was I doing here? Again, I was running to my mother to fix a problem for me. "I know you mean well, that you only want the best. But I have to make my own way. Now, it means doing a story on Carmen's murder. I need the gun to protect myself."

"From what, for God's sake? I'm your mother. You can tell me anything."

"I..." How much could I tell her? She was an incredibly intelligent and resourceful woman, and I knew she could help me. She was the mayor's administrative secretary, his right hand man, despite her gender. He never made a move without checking with her first. With all the resources available to her, no one held a better position to help me so quickly. With one phone call, she could arrange my F.O.I.D. On the other hand, if I told her everything, she'd worry, she'd try to talk me out of it, or she'd ridicule me. But I had no choice, and decided to take a chance and be forthright.

"Someone kidnapped Siddharma as a ransom for information in a box that Carmen Dellamorte had given me just before she died."

Her eyes widened with alarm. "Alex! My God! Does Edgar know about this?"

"He does."

Mom pursed her lips and fought back tears. "I just wanted to help you. I can't believe this job has turned into a…"

"Mom, please, I'll be fine."

"You're asking me for something I just can't do. I don't want you to have a job that requires a gun. It's not right." She wiped back a tear and she set her jaw firm.

"Can't or won't?"

"Won't."

"I promise to get a haircut if you get me the F.O.I.D."

She pursed her lips. "That's not funny." She regarded me curiously, as if I weren't the same daughter she'd known for the past thirty years. "You've changed, Alex. Why does this mean so much to you?"

I looked around her office, proud of how much my mother had accomplished with her life since Dad died. I wanted her to understand me. "It's my chance to prove myself."

"Edgar wouldn't have hired you if you weren't qualified, no matter what I said."

I smiled. It was nice of her to say that, but unfortunately, nobody else at the office believed it. "I think I know that, Mom, but I still need to prove it to everybody else. And a gun will protect me."

Mom sighed.

I walked around the desk and hugged her. It was my last-ditch effort. "I can get it in five weeks without your help, but by then it'll be too late."

"I just can't do it, Alex. You're asking me for something impossible."

I squeezed her harder. "It's important."

She shook her head once to the left and once to the right. It was the final no, and I knew from years of experience that no amount of persuasion would budge her. I wouldn't have a gun when I entered Parsifal's, and that was that. I released my hug.

Now what? The Wizard had told me that everything happens for a reason, that I should accept all circumstances without resistance. I thought hard. If Mom wouldn't give me access to a gun, did that mean the Universe was telling me I shouldn't have a gun?

Mom looked at me with tears brimming on her lashes. "I'm sorry."

I sat back in the chair in front of her desk and covered my face with my hands.

Suddenly the cherry wood door opened and Mayor Dryad rushed out. "Reenie. You gotta save me. My speechwriter doesn't understand my program."

Mom wiped her tears, blew her nose, and turned to face him. "Did you explain it to him?" He shrugged.

"Sit him down in your office, give him the history of the program, your idea of how you see it, how it connects to what you want?"

"Reenie, you know I don't have time for all that." Mayor Dryad noticed me. "Is this your daughter?"

I put my hands down on my lap and smiled at him.

"Why yes. Alex, say hello to Mayor Dryad."

I extended my hand. "Nice to see you again, Mr. Mayor."

"Hello, Alex. How's your job?"

"Fine, thank you."

"What's the name of your magazine?"

Why should the mayor of Chicago remember the name of the magazine I write for? Oh, well. "*Gypsy Magazine*."

"Oh, right."

Mom said, "I keep telling her she should become one of your speechwriters, don't you think, Robin?"

I glared at my mother, willing her to stop handling my life.

"Anytime you want the job, it's yours," the mayor said, with a broad, disingenuous smile.

"Thanks," I mumbled.

The mayor dropped his speech on my mother's desk. "See what you can do. Thanks. You're a doll." Then he left.

Mom patted the back of her hair bun.

"Mom, I–"

The phone rang. A look of anxiety crossed Mom's face as she listened to the person speaking on the other end.

"McDonald's? Old milk? Not in the museum! Oh dear." She covered the receiver. "McDonald's has been serving expired milk in the Field Museum. Can you believe it? Honey, I'm going to have to deal with this. Let's talk more tonight, okay?"

"Sure, Mom. No problem."

I left, worrying over how I'd rescue Siddharma without a gun. There was no one else to help me obtain a firearm. Besides, I'd wasted enough time already, and I needed to move forward. If I was going to enter the Order of the Tarot at the Fool's degree, it would be without a gun. I accepted this as my fate.

Chapter Thirty-One

Because the afternoon sun was still bright, the awning of Parsifal's Spa remained open, providing a splash of color on Oak Street. Inside, passionate Wagner music played as I waited at the counter for the receptionist to appear. Apparently, business was slower today than last Tuesday, when I interviewed Teresita.

The receptionist finally arrived, a woman in her twenties with long, straight blonde hair. I hadn't seen her last time.

"Can I have a massage with Jorge?"

She looked at the schedule.

"He's with a client now, but he could take you in about an hour. Would you like a haircut or manicure while you're waiting?"

I could use a trim. Perhaps that would provide me with an opportunity to see if Siddharma was here. I wished I had Tango's psychic abilities to determine her whereabouts, but it was clear I'd have to search for her in the conventional manner–with run-of-the-mill snooping.

"A haircut would be fine."

She smiled. "Antonia can take you."

"Wonderful."

I followed the receptionist down the short hall to another room, noticing small round stones scattered in the corners of low tables, under chairs, and on counters. Before I sat down in the beauty salon area, I asked if I could use the restroom. Maybe Siddharma was there.

No luck. Smooth stones glistened in the sink. I peeked out the door of the restroom. The hallway was clear and I tiptoed to the next door, then opened it. It looked like Teresita's office. No sign of my cat here either.

Before I had a chance to really snoop around, a woman with a beehive hairdo and wearing a funky spring green dress appeared in the doorway.

"What are you doing here?" she asked. "I've been waiting for you in the salon. This is the boss's office."

"I…uh…must have gotten lost. Sorry."

"Follow me," she said with an understanding smile, as she patted the back of her head.

Back in the salon area, I noticed the place wasn't nearly as full as last Tuesday, either–just two other women getting hair tints. There were several closed doors back here; Siddharma could be behind any one of them.

"We're always slow on Mondays," Antonia said, as if she could read my mind. She ran her fingers through my hair. "Wow, you've got beautiful hair, so thick and silky. You're not going to cut it off, are you?"

"No, just a trim. Maybe two inches?"

Antonia nodded. "Let's start with a wash."

As she led me to the sink, I tried to think of a way to sneak into one of the adjacent rooms, but Antonia was right behind me. In the next moment, I was having my scalp massaged under warm running water.

"Is the water too hot?" Antonia asked.

"No, it's perfect."

Antonia stroked my head vigorously as she worked in the shampoo with strong fingers. My mind kept turning over the kidnapping of my cat, Jorge's involvement, and how it related to Carmen's murder. I couldn't wait to talk to Jorge.

"Not too cold?" Antonia asked.

"No, it's great."

"You're the reporter who was with Carmen just before she died."

"Yes, how did you know?"

She turned off the water, and massaged in apricot-scented conditioner.

"Oh, everyone around here knows," she said. "I hope they find her killer soon."

"Mmm," I said, going back to my thoughts. Jorge wore a black turtleneck with dark slacks. Could he have returned unnoticed, poured the rubbing alcohol into a glass of champagne, even be the man who gave it to her? Why did he pick up Siddharma from Bruno two days ago?

After blotting my wet head with a towel, Antonia escorted me back to her station and trimmed my hair. Photographs of opera singers hung on the walls. I stared at one.

"Who's that playing Aida?"

"Teresita. In Paraguay."

With all the make-up, it was hard to recognize her. "Really?"

"It's amazing how far she's come."

"What do you mean?"

"She worked in a gun factory with the rest of her family, assembling them, before she made it big as a singer in Paraguay."

"Guns?" I straightened my back.

"Didn't she talk about that with you? She talks about it with me all the time. How she went from guns to songs."

It had to be in Adriano's gun factory! So that's how she knew him.

"Uh, now that you mention it, Teresita said something about Adriano Capezio discovering her and bringing her to Chicago. Like Cinderella."

Antonia laughed. "Yeah, a regular princess. What a voice. Such a shame she can't take her career further here. But she's got a knack for business. Most days you can't get a seat in this place."

I nodded, remembering how it was last Tuesday. "Her family still at that factory?"

"As far as I know."

A junior hair stylist interrupted Antonia to ask for advice on how to mix colors. In the meantime, I thought about Adriano Capezio, who manufactured Ilmatos in Paraguay. I now understood how he discovered Teresita. That meant she knew about his guns. She'd also noticed the box in the dressing room, and perhaps had figured out it contained material on Adriano. Maybe she called Adriano and told him all about it.

But why would she kill Carmen? And why did she have Jorge take my cat?

"She has a music degree from the University of Asunción," Antonia said, now blow-drying and styling my hair. "She was quite a sensation. Played at all the big places down there, even Buenos Aires."

"It's hard to believe she left all that."

Antonia leaned in closer. "Just between you and me, I think she ran away from trouble. She tells me a lot. I don't know. It's just small talk, but sometimes, she scares me."

Our eyes met in the mirror and I encouraged her to continue. "In what way does she scare you?"

"She gets this look of blind ambition that says she could do anything. She's good with guns, you know. The story goes that she shot her stepfather because he tried to rape her, and she ran away."

"Shot her stepfather?" That would explain her need to leave at the height of her operatic career in Paraguay.

Perhaps Adriano felt sorry for her and brought her to Chicago to escape prison in Paraguay. He was known for helping artists. Seeing such vocal talent in Teresita may have inspired him to bring her to a new place to sing. This would have made Teresita indebted to Adriano. If he had asked her to kill Carmen, she might have felt so grateful to him, she would have done anything.

Antonia continued. "It's hard to believe when she's telling the truth. She's always talking about how she made this place what it is. I don't know, it's just this feeling."

"What feeling?"

"About a year ago, she mentioned that Carmen told her if anything happened to her, she'd leave the place to Teresita. I got the impression she wanted to be the owner of Parsifal's."

That sounded like a motive for murder to me. "Have you told any of this to the police?"

"Oh, no. I'd feel silly telling them. Like they'd take it serious, or something. This is just small talk between us girls, right?"

"Well, actually, I think you should mention this to the police as soon as you can. It sounds very important."

"Really? I don't want to get her in trouble, or anything. Maybe I've said too much to you. Oh, dear."

I'd have to tell Joe all this as soon as I could.

Antonia was teasing my hair.

I asked, "By any chance, has anyone brought in a cat around here lately?"

Antonia blinked with surprise and she froze in mid-tease. "How did you know?"

Oh! It is true! I tried to remain nonchalant. "Where is that cat?"

Antonia smoothed out my hair and pointed toward one of the doors. "In there. Looks a little depressed, if you ask me. I don't know why Jorge brought it here."

I leapt from my chair and headed toward that door, but it was locked.

Antonia was right behind me. "What's the big deal?"

I heard a meow. She was alive! "Siddharma, it's okay. I'm here."

I turned to Antonia and motioned to the door. "Where's the key to this door?"

"Teresita's got it. Why?"

I let go of the doorknob and regrouped. Now that I knew Siddharma was here, I could breathe easier and resume the trail toward Carmen's murderer. I still wanted to talk to Jorge. With any luck, Antonia wouldn't have a chance to tell him about our conversation until after my massage. By then it wouldn't matter anyway because I would have gotten my answers and my cat. I was torn about leaving her, though, and it took every ounce of will I had to convince myself she would be safe for another hour. If I burst through the door now and grabbed her, I didn't think Jorge would answer my questions, and with Siddharma in my arms, I knew I wouldn't be able to think of anything else but my joy at having her again.

I turned around, pulled off the beauty bib, and handed it to Antonia. "I just have this sixth sense about cats," I lied. "The cat is all right, isn't it? As far as you know?"

Antonia nodded and shrugged.

"Well that's good. Is it time for my massage?"

She had a look of suspicious bewilderment, as if she wanted to ask me a few questions of her own, but she didn't voice any of them. I tried to act casual, like I was just a concerned cat-loving citizen who overreacted. After a few more heartbeats, she escorted me to Jorge's massage parlor.

"Thanks," I said, leaving a generous tip in her hand. "Love the haircut."

"You're welcome. I'll tell Jorge you're here."

I sat in an easy chair to wait for Jorge and regarded a flickering candle in the shape of a cat while inhaling the minty perfume in the air. Soothing classical music filled the space.

Jorge entered and recognized me immediately, but didn't seem surprised. He acted like I was only here for a massage and instructed me to undress. When he left me alone, I looked around. The room was filled with pictures of Jorge holding cats. Definitely a cat lover.

I removed my bra and panties, slid face down on the massage table in between the sheets, and rested my face on the padded donut. Did he know why I was here? What would happen when I asked him about my cat?

Jorge knocked to see if I was ready. I told him to come in.

"I've been expecting you," he said.

I craned my neck to look at him and noticed sweat on his brow. "So you know why I'm here?" I asked.

"Not for a Swedish massage?"

"I want to ask you a few questions."

Jorge shrugged and poured oil in his hands.

I regarded the two pillars in a corner, each topped with big, fat burning candles. The fountain, also in the shape of a cat, gurgled water. Everything seemed so peaceful on the outside, yet inside my emotions were on a battlefield.

Jorge poured warm oil on my back and applied friction gently.

I tried to get into the spirit of the massage. "Mmm, that

feels sooooo good. It's been too long since I've had a massage."
I waited for just the right moment to begin launching my questions.

He kneaded my right calf first, then down my right foot. Next, my left leg and thigh. He squirted almond-scented oil on my back. I felt two heated stones sliding slowly up and down either side of my spine.

"Ahhh."

"I have clients who come in once a week to release all the impurities and toxins from their systems."

"I certainly have a few of those."

As he chop-chopped my back, I looked at the door and noticed a black leather jacket hanging on a hook with something orange peeking out of its pocket. I lifted my shoulders higher to get a better look. It looked like a ski mask.

Something tugged at the back of my mind. I closed my eyes and remembered my conversation with Mindy and Joe the night we were ransacked. Mindy said the intruders to our apartments wore orange ski masks. Was Jorge one of the intruders?

Only one way to confirm my suspicions…pretend to know everything and bluff my way into a confession from Jorge.

I cleared my throat. "You know that cat you took from the Four Seasons Hotel two days ago?"

He stopped moving his hands. "How did you know about that?"

"I know a lot of things."

Now I scooted up to get a better look at him. He looked like he had just swallowed a fur ball.

"You kidnapped my cat as ransom for information related to a murder. Carmen's murder."

Jorge took his hands off my body, and I adjusted my position to face him, wrapping the sheet around my body.

He didn't deny it.

"You ransacked my apartment, as well as my landlord's, with Teresita. The next day, you took my cat to Resurrection Cemetery and you were supposed to ask Angel to kill it. But,

God bless him, he didn't. Why?"

He shook his head and took a step back.

"I've been asking myself this question for days. I believe you love cats too much and couldn't bring yourself to kill one. You gave Angel money to make it look like he'd kill my cat."

Jorge fought back tears. "I couldn't kill the cat. It was too much!"

"But you could kill Carmen?"

He stiffened his back and wiped back a tear. "I didn't kill Carmen."

I backtracked to ask more about my cat. "Why did Bruno Scavoro pick up the cat from the cemetery? How is he involved in this?"

"Bruno doesn't know the half of it. I called Adriano to tell him everything I knew. Adriano called Bruno to get the cat. Bruno was about to kill it, but I talked him out of it."

"So, *somebody* wanted to make it look like Adriano was Carmen's killer."

Jorge's eyes took on a hunted look.

"Why don't you tell me who that *somebody* was?"

Jorge walked to the door and opened it a crack. In the meantime, I slid off the massage bed, wrapped the sheet around myself even more tightly, and stepped over to his coat hanging behind the door to pull out the ski mask.

I waved it around. "You wore this the day you ransacked my apartment."

Jorge whirled around wild-eyed. "I knew it wouldn't work."

"What wouldn't work?" He was so close to confessing everything, I could feel it.

The door swung wide open. Before I could see who, Jorge ripped off the sheet from my body and wrapped it tightly around my head. He held me in place as I struggled, using me as a shield.

"Jorge!" I screamed. The sheet muffled my voice.

"Shoot her, and let's get out of here!" he said. "She knows everything."

As I struggled, I tried to elbow him, but he held me tightly. I was having trouble breathing.

"Hurry up! Come on!" Jorge shouted to the intruder.

The soft music played as background to my choking. I lifted one of my feet off the ground and kicked wildly.

Bang! Bang!

Jorge dropped me.

I caught my breath, unwrapped the sheet from my face, and gasped at the sight of two bloody holes shot through Jorge's head and heart. I felt sick, but didn't have time to throw up because the orange masked invader had a gun pointed at me.

"I know it's you, Teresita. You can take off your mask now."

Teresita kept her mask on, and said with a quavering in her voice, "I'd suggest you put something over yourself. Unless you want to be found naked."

It was definitely Teresita's distinctive Paraguayan accent. I was sitting on the floor nude with the bloody sheet nearby. I didn't really care how I looked; I just didn't want to die. I grabbed the sheet and stood up.

"What's going on?" Antonia shouted from what sounded like a few paces away. "I'm calling 911."

"Don't come in yet!" I warned to Antonia. Then to Teresita, I said, "You're not going to get away with this. I know why you killed Carmen."

Teresita lowered her gun. "Why is that?"

"So that you could become owner of Parsifal's."

Teresita laughed nervously and raised her gun again. "You don't know everything."

"I know enough to put you away for the rest of your life. After you kill me, are you going to kill Antonia?"

I tilted my head toward poor Jorge's bloody body. "Me? Antonia? Jorge? On top of Carmen?"

Her posture went limp, and she stood as if she were shot and waiting to fall. If it weren't for the gun in her grip, I'd lunge at her.

"You've got my cat here too. You masterminded the

kidnapping and made everyone believe Adriano took it because of the box. But Adriano had nothing to do with Carmen's murder. Somehow, you convinced Adriano, though, that I was a danger to him and that he could get the box back through my cat."

"That damn cat," she spit out with contempt. "Jorge was supposed to kill it, but he felt sorry for the cat, said the cat didn't do anything to anybody. I should have never trusted him. Jorge is a weak man."

She aimed the gun at him and for a second, I thought she'd shoot him again.

"The police are on their way," Antonia shouted through the door.

Thank Goddess!

Then Teresita waved the gun at me, and I feared the worst. When Antonia approached the doorway, Teresita turned around and fled the room. She must have figured she couldn't shoot us both.

"Stop her," I screamed to Antonia and anyone else who could hear me. "It's Teresita!"

I was beside myself. I didn't want her to get away. I followed her into the hallway and looked around for some sort of a weapon. I noticed three stones on the floor used for the massages. I scooped them up and hurled them toward Teresita. One bonked her on the head, but it didn't deter her. I grabbed more stones and hurled them. Antonia caught on fast and grabbed a few stones herself to throw at Teresita. I continued grabbing and throwing stones until she ran out the front door. But I couldn't follow because I was naked.

Teresita jumped into a maroon Thunderbird double-parked in front of the salon and drove off.

Chapter Thirty-Two

The spa bustled in chaos. Customers screamed, employees cried, and I grabbed a robe to wrap around my body.

My clothes still rested in a heap in Jorge's massage room, and I had to go back to retrieve them. Jorge lay crumpled on the floor, a pool of blood under his head. I felt sick, the sight of the gore making me lightheaded. I grabbed my clothes and dressed quickly, realizing I'd have to stay to answer questions from the police.

I passed by a mirror and noticed the amount of blood spattered on my clothes. The room swirled and my head reeled from dizziness. I collapsed into a chair, closed my eyes, and breathed deeply. I was alive. That was all that mattered. Teresita aimed a gun at me, but didn't shoot, and I had survived. When I opened my eyes, I thought of Siddharma and wanted to rush to her.

Antonia, looking shaken, stood in the doorway staring at Jorge.

"Are you all right?" I asked.

"Nothing like this has ever happened here before."

"I'm sure! But I need to ask you something. Can you help me open that door so we can get that cat?"

Antonia's expression changed into a look of disgust. "A cat? You're worried about a damn cat?"

She covered her face, leaned against the wall and slid down until she slumped to the floor. She looked at Jorge again and began screaming hysterically, as if the reality of the gruesome situation had just sunk in.

Siddharma would have to wait a little longer.

I stayed with her and eventually coaxed her out of the room into the reception area and onto a sofa.

"Just sit here for a minute, okay?"

She nodded in a shell-shocked way. I made her a cup of

tea and held her hand for a few minutes until she told me she'd be fine. Another employee took my spot to sit with Antonia, and I left them to get Siddharma.

I approached a manicurist and asked how I could enter the storage room. She pointed to the manager's office.

"Teresita keeps the key. Whenever we want something from the supply room, we have to ask her first."

"Thank you," I said, and headed to Teresita's office.

A siren blared outside and I hurried to find the key.

Her office door stood ajar. Inside it looked like an executive suite with dark mahogany wood furniture accented with brass cast hardware. The right side of her pedestal desk had a felt-lined drawer pulled open, now empty. I wondered if Teresita had pulled out her Ilmato from there. Still searching for the storeroom key, I opened her other drawers, looked over the top of her desk, went through her files in her cabinet secretary, and then rummaged through her bookcases filled with classical literature in English and Spanish. A brass chalice stood on one of the shelves. I peeked inside and discovered several keys. The one on top was attached to a leather strap, and it looked like it was used frequently.

I grabbed that key and headed toward the storage room. Just as I inserted the key into the lock, I felt a hand on my shoulder. I flinched, but when I turned around, I was relieved to see Joe. At first his expression was serious, but then he gave me a broad grin.

"Glad I could be here for the big moment."

I gave a triumphant smile to Joe, then flung open the door, and stepped into a room filled with beauty supplies. In a corner stood a cage holding a scrawny white cat that looked terrified.

"Siddharma!" I opened the wire door and reached for her. At first, she didn't seem to recognize me. I removed her gently and nuzzled her face to my cheek. "Oh, Siddharma!"

I never thought I'd feel this happy again and the joy welled up through my eyes.

"What a sight, huh?" Joe said, standing behind me with a smile from ear to ear.

It still felt unbelievable, like a dream sequence, and I squeezed Siddharma tightly to make sure she was really in my arms. "I thought I'd lost you, Siddharma baby. Nothing like this will ever happen again, I swear."

"Watch it," Joe said with a laugh. "You'll strangle her with that clinch hold."

"I can't help it." But as I said the words, I loosened my grip and stood up, Siddharma still in my arms. For her part, Siddharma didn't struggle and the terror in her face had been replaced with calm.

By this point, Antonia had closed the spa and everyone was trying to make themselves as comfortable as possible. Joe didn't say anything, but from his dour expression I knew we needed to talk.

"Why don't we go in the reception area," I said. "I can tell you what happened there."

Joe and another detective followed me to the front of the spa, which was still filled with customers waiting to be questioned by the police. We settled into three chairs with Siddharma on my lap.

"Tell us what happened," Joe said.

I told them how Antonia had explained that Teresita worked in a gun factory in Paraguay. At that, Joe's eyebrows shot up.

"Yes," I responded. "She was cutting my hair and telling me about Teresita's past life in Paraguay. It all makes sense now."

"Go on," Joe said.

"She grew up in Paraguay with a big family and felt fortunate to get a job in a gun factory, where Adriano has his guns custom-made. Apparently, she shot her stepfather with a gun from that factory because he was going to rape her. She escaped, with the help of Adriano Capezio, and started a new life here."

"We'll check this all out," Joe said, as the other detective took notes. "Go on."

"This brings me to what I learned during my massage." I

explained how Jorge wrapped the sheet around me and told the intruder to shoot me, and how, instead, Jorge was shot twice.

Joe and the other detective grimaced.

"You're lucky you weren't killed," Joe said.

"Don't I know it. That intruder was Teresita."

"You're sure?"

"She has a distinct accent. I'm sure."

"What did she say?"

"I was just babbling, trying to mark time waiting until someone walked by. I told her I knew she and Jorge kidnapped my cat. But Jorge is a cat lover. He couldn't kill Siddharma."

"Then what happened?"

"Then Antonia walked by in the nick of time. She saved my life. How is she doing?"

"Two other detectives are questioning her."

I stroked Siddharma on my lap. I felt that an army of angels was looking after me, that my life and Siddharma's were spared so that we could help the Universe in our own way. It was time to wrap up the loose ends so we could find Carmen's murderer.

I told Joe about the ski mask in Jorge's jacket, how I told him I knew he ransacked my landlord's and my apartment, and how he didn't deny any of it.

"It sounds like you're right. Any idea why Teresita shot Jorge?"

"She was mad at him for not killing my cat."

"The cat did bring you here," Joe said. He looked at the other detective who nodded.

"But we still don't know for sure who killed Carmen."

Joe had a troubled look. "I might as well tell you what I just found out this afternoon."

"What?"

"Castrato is Carmen's brother."

"What?" I gasped. "Are you kidding?" I immediately felt idiotic that I had missed it during my interviews. He lived with her, shared her clothes, listened to her confessions about her father. *Their* father. The signs were there. If only I had looked closer, tried harder.

"Alex? Are you listening?"

"Yeah, I…I… Why would they keep that a secret?"

"What I could get from the rest of the family is that the father disowned him years ago by removing him from his will. He couldn't stand the idea of having a son who really wanted to be a daughter."

"Adriano removed Castrato, his own son, from his will? That's terrible."

Joe sighed. "It's perfectly legal. Actually happens more often than you think."

"God! That explains a lot about Castrato. Getting removed from a father's will would drive anybody crazy. It's like getting disowned. Not to mention the fortune he must have lost."

Joe grunted.

It shed new light on Castrato's relationship with Carmen. I recalled bits of my conversation with Castrato. Suddenly, his words "soulmate…felt like we knew each other for centuries…was like a sister to me" all made sense.

"Castrato could be her killer," I said.

"It's possible," Joe said.

"We found Carmen's most recent will, in which she left everything to Castrato. But she was going to reunite with her long-lost daughter in Italy. Maybe Castrato thought Carmen would remove him from her will too."

Joe considered this. "But why would he work with Teresita and Jorge?"

"I don't know."

"Any idea who might know more?"

I sighed and patted Siddharma's fur for several moments. "I've been trying to interview Felix Vasilakis, the assistant conductor, for over a week. I can catch him at the fundraiser tomorrow."

Joe looked at his hands. "I know you won't like hearing this, but I don't think you should go."

For once I wasn't upset with Joe's advice. "But you know I wouldn't miss it for all the lotus tea in Asia. Castrato is the leading act. He's got to be there."

Joe never looked more concerned for me, and I was never more convinced of my decision. "I have to go."

Chapter Thirty-Three

Day Ten: Tuesday, April 1

The next morning, a Tuesday, clouds covered the sky and the wind blew strong gusts, making the leafless trees sway like a chorus with its arms raised. Siddharma slept with me the entire night, allowing me to cuddle her at will, and this was a change. Before her kidnapping, she'd never stand for it. I awoke first and watched her for several minutes, saying a long prayer of thanks. She awoke, stretched her legs, and hopped out of bed as if she knew the day demanded much and wouldn't allow us the luxury of lingering.

As soon as she left my arms, the fear of what lay ahead intensified. I worried that Castrato would abandon his plans at the fundraiser and flee the country. I also worried about being there without a gun.

After I exercised my body with yoga stretches and my mind with a morning meditation, I worked with my Tarot cards for twenty-two minutes at the kitchen table. As I sipped lotus tea and contemplated the intricate detail on the cards' artwork, the classical music station featured Italian baroque. During the last eight days that I've been working with the Tarot, I noticed how they accessed my intuition, allowing me to feel more sure about my hunches. Siddharma watched me study the cards.

I settled on the Fool card, recalling the visualization I experienced at Claire's home, where the wolf taunted me as I climbed a steep staircase. That shadowy wolf leered at my efforts, filling my knapsack with fear and self-doubt, yet it had told me Siddharma was alive and reassured me that I should continue my search for her. Finding Siddharma with the help of the cards strengthened my trust in their power.

It was ten o'clock. In five hours I'd be at the Chicago Lyric Opera House, facing Castrato. I still didn't know how he worked with Teresita and Jorge to kill Carmen, but I sensed a showdown and decided that, before the big night, I wanted to visit The Wizard.

After eating a protein bar, I swallowed two antibiotics for the waning infection in my finger and drove the mile to The Wizard's studio. I entered slowly. His wife stood in the front, dusting off a few crystals–amethyst, quartz, turquoise, jade.

"He's expecting you in the kitchen," she said, looking up from her dusting. I watched her for another moment, then stepped through the swinging door that led into the small hallway. The Wizard stood in front of the stove, his back to me. He lifted a pot of freshly boiled water and poured it into a sea-green teapot, dunked a green teabag twelve times, then set the teapot to steep while he arranged two cups on the table, along with sugar and a tiny plate of thin lemon slices.

He looked me in the face. "So, what happened?"

"Don't you know?"

"It'll help you to talk about it."

"You predicted a married man would seduce me, and it came true. I came so close to submitting to my personal desires."

The Wizard nodded with a look of compassion.

"I never wanted to be in love with him. I knew it would be bad for me, yet I felt powerless. Until the very end."

The Wizard smiled. "That is what counts. We are always tested to strengthen our soul, to prepare us for greater tasks. You have walked through the crucible and survived. How's that infection in your finger?"

"It's better."

"Nothing happens by accident. You did well, and are now ready to proceed."

"To proceed to what?"

The Wizard took a sip of his tea and invited me to sip mine. I ripped open a packet of sugar, poured it into my cup of dark tea, and drank. The hot liquid went down smooth.

"Why do you think you are involved in this murder?"

"I don't know. To enter into the Order of the Tarot at the Fool's degree."

"True, but as I said, nothing happens by accident. Look at it as if you were chosen for this task. Why you?"

It's a question I've been asking myself ever since Carmen gave me the box. "I wanted to do something meaningful that would affect a positive change."

"Anything else?"

I thought hard. "Bringing Carmen's killers to justice would save the Lyric Opera House." I continued to struggle, groping in the dark for a reason. "And it would make me feel worthy of passing a test given to me by my...father."

The Wizard nodded. "Do you understand who your father is?"

I shook my head. I thought I knew who he was, but the way The Wizard phrased his question made me doubt myself. "A famous concert violinist?"

The Wizard stared into his cup of tea. "The time has come for me to tell you more about Alexander Vilkas."

I opened my eyes wide. "You knew him?"

"Oh, yes. A great man. Very few knew how great. He worked quietly, not attracting attention."

"But he was a celebrity violinist. In the papers all the time."

"You could say he led a double life, very much like you."

The shock of this news was overwhelming, yet I also felt elation. As though confirming something I had sensed all my life. "Did my mother know?"

The Wizard shook his head. "It's better she not find out."

"What did he do?"

The Wizard smiled. "He was a detective of the paranormal. He chased vampires, mummies, black magicians, evil Wizards, and worked with a Cabal of Masters for the Good to bring them to justice."

"What?" This was incredible!

"You are following in his footsteps. He knew you would when you were born. That is why he named you after himself."

My hands flew to my face and tears squirted from my eyes at the thought of my father knowing so much about me on the day of my birth. I couldn't believe this, yet I did. "How could he know?"

"You have a special relationship with your father, like few between fathers and daughters. He has always been with you, guiding you, and he is here to help you follow his path."

"Here? Right now? Do you see him?" I looked around the kitchen, but only saw the table, the oven, the tea.

The Wizard nodded. "There may come a day when you will see him, too."

After several more moments, The Wizard asked, "No questions?"

My mind was reeling. "How did you know him?"

The Wizard took another sip of his tea. "What I am about to tell you must never cross your lips for as long as you live. Can you agree to that?"

I nodded.

"I am a part of the Cabal of Masters for the Good. There are twenty-two of us in the world, all at strategic points around the globe. We have all passed through the twenty-two degrees of the Order of the Tarot and have reached spiritual enlightenment. Each owns a mythical crystal skull that has been passed down in our families from generation to generation. As you know, my crystal skull is now at the Chicago Field Museum. Whenever I need to consult it, I go there."

My God! I knew of the crystal skull. A year ago Detective Joe Burke found it in my car and I became a suspect for the murder of Chicago's first Hispanic mayor. Since then, Robin Dryad became mayor and my mother became the mayor's administrative secretary. I had written a story on it for *Gypsy Magazine*, but I had never imagined the skull and The Wizard were connected to my father and my destiny.

"Why haven't you told me about this sooner?"

"You were not ready."

"And now I am?"

He put down his cup, covered my fist with an open palm, then added, "You are the one. What you bring to this task, only you can do. Your father has groomed you for this position, and I have helped. Now your father and others will assist you."

"Assist me in what?"

"Everything in its own time. Your development will mirror each Major Arcana as you write about it. You are now at the Fool stage. Your folly, however, is of inexperience, not dull wit. With each Arcana you explore, your experience will increase."

"Experience of what?"

The Wizard took another sip of tea. "How the universe works. Remember that army of 50,000 horses I spoke to you about?"

"You mean the 50,000 thoughts in a day."

"Yes, imagine if they all ran in the same direction, how much you could accomplish. The road to success in any endeavor is concentration."

I felt like my mind climbed a steep staircase, as I struggled to comprehend all that The Wizard explained. I wanted to sit here for hours and ask more questions about my father.

"Time is running short," The Wizard said, as if he read my mind. "We will talk at length about your father another day. Now we must prepare for what lies ahead, tonight, for you. Are you ready?"

"I couldn't get a gun."

"No?" The Wizard thought for a moment. "Ah, yes, I understand now. You once were on the other side of a gun, and now you must work out that karma. The Universe believes this is the best way for you to do it."

"Won't it just get me killed?"

"That is always a risk."

I remember reading somewhere that the only thing you can take with you when you die is your karma. "Did I...did I...kill people in another life?"

The Wizard nodded.

"Innocent people?"

"Are you sure you want to know?"

"I guess that means yes," I sighed. "Maybe that's why I

can't use one now. Even to save my own life."

The Wizard smiled. "You are following in your father's footsteps. At the beginning, he operated without a gun as well. Which reminds me, you will need something for your protection. Your father left you a gift, and now is the time for you to receive it."

As The Wizard stepped toward the oak cabinet and pulled out a small leather box, my heart swelled with joy at the thought of my father envisioning this moment twenty years ago, before his death. I could feel his presence, his smile as he stood over me to witness this occasion, which to me, took on a ceremonial significance.

The Wizard opened the box and pulled out a thin, gold chain with a medallion, then handed it to me. I held it in my palm and looked at the inscription. "It's St. Casimir!"

"Each of our detectives wears a medallion with a symbol that is significant to them. Your father chose St. Casimir because of his Lithuanian heritage. He wanted you to do the same, but of course you are free to choose another. It is most important that the symbol be significant to you."

I made a fist around the medallion, making it my own. "No, I want this one. I've always known something special would happen on March 4th, the Feast of St. Casimir."

I unclasped the chain and handed it to The Wizard. He stood behind me as he fastened it around my neck. "Alexandria Vilkas. You are now initiated into the spiritual detective business, one of a select group of detectives around the globe, all working with a Master from the Cabal of Good. Your mission is to pierce the veil of death and bring balance and justice to this world."

I closed my eyes, feeling the weight of the medallion on my neck, and knew that I had found my mission in life.

When I opened my eyes and turned to face The Wizard, he said, "Let's do a little meditation, to prepare you for the task ahead."

I agreed.

He led me to another room, the color of turquoise. The

ceiling had a fresco of a lotus blossom with the brass chandelier in its center. On one wall hung a banner of the chakras system. The Wizard approached the banner and pointed to the fourth chakra–a green wheel. "This is the heart center, and our meditation will open your heart today."

We sat cross-legged, facing each other, on two orange pillows.

Smiling, he said, "Close your eyes."

I did, and fell into the meditation.

"Breathe in. Breathe out. Focus on your heart. You are taking in a loving, sustaining Life Force that is expanding your heart."

I imagined the love in my heart heating up my entire chest area, expanding further in an effortless manner.

"Very good, Alex. Now, behind you, visualize all who are available to help you in your quest..."

I saw my mother and Alyce, Lt. Joe Burke, Tony, and Edgar Sheldon.

"...and those who may have passed on to a new life on the Other Side."

I visualized Carmen in the costume she wore for her last performance, and then I saw my father, standing in the last position behind everyone.

"Good. This is your Council, the people you will consult to help you solve this mystery, if they so desire. And they will. You have raised your energy level high enough for them to notice and attract them."

After a few more minutes, The Wizard concluded the meditation. My hand flew to the medallion, and I thought of the Fool and his knapsack–envisioning myself carrying it with Encouragement from the Wizard and St. Casimir, versus Fear and Self-Doubt. I had a sense it would be my most powerful tool, the one I'd treasure the most. How we clung to the few words of encouragement we receive in our lifetime, their power stamped upon us through eternity.

Chapter Thirty-four

After leaving The Wizard's studio, I drove home. There wasn't nearly enough time to process all the emotions I felt about the news of my father–joy and pride over all he'd accomplished, blended with anger and resentment at not knowing about his double life sooner. Nevertheless, the influence of his medallion on my bosom fortified me, giving me a newfound pluck I hadn't known I possessed.

Once I arrived home, I called Denise Johnson, the Lyric's administrator, and had a long conversation with her. She admitted she knew Carmen wanted to change her will and leave everything to her daughter, but that she never had a chance to before her death. We also established that she was with Bruno during the length of the second act and not a suspect in the murder. Nevertheless, I hoped she would help arrange an interview with Felix Vasilakis. By the time I finished explaining everything, she understood how a portion of the Lyric's funding from Adriano Capezio came from the sales of arms.

At first she couldn't believe it. "That is absolutely ridiculous," she said. "Adriano is our biggest donor, our greatest supporter."

Then she was in shock. "My God! What will we do?"

Then she was angry. "How dare he place our opera house in such a precarious position? The nerve of him! Doesn't he realize what this could do to us?"

That was when I asked, "Wouldn't it look better if you agreed to help *Gypsy Magazine* as soon as you discovered the Lyric's funding came from the sale of Ilmatos?"

After a moment's pause, Denise answered, "And will you write that once I knew about the arms deal, I vehemently denounced it?"

"Absolutely. If you help me land the interview with Felix

Vasilakis."

And so my interview with Felix Vasilakis had finally been arranged. Less than two hours later, I arrived at the Lyric. I had parked my car in a lot on Madison Avenue and quickened my pace crossing Wacker Drive. The temperature plummeted suddenly, and as the wind picked up speed, wee particles of ice fell intermittently. Shielding my eyes, I looked up to see the tiny ice bombs fall from the sky. Most on the street were caught unaware, like it was an April Fool's Day prank from the weather demons. Traffic slowed.

From the outside, the forty-five-story skyscraper looked like a majestic fortress, and the color of the roiling clouds above matched the gray limestone. A cornucopia of engraved comedy/tragedy masks and instruments ran along the entire length of the portico. I thought of Alyce's code name for this episode–Opera-tion Lyric House–as I felt a prick of anxiety over my upcoming interview with Felix.

Denise Johnson greeted me in the lobby, a woman in her sixties with gray-streaked hair and a pillow-soft bust. "I haven't told anyone about your visit," she said. "It would make them, you know, a little nervous, having a reporter here. But I suppose there's no hiding you now, is there?"

She helped me remove my coat and hang it up in the coat-check room, seeming solicitous in her manner.

"I'll try to be as discreet as possible," I said.

"We will meet with resistance from Felix Vasilakis," Denise said, but from the look in her eye, I could tell that if she couldn't get Felix to talk to me, nobody could. When Tony arrived a minute later with his cameras, Denise gave a dry laugh, perhaps out of excitement or uneasiness at what she imagined lay ahead. After I introduced Tony to Denise, we followed her from the lobby through the auditorium, backstage, and into the principals' dressing rooms.

Denise rapped her knuckles lightly against the assistant director's door. We stood for several awkward seconds, the three of us glancing nervously at each other. Felix's dressing room was next to the one Carmen had used ten days ago. No yellow police tape was draped across her entryway, I noticed. Perhaps the forensic specialists had gotten all they could out of the room by now.

"Maestro? Are you in there?" Denise tried the door again, but it was locked.

"Just a minute," we heard. "I'll be right there."

Finally, Felix Vasilakis opened the door. When his eyes rested on me, I knew he couldn't pinpoint how we had met before. Then a look of recognition dawned on him as Denise introduced us. He wasn't pleased, yet he took my offered hand to shake it.

"Alexandria is here to do an article on our opera house for her magazine," Denise said with a note of firmness. "For *Gypsy Magazine*."

"It's about Carmen Dellamorte's death," I added.

Felix let go of my hand like he had just touched a rotten fish. "Really? I thought I said everything there was to say to the police."

Felix looked at Tony and me, then said, "I'm sorry, but I have no time for granting an interview. The show begins in less than three hours. I have too much to do."

"I understand, Mr. Vasilakis," I said, "but we're trying to determine who murdered Carmen. Surely, you'd have no objection to helping."

"You are not the police, and I do not have to talk to you. Really!" He was about to close the door.

Denise caught my eye, then stepped forward. "I'm going to have to order you to speak to Alexandria Vilkas. You don't have an option."

The look Felix sent to Denise could have summoned a chorus of devils from Hades, but Denise stood her ground. Now Tony sent me a questioning look, as if to ask, "How did you get Denise to do that?"

I mouthed back, "I'll tell you later."

"Order me?" Felix huffed. "Or else what?"

"Don't push me, Mr. Vasilakis. Assistant conductors are a dime a dozen. I have a stack of resumés from eager conductors around the world who would do anything to work here. Please. We need to get to the bottom of finding Carmen's murderer."

Felix looked crushed, but Denise's tactic worked. "Very well," he said. "Since you put it that way." He showed me to a soft burgundy chair. The room looked exactly like Carmen's next door down to the beige walls, turquoise trim, piano, private bathroom, and vanity mirror. "Will you be covering the performance?"

"Yes."

"Then you know we have little time to talk."

I nodded as I dug out my reporter's notebook and put my tape recorder on the ottoman that matched my burgundy chair. While Tony stood by the piano fiddling with his cameras, Felix and Denise sat on the couch to my right.

Felix pulled each sleeve of his black turtleneck down to his wrist and adjusted his collar.

"Ten days ago, I was interviewing Carmen next door for an article on Tarot cards," I began.

Felix harrumphed, "When I walked in, right?"

"Yes."

"And so why, exactly, are you here?" he asked, glancing alternately at Denise and me.

Denise jumped in. "Alex Vilkas called me this afternoon to talk about including you and our opera house in her story. We all know about your close relationship with Carmen."

"And Castrato, her roommate," I added, studying Felix for his reaction. I wanted to have him talk about Castrato as soon as possible.

Felix shook his head and covered his eyes. "I suppose you've heard I spent a fair amount of time with them," he said. "You want to know about the extent of my relationship with them?"

"Yes," I said, as I dug into my purse and pulled out my pack of Tarot cards, laying them next to the tape recorder. It was the first time I used these cards during an interview like this and I worried about the effect they would have. But if I was going to be a spiritual detective of the paranormal, I might as well start acting like one and use all the weapons available to me. In my case, the Tarot cards became my Magnum .45.

"What in the world do you expect to do with those cards?" Felix asked, recoiling at the sight of them.

Already they were working to intensify the effect of the interview. Before I could answer, Denise interrupted. "I was thinking, Maestro, that maybe you could get your cards read here."

I caught Felix's gaze. "The idea is I'll read your cards to learn all I can from you about Carmen's death."

"I've heard of nothing more ridiculous," Felix exclaimed, indignant. "I won't stand for it."

"The circumstances are highly unusual," Denise said. "We're desperate to find Carmen's killer. Don't you see what a precarious state our company is in until we do? Alexandria believes the cards will help draw out the truth."

"Nothing in my contract with the Lyric says I have to undergo a Tarot card reading to keep my job," Felix said between clenched teeth. "I'm going to take this up with the musician's union."

"I'm sorry to have to do this," Denise said. "But you've left me no other recourse. You'll be fired this evening if you don't have this interview with Alexandria. *With* the cards."

Inwardly, I cheered for Denise. She had a way. Felix formed his mouth into a pucker as if he were about to whistle, but only blew out a stream of air. Then he stroked the lonely strands of hair on his shining scalp and massaged the back of his neck, swinging his head downward. By this time, Tony had organized his cameras and was furiously snapping pictures. His clicks sounded like a Spanish flamenco dancer tapping the hardwood floor with her heels. When Felix looked up, he grimaced.

Without warning he stood up and pointed to the door. "No pictures! No photos! No audience! Everybody out! I want to be alone when I speak to this…this…woman with her cards!"

Denise stood up and Tony stopped clicking. I looked at both of them and nodded. "Perhaps I should be alone with

Felix."

"Are you sure?" Tony asked.

I looked at Denise who winked her left eye, a signal that I took to mean I shouldn't worry and that I'd get what I wanted.

"Yes, I'm sure. Felix is right. We should be alone."

"I'll be just outside this door if you need me," Tony said, as he and Denise stepped out.

Once they left, Felix and I sat down, both of us sighing for our own reasons. I grabbed the Rider-Waite Tarot, briefly shuffled them with a prayer, and handed them to Felix.

"Please mix them until you feel they are ready to help us talk."

With reluctance, Felix took the cards and shuffled them, never taking his eyes off me. Each of his movements with the cards felt like a slap to me, as his manner was brusque, just verging on violence.

He stopped and placed the deck on the ottoman. I asked him to cut the cards with his left hand. I put them back together and laid out five in a row. The Fool appeared first, followed by the Lovers, three of Swords, Death, and nine of Swords. I noticed a bead of sweat had formed on Felix's forehead before I closed my eyes to meditate upon the cards' message. To bring my mind to stillness, I pushed away lingering feelings of unease.

When I opened my eyes, I said, "With these five cards I know what happened to Carmen, and I need you to verify the truth."

Felix looked at the cards with fear. "What do they say?"

"The first card is the Fool and he represents Castrato. Sometimes the Fool suggests taking risks with childlike innocence, signifying a period marked by nervous energy and uncertain conditions. A Fool also represents a bisexual or homosexual person who influences the situation."

Felix sat motionless, then cleared his throat, and nodded. "Yes, that's correct," he said with a note of resignation.

I continued. "The second card is The Lovers, signifying Castrato and someone else, which I believe to be you. Your love was betrayed, which resulted in Carmen's death. That is why we see the Death card."

"My God," he said. "I can't believe it."

"The next card, the nine of Swords, shows a woman sitting in bed, worrying with nine swords hanging over her. She can't believe what happened. In this case, however, this card also represents you."

Felix looked at the spread with incredulity. "It's true! I haven't been able to sleep for the past ten days."

"The cards tell me you and Castrato are lovers. Someone came between you to cause much pain–the Three of Swords."

"No. Yes. No."

I sat still, my hands now on my lap away from the cards as I regarded Felix in as gentle a manner as possible. I breathed slowly and deeply to bring calm to the room; Felix twitched his hands in his lap, struggling over what he could tell me.

He picked up The Lovers card and studied it for several moments. "I suppose there's no hiding it, is there?"

I bit at my upper lip and nodded, afraid to break the spell of the confession to come.

"It was Teresita. She came between us. I never did like her, but Castrato adored her. When Carmen heard her daughter lived in Florence, Teresita planted the seed of reunion. She kept at it with Carmen–how wonderful that Katarina wanted to be with her mother, a new opportunity for Carmen. Then, when Carmen realized Macbeth would be her last opera, she decided she had no more excuses to stay away from her daughter."

"There's more, isn't there?"

"There's something about Castrato and Carmen that few realize."

"I believe you are about to tell me that they are brother and sister."

Felix looked at me with incredulity, then nodded. "Their father, Adriano…" He shook his head back and forth. "Castrato was torn over him. He never really forgave him for removing him from his will…I don't know what possessed a father to remove his own son from his will. I've never heard of such brutality. You've no idea how that has torn at Castrato, how it changed him, shaped him to who he is today. He took it as the ultimate rejection, and the pain he felt was a constant reminder of how he could never please his father. Eventually, he directed the pain against his father."

I nodded in understanding. "It could go nowhere else."

I felt the anger emanate from Felix in a strong wave, his indignation against Adriano on Castrato's behalf filling the room. I soaked it in and understood deeply how much Castrato suffered over this.

Felix cleared his throat and continued. "Teresita knew this about Castrato, yet she continued to tell Carmen to reunite with her daughter. Castrato became horrified over this because he knew where it would lead–Carmen would take him out of her will and leave everything to her daughter. I'm not saying it's wrong for a mother to get back together with her daughter, it's just that Carmen was all the family Castrato had."

I considered this information and turned it over in my mind, seeing from Castrato's viewpoint how he would feel betrayed again by being removed from his sister's will. It was a strong motive.

Felix shut his eyes. His eyelids trembled. He balled his hands into fists and pounded them together. "I love him. I can't betray him."

I recalled The Wizard's words from a previous conversation. "To see the truth more clearly, sometimes it is necessary to step away from the center of the storm and move to the edge." Felix was in a state of confusion and my intent was not to break his spirit, but to guide him to revealing all that he understood about Carmen's death. I moved our focus to a wider angle of the problem.

"After you left Carmen's dressing room, what did you do?"

"The police have already asked me all this."

"But you haven't told them everything." I tilted my head toward the spread.

Felix tightened his lips and lowered his eyelids.

"The belladonna plant. I was with Carmen when you brought it in, and Carmen asked you to get rid of it. Where did you put it?"

"I threw it out."

"Where?"

"I took the elevator to the fourth floor, the chorus dressing room. It's customary to give them a little pep talk."

"You still had the plant."

"I had a lot on my mind and left it on the first table I could find, one of the sinks where the choristers do their make-up. I didn't give it a second thought until later when I learned Donacella's kitten had died." Felix grimaced at the memory and shook his head. "It was only then that I realized her kitten must have nibbled on the plant."

"Do you remember seeing Donacella in the chorus room?"

"She was bragging to them about her curse to Carmen. In fact, she was shouting 'Macbeth, Macbeth, Macbeth' over and over up there. I thought she was going mad herself." He threw me a "and you see where that went" sort of look.

I nodded, pleased at his rush of words. He had them dammed up inside and they were waiting to come out.

"Where did you go after you left the plant on the fourth floor?"

"The musician's lounge. I spoke with Maestro and stayed nearby for most of the performance."

"Exactly where?"

"The orchestra pit."

"I saw the plant in Carmen's dressing room right after the performance. How did it get back down from the fourth floor?"

For the first time since my arrival, Felix's face brightened. "You know, I noticed that, too, and even asked about it. I was told one of the choristers returned it to Carmen's dressing room. She noticed Carmen's name on the tag, and decided it belonged to Carmen." That explained how the plant was returned to Carmen's dressing room.

"What were you doing during intermission?"

Felix's eyes widened, then he closed his eyes and rubbed

his temples. "I was in Carmen's dressing room with Castrato and several others from the cast. Castrato noticed the bottle of champagne from his father–you know, the one that said, 'To make the poison go down easier. Love, Dad.' He roared with laughter, and I thought he really had gone insane at that moment. He opened it with zeal and convinced Carmen to take a sip with him. She didn't want to because she still had to go back onstage, but he insisted. Finally, she agreed to take a sip with him after her last song. I never told this to the police. I just didn't believe it was really Castrato. I wanted to protect him and I knew how it would look. But now…"

Felix sent me a pleading look and I nodded my acknowledgement of how difficult this has all been for him. All he said made sense and confirmed my suspicions of Castrato.

"You never went backstage?"

"Only after Carmen fell. I rushed up to see what had happened. Unbelievable, surreal. Never in all my days has something like this ever happened." He shook his head. "It's a defining moment…catastrophic! Everyone immediately blamed Donacella, of course, and when she went onstage with the dead kitten…" He sighed. "To think that Carmen's death will result in the end of this House. We are cursed."

"The public still believes Donacella's curse killed Carmen, it's true. But we can play a role in changing the public's perception of the facts so that the truth can come out."

Felix looked at his watch. It was after five o'clock, and the performance would begin in two hours. "Is that all then?" Felix stood up, towering over me.

I still felt our conversation was incomplete, that he had more to tell me, but I turned off the tape-recorder, gathered the cards, and proceeded to place them back in the box. The Emperor card fell from the Tarot pack.

I picked up the card. "Just one more question." I peered at the Emperor sitting on his throne. "Look closely at this man. Who do you see?"

Felix hesitantly took the card and studied it. "I don't know what you mean."

"The Emperor signifies Adriano Capezio. What can you tell me about him?"

He stood up and walked to the piano, leaned against it, then hit two notes. "Nobody likes Adriano in the opera world, or will cross him either. When I came to the Lyric, I had Adriano's sponsorship in my hands–more powerful than any baton."

"It's always who you know in opera. So you're in his debt."

Felix struck a minor chord on the piano, then added, "We all are."

"Have you noticed Castrato spending more time with his father lately?"

Felix pulled out the stool from the piano, sat upon it, and plunked out a little tune with one finger. "There was a reconciliation this past year. Adriano reached out to Castrato, even asked him to join his business. At first Castrato was happy about that, but then he said his father really hadn't changed on the inside, that everything he did was just for show."

"Do you know what sort of business relationship they had?"

He plunked a few more notes on the piano. "Those dreadful guns, the Ilmatos. I never thought Castrato would stoop to selling firearms."

So Castrato *was* in his father's business. "Why do you think he did?"

"He was trying to please his father. There's…" He wanted to say more, but checked himself. He balled his hands into fists and pounded on the piano.

"Go on."

"There's some sort of a…sale tonight. I…" He choked on the words and slumped over the keyboard with a clang, as his body shook in sobs. He had delivered Castrato to me and now felt guilty over betraying his lover.

"What sale?"

"I…I don't know. I just heard Castrato talk about it with

Teresita."

Felix had confirmed that Castrato joined his father in the arms business. He had most of the pieces of the puzzle, yet he couldn't bring himself to put them together. But I could. Teresita poisoned Castrato's mind against Adriano for taking him out of his will, then she poisoned Castrato's mind against Carmen. She incited him to kill his sister and frame his father. Castrato sold the Ilmatos illegally to implicate his father. He'd inherit half of Carmen's fortune and he'd share it with Teresita.

I still had to ask Felix one more question. "Who do you think killed Carmen?"

He choked out the words in sobs. "I...still want to believe it was Adriano."

I stood up and breathed slowly, waiting for Felix to compose himself. When he looked at me with swollen red eyes, I thanked him and left, wanting to find Adriano Capezio. Although I didn't believe Adriano was the killer anymore, I knew he could tell me more about his son Castrato.

Chapter Thirty-Five

As I stepped out of Felix's dressing room, I found Tony waiting for me, sitting on the floor in the hallway, eyes closed. From the looks of it, he fell asleep, and for some reason, I couldn't have been happier seeing him snore softly with his mouth open. Gently, I touched his shoulder. "You're still here?" I asked in a low voice.

He opened his eyes and, after rubbing them, smiled. "Sorry, not much of a guard, am I?"

I extended my hand to help him up. "Good enough for me. Thanks for sticking around."

"No problem. So how'd it go?"

"Fine, it went fine. Now I need to find Adriano Capezio."

"You think he did it?"

"No, I think it was Castrato at Teresita's urging. But I need to hear from Adriano why he disowned his son and took him out of his will."

Tony picked up his cameras and followed me in my search, but after spending about twenty minutes walking around the place, talking to Denise Johnson and others, it became clear Adriano had not arrived yet. We told several people we hoped to talk to him, then headed back to the auditorium to wait.

Tony took pictures backstage in an attempt to capture Carmen's ghost in her final steps. He shrugged his shoulders and shook his head at his cameras. "What a waste, but hey, it's what the boss wants."

"Just think about it," I said, trying to cheer him up. "If you see her, you really will live out our magazine's motto–to pierce the veil of death."

At least Tony had a smile on his face before he walked behind the curtains. In the meantime, I thought about Carmen's last moments and how Castrato and Teresita had poisoned her.

Silvia Foti

Alone, in the same chair I sat in ten days ago, I turned around and looked at the theater's 3,500 seats, wondering what it felt like to perform before a crowd that size.

I imagined Carmen joyously singing her heart out to the full house, then moments later feeling betrayed. I touched the medallion hanging on my neck and understood Carmen's desperation, as well as the extreme burning pain in her esophagus and abdomen as the rubbing alcohol ate away at her delicate pink tissue, leading to hemorrhage. I coughed and rubbed my throat, sharing the confusion and dizziness she endured. Did she know her brother poisoned her champagne?

As I released the medallion, my temporary connection to Carmen's mind and heart ceased. Was it possible the medallion heightened my empathy for Carmen to such an extent that I truly felt her emotions? It seemed impossible, like nothing I'd ever experienced before. My mind reeled, thrilled with the discovery of this new power, imagining how it could help me understand people better. Would it help me in other instances, or was this just a fluke?

At that critical moment, the weight of my Fool's test to enter into the Order of the Tarot bore down upon me. With this medallion and its vested powers, I realized The Wizard expected me to find the proof necessary to convict Carmen's murderers. Although I was convinced Castrato and Teresita killed Carmen, I still had no concrete proof.

I sat still and closed my eyes to think. One of The Wizard's teachings unfolded in my mind—to find the right answers, you had to ask the right questions. What would be exactly the right question? I opened my eyes and stared at the stage, imagining again Carmen's final moments. How had Castrato changed so quickly from his black leather outfit as a witch to the one he wore as a spectator with turtleneck and slacks leaning in the doorway, waiting for his sister with a glass of poisoned champagne?

Only one way to find out—retrace his steps. I left my seat and went backstage to walk from the stage doorway to Castrato's dressing room. As I stepped behind the curtain, I

258

noticed Tony engrossed in snapping pictures backstage. He didn't notice me, and I hesitated to interrupt him. I turned back to my own task. I assumed Castrato stood somewhere backstage before the final scene and imagined several other cast members, as well. Most would be focused on the performance and wouldn't notice Castrato slipping away. I walked quickly from my position backstage to Castrato's dressing room, waited a few moments to allow for him to change, then walked back to the doorway. If everything went smoothly, which apparently it had, Castrato, dressed as a witch, could run to his dressing room, change into a man wearing a black turtleneck and slacks, and be back at the doorway standing with a glass of champagne waiting for Carmen, all in less than two minutes. Carmen would have noticed him in the doorway and approached…or perhaps he had called her over in some way without being noticed by anyone else.

Another thirty seconds for Carmen to sip the poisoned liquid and kiss her brother. When she handed the glass back, Castrato returned to her room to drop off the glass, then stepped into his room to change back into his witch's outfit. If he kept on his pantyhose he could change back into his black leather in less than a minute. At that point, he could walk slowly down the corridor to wait in the wings for the death of Carmen as the poison did its dirty work. From start to finish, the diabolical plan conceivably occurred in about five minutes. But where was my proof?

I stepped to the center of the stage and looked around when a booming voice startled me. "Mizz Alexandria Vilkas! I understand you've been looking for me."

When I turned to face Adriano Capezio walking down the center aisle toward the stage, I saw exactly what I expected to confront, an angry and overbearing man who looked like he hadn't slept in days. I steeled myself for what I knew would be an unpleasant conversation.

"How dare you," he began, now turning the corner of the aisle and heading for the side entrance to climb onto the stage. Unable to stand still, I paced while waiting for him to approach. How would I tell him about his son? Did he already know?

In the next moment, he towered over me. I took a step back, hoping the movement would slow down his rage, but it seemed to only fuel it. As he took another step toward me, he crossed his arm to his hip under his jacket, and pulled out a gun. My God! I summoned my Council from the Other Side, my Father and Carmen, and any others they related to because I thought I'd join them very soon.

He held it four inches away from my third-eye chakra, which probably stopped spinning because my mind went blank. He wouldn't dare shoot me on stage, not like this. Please not like this. Yet he seemed insanely enraged.

"Do you know what this is?" He screamed the question and I almost swooned as I stumbled backward, but I recovered my balance.

"What is it?" I asked, trying to make time. I hadn't seen Tony in the last few minutes. Where had he gone?

"It's everything–my livelihood, my passage to all I've ever wanted. With this, I've nurtured my daughter's career in opera, made sure she'd become the diva I knew she could be."

My mind raced. Why was he telling me this? He was building up to something, but I couldn't be sure what it was. A confession?

He lowered the gun until it pointed to my heart, rammed it into the center of my bosom, right into the medallion, which I feared would not stop the bullet. Not here! Not now! I closed my eyes and said a prayer of thanks to all those who have guided me to this moment and who would usher me into the afterlife. There was nothing else for me to do. I slowed my breath and then felt the pressure removed from my chest.

When I opened my eyes to verify if I had really passed to the other side, I was shocked to see Adriano pointing the gun to his own temple. A sense of relief instantly washed over me as I realized he never intended to kill me, yet in the next moment, terror at what would happen overwhelmed me. I locked eyes with him, noting his fear and desperation.

"I killed her, alright? It was me. Put that in your fuckin' book. I'm confessing to the murder of my daughter, Carmen Dellamorte."

He pushed the gun further into his right temple, causing the skin around the muzzle to bunch up. His confession made no sense at all.

"Please. Don't." I took a step toward him.

His body shook with rage and fear, his face drenched in sweat. "Nothing is left. It's all been taken away."

I made a supreme effort to calm myself to bring a sense of calm to him.

Then, as if an internal switch operating Adriano's life force had been turned off, he went limp and dropped the gun. As it hit the floor a shot rang out, but no one was hurt. He covered his face with his hands and began to shake.

I steered Adriano to a raised platform on the stage so he could sit down. I took several deep breaths while I waited for Adriano to compose himself.

"I know you didn't kill Carmen."

He shook his head. "There's nothing left for me. Denise Johnson just fired me from the Lyric's Board of Directors. Said the money from my firearms wasn't good enough for her opera house."

I touched his right arm and fathomed how his removal from the Lyric's board precipitated his false confession.

"There's nothing else for me to live for. Carmen's been threatening suicide ever since she was a teen-ager. She might have poured in the poison herself, but I pushed her to do it. That's why I'm taking the blame."

He stared out across the stage catatonically.

"You didn't kill her. It was Castrato."

Adriano laughed hollowly. "Yeah, right. He's not capable of it. He couldn't have. It was a suicide. And it was my fault."

"Is it true you removed him from your will?"

Adriano ran his fingers through his hair. "That has nothing to do with this. It happened a long time ago, after he decided to become a woman."

"How long ago?"

"If you haven't noticed, he's got a gender identity disorder. He's prone to making up facts, can't quite figure out what's real. He kept saying he's a woman and kept dressing like one. I thought if I took him out of the will, it would knock some sense into him."

"When did you do that?"

"In college. When he dreamed up his castration."

"Dreamed up?"

Adriano laughed. "Yeah, he made it up. He's got balls, believe me."

"What are you saying? That he wasn't castrated?"

"Turned out he had quite a gift for singing the high-voice roles. Somebody noticed he had a brilliant falsetto voice. Opera companies loved calling him Castrato, and he went along with it."

"And you didn't approve."

"I wanted him to be a man. That's when I took him out of the will. I wanted him to stop that nonsense."

I considered this. Both of his children achieved what he had always wanted–to become opera stars. Yet he didn't approve of the path his son had taken. It was too bad.

"Yet now he's working with you? How did that happen?"

"About a year ago, he asked me if he could join my business, thought it would help us reunite."

"All of a sudden? Didn't that seem strange?"

"It was strange, but I figured what the hell. I haven't had a chance to be much of a father to him."

The timing made a lot of sense. "That was about the time Carmen began talking about reuniting with her own daughter in Italy, wasn't it?"

Adriano's eyes widened. "You know about that? Yeah, you're right."

"Did you also know that Castrato thought she would remove him from her will too?"

"No, I didn't."

"All this drove him over the edge, with Teresita's help."

Adriano considered this.

"He planned this with Teresita and wanted to blame you."

"How?"

"They've been selling your Ilmatos to other people. But they told Carmen *you* were selling firearms illegally. This was planned in advance so it would look like you had something to hide. They wanted to make it look like you would kill your daughter to protect your business."

"What?" Adriano asked. He looked like he was waking up from a drunken stupor.

I sat still, hoping Adriano would make the necessary connections.

"Shit. My crew noticed a few Ilmatos missing. All this time I thought my son wanted to get on my good side. This…"

But before he could finish his thought, Tony came rushing toward us. "Guess what," he said, barely containing his excitement. "I saw Carmen."

"What?" I said incredulously.

Tony lifted one of the three cameras hanging from his neck. "Through this one. Her ghost. She's here. It's unbelievable."

Adriano's face contorted into a look of skepticism. "Get outta here."

As for me, I had my own share of skepticism of what Tony really saw through his camera, but didn't dare voice it. If Tony believed in what he saw, who was I to tell him otherwise?

Tony pointed toward stage left. "She stands right there, backstage, smiling and looking around, like there was a crowd around her. Then she walks to that door in the back. That must have been right after her last scene, as she headed to her dressing room."

"Then what does she do?" Adriano asked.

"She returns, stops at the doorway, takes a drink someone had offered, smiles, gives a kiss to that person, and moves to watch the action onstage. She hugs her stomach, looks at the doorway she came from with anguish, then walks onstage and falls to her death."

All of this I had told Tony earlier. So far he saw only what I described to him, which is why I had a hard time believing he saw anything.

Adriano stood up. "Let me see that camera."

Tony handed it over.

Adriano looked through the lens. Soon he started to walk with it, as if pulled by an invisible force.

"Do you actually see something?" I asked. It was one thing for Tony to be convinced he saw something, but quite another for Adriano to act like he was seeing his daughter's ghost.

"Oh, God! It is her. I can't believe it. Oh, honey, I'm so sorry. What? Really?"

I wanted to grab that camera and see for myself, but restrained myself. Adriano looked to be on the verge of a revelation.

Adriano put down the camera and gulped. "It can't be."

"What did she say?" I asked.

He shook his head. "It wasn't suicide after all. She wanted to live. She said to look in the sarcophagus for the proof."

"What sarcophagus?" Tony and I asked in unison.

"On the sixth floor in the props room," Adriano said matter-of-factly. He stood waiting, rather impatiently, for us to follow him, yet Tony and I both hesitated.

Did Adriano really see Carmen through the lens, or was he sending us on a wild goose chase? His hands shook and he seemed in earnest. Maybe he saw the image he needed to see. But what was with the sarcophagus? It didn't make sense, until I recited the poem written by John Keats left by Carmen.

"This living hand, now warm and capable

of earnest grasping, would, if it were cold

And in the icy silence of the tomb,

So haunt thy days and chill thy dreaming nights."

"So?" Tony asked.

"Don't you see? Carmen left four notes referring to a tomb. Remember how I thought she left a clue in a tomb?"

"Yeah, like when I found you at the cemetery," Tony said.

"There was nothing there."

"Exactly. That's because sarcophagus is another word for tomb," I said. "She left a letter in the sarcophagus right here."

I wanted to look through Tony's camera and verify Carmen's ghost for myself, but knew we didn't have a moment to spare.

Chapter Thirty-Six

Tony shook his head and looked through his phantasmagoric camera, entranced by what he saw. "I can't leave her, not yet. She might not return."

I wanted to strangle Tony. He'd already seen plenty of Carmen through his ghost camera. Why did he need to stick around for more? "You have to come with me. This is important."

Adriano stood beside Tony. "Seeing my daughter like this... I can't leave either. It might be my last chance to talk to her. Whatever is in that sarcophagus can wait."

I felt like screaming at them, unable to believe they'd become so enchanted by the vision of Carmen's ghost. What was she doing to them? But then again, if I had a chance to see my father's spirit, I probably wouldn't be able to break away either. I couldn't wait for the spell to break. The fundraiser was about to start, and I had to see if Carmen had left a clue upstairs.

Perhaps I didn't need them with me, after all. It was just an elevator up a few floors, an inspection of the sarcophagus, and a return to the fundraiser. What could go wrong? I left them; Adriano peering over Tony's shoulder waiting his turn to look through the camera while Tony clicked away.

As I rode the elevator up to the sixth floor, I braced myself for what I would find. Ever since Carmen had given me that box of material about her father, I'd convinced myself she wanted to tell me something. She suspected her life might be in danger and had left a clue, an insurance policy of sorts. By The Wizard's calculation, today was the tenth day of my test to enter the Order of the Tarot at the Fool level, and this case would come to an end soon one way or another.

The elevator stopped on the sixth floor. As I stepped out, I was shocked to see Beata about eight feet away. She didn't notice me because her back was to me, and she was absorbed in reading something. She stood before the gray stony tomb that lay flat on the wooden floor. It stood isolated from the other props–a wind machine, a rickshaw, and thousands of items on shelves such as dishes, toys, and books. It was much like a grandmother's attic. The lid of the sarcophagus had been pushed off.

I suspected Beata had shoved aside the lid to this tomb and found the sheet of paper she was still reading. She beat me to it! How dare she show up like this? And how did she figure out Carmen left something in this tomb?

When the elevator door closed with a thump, Beata whirled around and gawked in disbelief. "Alex, what are you–"

"I was just about to ask you the same thing. Is that a letter from Carmen?"

She held it closer to her breast. "As a matter of fact, it is. I spent the last three days sorting through all the material in the box left by Carmen, just like Alyce asked me to. In an entry in Carmen's diary, she wrote about visiting the props room. As soon as I figured it out, I rushed over here."

"And how exactly did you figure it out? I went through every single piece of paper in that box, and there was no mention of this sarcophagus."

Beata shrugged her shoulders. "You must have missed it. It was right there in her diary."

It was then that I noticed the missing page from Carmen's diary. Beata held it in her hands along with the letter.

"That diary page! You ripped it out! Before I had a chance to copy everything."

Beata looked at the pages in her hand, perhaps realizing the evidence was all too clear. "So what if I did? It's just one page."

I took a step closer to Beata. "Withholding the evidence from the police is a crime. Even I didn't think you'd stoop that low. Give it to me. Now."

Beata stood still for a long moment, perhaps weighing her options. Finally, she handed over the diary page, which I snatched greedily and inspected. It matched perfectly to Carmen's latest journal measuring nine inches by six inches. The corner of the page had the same curlicue swirl as the others and the handwriting coincided with that of the diva. Both sides of the page were filled with Carmen's words. She had written about her father, how she feared him. I remembered reading this page earlier before I found the diva's poetry. If Beata hadn't ripped it out, and if I'd had a chance to reread it more carefully, as I did with the rest of Carmen's material, I might have figured it out too.

Carmen wrote on March 2, "If anything should happen to me, I need to leave my suspicions in a safe place. But who shall I trust? I am surrounded by villains. Until I find someone I can depend on, I'll bury my thoughts in a special chamber, a prop that someone dear to my singing heart could unlock."

Originally, when I read the passage, I thought Carmen would have simply stated her suspicions to someone close to her, that her "special chamber" was a metaphor for her heart. However, this time when I read the passage, I knew Carmen obviously meant the special chamber was the sarcophagus in the opera house's prop room.

The timing of Carmen's plan now made sense. Right after writing this entry in her journal, I called her to do an interview on Tarot cards. She was so desperate to leave a clue to someone, she chose me, a stranger who entered her life at a critical moment. Shortly after our first phone conversation, she wrote the letter outlining her suspicions, and hid it in this secret tomb. Next, she devised a way to have me find it.

The only time we could meet during her hectic schedule was two hours before her last performance. Carmen knew we wouldn't be alone in the dressing room, so she couldn't just blurt everything out to me. She had to give me the information in a hidden fashion, and hope that I would put the pieces of the puzzle together. In preparation for our interview, Carmen gathered the material on her father, which she had been saving for years, and placed it all in a box. Inside that box, she placed four clues of written poetry with the word "tomb" on them.

From those poetry passages, the entry in her diary, and from what she told me during our interview, she expected me to find the letter outlining her suspicions in the opera's prop room.

And to think that six days ago I had dismissed as paranoia my suspicions that Beata had ripped out a page of Carmen's diary.

"You are going to give me that letter, aren't you," I said to Beata. My voice shook.

She folded it into thirds and placed it back into the envelope. "The answers are right here–Carmen's murderer and motive. Without this, you couldn't write the story or launch your series."

"What do you mean?" Silently, I seethed.

Beata stroked the envelope. She really meant to keep it from me. I considered lunging for her, but at this point that seemed a bit extreme.

"It's not fair," she said. "You get all the good stories. All along, you've been trying to get rid of me, even disparaging me to Alyce."

She was trying to steal my story, even tampering with my evidence, and then blaming me for reacting. The anger surged through me, and I thought I wouldn't be able to control it. "Give me that letter," I said through clenched teeth. "You're completely out of line."

"Oh, just like that slap you gave me the other day? I can't believe Alyce didn't fire you on the spot. But since I found this letter myself, it occurred to me that I could write the story without you."

"What?"

Beata flipped back her hair. "Alyce thinks you've gone over the edge. Well, almost. She doesn't need much more to be convinced. The story, the series, will be all mine."

"Beata," I said slowly. "You don't know what you're doing."

She looked at me defiantly. "I've been talking to Bruno about you too."

"Oh, have you?" I clenched my fists, ready to pound them

on Beata. She had always been a thorn in my side, constantly competing with me, thinking of ways to make me look bad in front of Alyce. If I lunged now, I could topple her. With all my yoga training, my body was agile and strong. I could knock her out, then leave her body in the sarcophagus. In a few hours, after I'd confronted Castrato, I'd let people know she was up here resting in a tomb.

Then something else occurred to me. A shining clarity lightened my mind, like an epiphany, a sign that there was a better way to get that letter.

"I know what the letter says," I said.

"Oh really?" she said sarcastically.

"It was written on March 4th, right?"

Beata pulled out the letter from the envelope to check. She blinked with surprise. "Yes, you're right."

Until that moment, I wasn't completely sure.

Beata rolled her eyes. "Look, maybe you're right after all. I know Alyce would want me to show you the letter anyway."

Why the quick change of heart? I decided to play along with Beata, believing she'd now give me the letter.

"Despite your ripping out the diary page, I'll admit I haven't been treating you fairly and I'm willing to start over. That is, if you're willing to work with me. If this series continues, there will be plenty of material for both of us." I took a deep breath and said, "I'm sorry."

"You don't really mean it; you just want the letter."

I sighed. "Okay, you're right. But we are a team, aren't we? Like you said, Alyce would want you to show it to me."

I stepped up closer to Beata and extended my arm. With a reluctant smile, she extended her own and we both chanted, "To Pierce the Veil of Death!"

Beata handed me the letter and I took it as if I were accepting a delicate piece of china.

March 4th
Dear Alexandria,
If you are reading this letter, it is because the horrible

plan to kill me has succeeded, and I have found a way for you to find it.

I am alone in my bedroom reading my Tarot cards by candlelight. Teresita and Castrato didn't know I was home and I have been listening to their conversation. My cards were right. They warned me Teresita and Castrato wanted to kill me.

I have little time to explain everything. I leave you my final suspicions, as you are the last person I can trust with my thoughts. It is most unfortunate, but true.

Castrato, Roberto Andretti, is my brother. Teresita and Roberto have both conspired to kill me.

They are after my estate, now worth $22 million. Castrato believes I will remove him from my will and leave everything to my daughter, Katarina Mendoza. This is not true. I have kept him in my will all along, and never planned to remove him. My daughter married a wealthy man and is taken care of. However, if it turns out my brother kills me, I leave him nothing.

Teresita has poisoned his mind, having him believe I no longer loved him. She wants Parsifal's. I have tried to explain this to my brother, but he does not believe me.

I don't know how they will do it, but they will blame my father, Adriano Capezio. This, too, is Teresita's idea, for she knows how Roberto feels about being removed from his father's will. Castrato has joined our father's gun business and has been trying to convince me we should write a book about our father, exposing how he makes his money and what kind of a father he has been to us. He wants me to hire a ghostwriter for the book. That is you, Alexandria Vilkas. When you called me for the interview of Tarot cards, I took it as a special sign.

Castrato has been selling guns to people who should not own them. This too he will blame on our father.

I will hide this letter in the safest place I could find at the Lyric, and pray that you will never see it, unless Roberto's and Teresita's plan to kill me succeeds.

I want you to tell Denise Johnson that I bequeath my entire estate to the Lyric. I want to leave what I can to the institution that has helped my career blossom. In fact, you should give this letter to Denise as soon as possible. She will know what to do next.

If it is in my power to help the Lyric from the Other Side, I will do all I can. Even now, I am with the Lyric.

God bless,
Carmen Dellamorte

I folded the letter into thirds and slipped it into the envelope with a strong sense of satisfaction. It vindicated my suspicions about Castrato being the murderer and how he planned to cover up his evil deed. This was the proof I needed.

"We need to call the police and bring this letter to Denise right away," I said.

Beata looked at her watch. "It's five minutes to seven. You think we can show this letter to Denise before the show begins?"

"We're going to have to. The only reason Castrato is here is to sell those guns at this event. If we don't catch him here, he's likely to make his escape and never show up again."

Beata nodded and waited for me to call Lt. Joe Burke.

"Where are you?" I asked Joe once he'd answered. "I thought you'd be at the Lyric by now."

Joe had an edge of impatience creeping into his voice. "We got stopped by a nine-car pile-up on Lake Shore Drive. The hailstorm. What's going on?"

I told Joe about the letter Beata found in the sarcophagus, the interview with Adriano, and how Felix Vasilakis suspected there would be a sale of Ilmatos this evening.

Joe sighed heavily. "I'll be there in a few minutes. Don't do anything crazy before we get there, all right?"

"Who me?" I hung up, hoping Joe would be here soon, because I wanted him to be the one to confront Castrato and find the stash of Ilmatos.

Beata and I stepped onto the elevator, both of one mind. On the one hand, I felt relief that the two of us had set aside our differences, but on the other hand, I couldn't shake the feeling our friendship would be short-lived.

Chapter Thirty-Seven

We arrived at the lobby downstairs with a few minutes to spare before the show began. The Rice Grand Foyer was filled with three hundred of Chicago's cultural elite, women in elegant gowns and men in tuxes. It was a small crowd, but these were the Lyric's biggest donors and they came to support this town's only opera house. There had never been a fundraiser this urgently prepared at the Lyric, and I was sure that by the time it ended, the fundraiser would be talked about for decades.

Off to the side stood tables dressed in white linen, silver candles, and appetizers. The floor's pink marble gleamed, as did the gold fixtures and brass railings throughout the foyer. No matter how many times I'd been here, it always took my breath away. The forty-foot-high columns topped with carved capitals covered in gold leaf and the comedy/tragedy masks added to the dramatic effect. Many in the audience held a glass of champagne and were avidly chatting about whether this fundraiser could save the Lyric Opera House. I hoped the letter I held in my hand would be the key.

We couldn't see Denise Johnson anywhere, but figured she'd show up soon. Beata disappeared to find a drink.

I looked around to see if I could recognize Castrato in his costume and makeup. Would Teresita be here too? I felt nervous.

The imposing double staircase leading up from the grand foyer to the mezzanine served as the stage for tonight's performance. Orchestra and chorus members had arranged themselves on the stairs. From my position, I could see the entire lobby and the performers on the staircase. Beata returned, and waved to someone.

"Oh, look! There's Bruno," Beata said with a big smile. "He's motioning for me to come over. I just have to say hello."

I grabbed her arm. "Not now! We have to find Denise to

give her this letter."

Beata looked around, as if searching for Denise. "Look, she's not here yet. If you see her, give her the letter. In the meantime, I'll be right back. Don't worry. Everything's under control."

So much for teamwork on our story. Beata dashed to Bruno's side and, despite myself, I watched to see what would happen while still keeping an eye out for Denise. I bridled when Bruno gave a lusty pat to Beata's buns. She returned the gesture with a peck on his cheek. He put his arm around her and whispered in her ear. Beata snuggled up even closer.

It was at that moment that Bruno's wife, Angelina Scavoro, chose to make her entrance. She defined elegance in a shimmering blue gown, with a satin shawl draped theatrically around her shoulders. Her face flushed with indignation as she saw her husband's arm tightly around Beata's waist. Beata had her back to Bruno's wife and so did not see her coming. If she had, she would have wilted from the scorching gaze of Angelina. She marched toward the unsuspecting couple, threw up her hands in disgusted resignation, and apparently demanded an explanation from him. Bruno released Beata from his grip and held out his supplicating arms toward his wife.

Although I couldn't hear what Angelina said, I could certainly imagine it, particularly with her furious gestures. Bruno said something to Beata, but before she could step away, Angelina slapped Beata's cheek. Everyone seemed to notice and glance away hurriedly. Beata headed in my direction, looking chagrined. As for Bruno, he looked like he had a case of intense heartburn.

At that moment, I pitied Beata. She had a hangdog expression as she rubbed her right cheek. I knew exactly how she felt for Bruno, and I also knew there was no chance he shared her feelings. I knew firsthand what a weasel he was.

"I hate to say I told you so," I said.

"Then don't. As soon as she leaves, he'll be calling me."

I shook my head and was about to give her more advice about Bruno, like how he wasn't worth the effort, how he was never going to leave his wife, how he wasn't just a two-timer, he was a multi-timer, but I changed my mind. She would never believe me. Besides, there were more pressing matters to address. We had to find Denise Johnson. Where was she?

The orchestra's tuning wound down and the star performers arranged themselves into position on the platform of the double staircase. Castrato appeared, dressed in his black leather finest, to play the role of Hecate. Two other witches were straightening their black leather outfits. All three performers found their places around a big black cauldron, preparing to re-enact the famous scene of Macbeth. Castrato had no idea I knew he killed his sister. The letter practically burned in my hand, as I itched to hand it to Denise. I wondered what Carmen meant when she said Denise would know what to do next.

Felix Vasilakis stood behind the witches, in front of the orchestra, filling in for the maestro. The orchestra sat on the east flank of the double-staircase; the chorus on the west.

Finally, Denise appeared, her heels clicking on the marble floor as she hastily strode toward the stage. Beata and I made a beeline toward her. I handed Denise the envelope with the letter and urged her to read it.

"Right now?" She looked perturbed.

"Yes, it's from Carmen Delamorte. We found it a few minutes ago in the sarcophagus on the sixth floor. She specifically requested that I give it to you as soon as I found it."

Denise looked curious. Perhaps she wanted to ask more questions, but because there was so little time, she read it quickly. "Oh, my!" she gasped when she finished. "This changes everything, doesn't it?"

She looked out across the audience, then to the platform and set a hard gaze upon Castrato.

She said, "I never imagined it was him." Her mouth formed a tight line as if she were holding straight pins while she considered what to do next. "I assume the police are on their way?"

"Yes, I've just called. They should be here any minute.

What are you going to do?"

"Just leave it to me. It's time for the show to begin."

As the administrator, she took complete control of the operations at the Lyric, and I felt relieved that she now knew as much as I did about how Carmen died. It was oddly comforting to know that she had died by the hand of a man, and not by some supernatural, illogical curse. Yet I also had an intense pang of worry. Joe should be here already.

Denise stepped onto the landing and cleared her throat. The audience hushed and a loaded silence filled the room. Denise launched her opening comments.

"I want to thank you all for being gathered here today at our memorial fundraiser to save the Lyric Opera House. Our doors first opened November 6, 1929, slightly more than one week after the stock market crashed in October of that year. The economic collapse was devastating, and it closed the Lyric's doors for more than twenty-five years, until 1955. Most of you know that was the same year Maria Callas made her debut here."

The crowd applauded in appreciation at the mention of one of opera's all-time favorite divas.

"Since then we've remained open to a tradition of excellent opera. In all those years, we've never faced the calamity we had ten days ago, when our beloved Carmen Dellamorte died onstage shortly after her understudy muttered the curse by mentioning the name of the play three times."

People in the crowd murmured loudly at the near-mention of Macbeth.

"The murder and the curse frightened our performers and investors to such a degree that we considered closing our doors again, even though we all knew that curse was just a superstition. It did not kill Carmen, I'm sure of it. Thus the only solution to saving our opera house and dispelling the illogical fears of the curse was to find the murderer. And I have just learned that the murderer is right here."

Now audience members gasped, myself included. Is this what Carmen meant by Denise knowing what to do next? I didn't want Denise to tip our hand so fast—not without the police here first. With a flourish, Denise pulled out the letter and glanced at me for some sign of reassurance. I reciprocated with a signal of cutting my throat to let her know I didn't think she should read the letter out loud. But she thought otherwise and sped forward like an out-of-control train.

"Alexandria Vilkas and her colleague Beata Szybowski found this letter, written by Carmen on March 4th. Carmen hid it in the Lyric's prop sarcophagus. This letter, ladies and gentlemen, outlines the sinister plan of her murderers."

People gasped, again.

While Denise read Carmen's letter, I kept my eye on Castrato. He turned with a look of shock toward one of the chorus members. She mouthed something back to him, but I couldn't make out what she said. All the chorus members were wearing heavy make-up and wigs, and that's why I didn't recognize Teresita at first. But when she began signaling to Castrato, I realized it was she.

When Denise finished reading the letter, all eyes turned to Castrato.

Castrato looked straight at Denise and screamed, "Bitch!"

I almost had to agree. Denise read that letter to generate drama at this fundraiser, and it came at a steep price.

Castrato hiked up his skirt and ran toward the exit door, but the crowd closed in on him, forcing him to retreat to the staircase. Teresita leapt forward, reached into the witch's cauldron, and lifted out a black bag, opened it, and pulled out two Ilmatos.

"*Putana*!" she screamed to Castrato. "I knew you'd fail! Your big contact never showed up, and now this. I always have to fix everything."

She handed him a gun and they both headed toward the exit, their weapons raised high. They were about to escape. Where were the police? Denise looked about to faint.

No one in the crowd dared stop them.

Except Adriano. He stood near a bar at the lobby entrance and pulled out his own Ilmato as he stepped forward to halt

Castrato and Teresita. He aimed the gun at Castrato.

"Son, I've made a lot of mistakes in my life, but I swear to God. If you take one more step, I'll shoot you."

Castrato looked terrified. Teresita pushed him back toward the stairs and instructed, "You go up the west flank, and I'll take the east one."

Chorus and orchestra members moved out of the way, perhaps too scared to try to stop them. I stood frozen in my spot, like most others, aghast and dumbfounded. I noticed a few people pulling out their cell phones. The police would be here any minute. Then we heard the steady click, click, click of Tony snapping pictures. I didn't know how he could help, but I was happy he was here.

I looked up the staircase and watched Castrato on the mezzanine landing, holding his gun over the railing.

As Tony snapped more pictures, Castrato fired at him, hitting one of his cameras. It fell to the ground and shattered. It was the phantasmagoric camera! This caused Castrato to gape in awe, as if he didn't expect to hit anything after all. Then he seemed confused and stopped shooting. Tony stepped further back.

"Alexandria Vilkas!" Castrato yelled. "I want to tell you my side of the story. Come up here now. I promise I won't shoot."

I was terrified out of my mind, but knew this moment was part of my test. The Wizard and my father would want me to go up there and talk to Castrato, and I had to believe they wouldn't let any harm come to me. I ascended the west flank. Castrato held his fire.

People scattered to hug the walls, and several jammed the lobby doors. Ducking down, using the railing as my protection in case Castrato changed his mind about using his gun against me, I proceeded to climb the stairs. I still had my purse with me, having slipped my Tarot cards into it, and carried it across my body like accessorized armor.

Slowly I climbed another stair in a crouched position, too scared to stand tall and expose myself to Castrato's line of fire.

My legs cramped, and each stair became more difficult to climb than the previous one, but I never considered turning back. I was now at the top stair, about five yards from Castrato.

"Don't worry, I won't shoot you," Castrato said, although he aimed his gun at me.

I gulped and asked, "Why didn't you tell me you were Carmen's brother?"

He held his gun rigidly, pointed toward me. His face was etched in desperation, as if he longed to tell me something.

"Why?" I asked again.

"After my father disowned me, I convinced myself I didn't have a father. I had repeated that story so often it eventually became the truth. I…I just didn't want to remember."

"Remember what?" I asked.

"The…the bathroom. His rage. He was always screaming at me. I was never good enough. I'd crouch in the bathroom with the door locked, trying to block out his yelling and pounding. He hated that I–well, the funny thing is I noticed he never yelled at my sister. If I could wear her clothes, be a girl, I'd…he'd love me more. Then he took me out of his will. And when Carmen was going to do the same…"

I sighed deeply.

Castrato stared at me. "I'll never forgive him or Carmen for abandoning me."

I shook my head. "Teresita poisoned your mind. Carmen was never going to take you out of her will. Teresita made that up so you would kill Carmen. She always resented Carmen's position as a diva. And your father is proud of you–you're an accomplished opera star, what your father always wanted, but couldn't become himself."

Castrato looked down from the balcony at Adriano, whose face was wet from a stream of tears. By now, Teresita had reached us and had overheard most of our conversation. "Pig! You deserve to die! You should have killed your sister sooner, instead of waiting for the last second."

Castrato cast a glance of disgust at Teresita.

"I killed my sister and framed my father all because of

you. And all for nothing!" he said.

The severe futility of his actions hit him, and something must have snapped inside. He raised his gun, aimed it at Teresita, and shot her. Teresita gave a startled motion and fell to the ground like a limp rag doll.

When Castrato looked up, a mask of terror crossed his face. He stretched out his arms and reached longingly into the cavernous space in front of him, as if he were grasping at something.

"Carmen!" he bellowed.

Was he seeing the ghost of Carmen?

"Carmen? Is that you? Oh, it is you! You've come back!"

He nodded, as if he heard something from her.

He screamed in agony, stretching his arms out further past the railing.

"Carmen," he whimpered. "I'm sorry. I'm so sorry."

I sensed he'd lean so far over the railing, he'd topple over. Impulsively, I lunged forward, ready to grab him should he fall. But I wasn't quick enough–he flopped right over the railing and I somehow grabbed a fistful of his leather skirt.

With me holding on to his skirt, Castrato managed to cling to the railing, his legs dangling about fifteen feet from the marble floor. I tried to hoist him back up, but I wasn't strong enough. I reached farther down and grabbed his waist to pull him up by the belt of his skirt. We were both struggling, and as I leaned out, I felt Castrato slip further. I was bent in half over the railing and I tried to keep one foot on the floor as I pulled Castrato, but I couldn't. In the next second, both my feet left the floor and I felt myself tip over the railing.

The crowd was screaming. Why wasn't anybody helping us?

In that instant, Joe arrived with several police officers. They rushed past the crowd and scrambled up the stairs. If Castrato and I could just hold on for a few more seconds, we'd be saved.

As I dangled, I still had managed to keep my purse slung over my back, but it swung open, its contents spilling out and scattering to the floor. My Tarot deck tumbled down until all the cards lay splayed below. As I tried to adjust my grip, Joe grabbed the arms of Castrato and lifted. Castrato's skirt slipped down his waist a notch.

Then Castrato writhed, causing his skirt to slide off completely, me along with it. I fell to the marble floor, holding Castrato's skirt, underwear, and pantyhose, landing first on my feet, then slipping on one of the Tarot cards scattered underneath.

I caught my breath, then looked up in a daze. My legs shrieked with pain and I wondered if I'd broken one or both of them.

Police escorted Castrato down the staircase in handcuffs, revealing that, indeed, he still had all of his equipment, that he wasn't castrated at all.

"Castrato has balls!" screamed a woman.

As another police officer lead Castrato away, Joe came to my side. "I can't believe you're still alive."

I met his eyes. "It was Teresita's mastermind. Like Lady Macbeth."

Joe looked at me with concern. "That was a long drop."

I was sore everywhere and didn't feel ready to stand up yet, but I was in one piece. I wiggled my toes and bent my knees, all good signs. I shook my head. "My guardian angel must have been working overtime."

Joe noticed the cards around me, gave me a quizzical look, and bent to gather them. Tony, silently beside us, helped Joe pick up the cards.

"Can't wait to see your pictures," I said to Tony.

Tony looked down at a shattered camera. "This is the one that had Carmen's pictures."

"Oh, I'm so sorry," I said softly.

Tony nodded. "It's not the camera, it's what was inside, a picture of a real ghost. Now, nobody will believe me."

"Do you believe?"

Tony nodded, then smiled reluctantly.

"That's all that matters."

The paramedics arrived, helped me onto a gurney, and rolled me toward the ambulance. Tony walked next to me at one side, Joe at the other. The ambulance siren light swirled, casting its red beam across the gray limestone.

"You were supposed to wait for me," Joe said. He handed me my deck of Tarot cards.

I took the deck with my left hand and covered it with my right, caressing it and sending a prayer to Goddess. I kissed the deck and returned Joe's gaze.

"Following the Fool is my destiny."

Postlude

At the beginning of May, almost a month after we solved the diva's murder mystery, my story appeared in *Gypsy Magazine*. On the day it published, I had lunch with The Wizard at his studio on Archer Avenue, reviewing some of the particulars.

When I had handed in my piece to Alyce, she was very pleased. So pleased she red-lined it all over the place…I mean there was more red ink on my draft than blood draining from a freshly pierced corpse. Of course, she "massaged" some of the quotes, fabricated a few transitions, and rearranged some of the key events. This meant, she said, she cared about it. I had a hard time seeing it that way, but on the editorial masthead of the magazine, I was the writer–under the publisher, under the editor, under the managing editor, under the advertising representative, even under the designer, but above the copyeditor.

I sighed when the teakettle whistled. Maybe Alyce knew what she was doing. The result was the successful launch of my murder mystery series in the magazine, which included an extra print run and a substantial increase in subscriptions. For now, I sparkled as the Golden Girl on *Gypsy Magazine*.

"Congratulations, Alexandria," The Wizard said, placing the tea tray on the kitchen table. "We shall celebrate."

As we sipped our tea, I told The Wizard about what had happened since I handed in my story. Castrato received lifetime imprisonment. His lawyer pleaded insanity, waving medical documents as proof of Castrato's personality disorder, but the condition was so new and untested by psychology experts that the judge dismissed the insanity plea for lack of evidence.

"How was he able to sing in that special manner of his if

he wasn't castrated?"

"He's a contra-tenor. It's something quite new, and experts are comparing the tone to how they believe castratos sang."

"What is going on with Carmen's father now?"

I told The Wizard how Adriano Capezio relinquished the gun manufacturing plant in Paraguay to the U.S. Navy, and how his mistress, Donacella Dimitriano, was on her way toward a brilliant career as a dramatic soprano. In some ways, she replaced the role that Carmen played in Adriano's life.

"But best of all, Siddharma is back home," I said, sipping from my cup of tea.

"And how is your poor kitty?" The Wizard asked, dunking a ladyfinger into his tea.

"She's fine, for the most part. A little shaken up."

"You will have to ease Siddharma's trauma."

"How?"

"Talk more to her, as if she were a person. Give her a special present, something to wear."

"You mean like a necklace?"

"Yes, that might be appropriate."

I thought about the friendship bracelets I used to exchange as a girl with childhood friends, and saw myself beading one up for Siddharma.

"And the daughter of Carmen?" he asked.

"Katarina Mendoza? She flew in from Florence and visited me at *Gypsy Magazine*. She asked me for the material that Carmen had given me. I told her the originals were still with the police, but I gave her copies of everything. I asked her if she would contest the inheritance her mother left to the Lyric. She said she won't…she's married to a very wealthy man and doesn't need the money."

The Wizard smiled. "That's good. What happened to that new boyfriend I warned you about?"

"Bruno Scavoro? I'm so over him. He's having an affair with another writer at the magazine."

"You'll be better off."

"I know."

We sat in silence for a few moments, drinking our tea.

I asked, "Is there really something after life on earth?"

The Wizard sat back in his chair, the better to assess me. He gave me an I-can't-believe-you-just-asked-such-a-silly-question look.

"You know, it's funny. I know we've been studying the Tarot cards for over a year so I could enter into the Order of the Tarot and that I'm following in my father's footsteps as a detective of the paranormal. But I still haven't witnessed a real, honest-to-goodness supernatural event. Don't get me wrong. I've interviewed dozens of people who say they've seen something supernatural. Even our photographer claims he saw the ghost of Carmen through his camera. I just...I don't know...I need to see it myself. What if the others are just delusional, wishing they're seeing something?"

The Wizard's gaze flitted across the kitchen, then back to me. "Many reporters write about subjects they have little knowledge of. But if their interest in the matter is high, they still write informative pieces. It is good to have a motive when writing murder mysteries, no?"

"What do you mean?"

"You are searching for proof of God's existence. That is your premise for staying with *Gypsy Magazine*. You are the Fool on the journey toward Enlightenment, seeking knowledge."

"Yes, you might be right." It was true. I did want to know what happens to us after we die. I was so glad that I had passed my first test and was received into the Order of the Tarot. By passing each degree, I'd be one step closer to seeing the face of God.

Staring at my cup of tea, I thought of the third card in my three-card spread, the one I drew at the very beginning of this assignment, the Three of Cups (The Dressing of the Sacred Spring). This card signifies a celebration of good fortune, an acknowledgement of blessings. It is the realization of a dream, creativity, fertility, and good cheer. Offerings to the Goddess of the Spring are practiced in May and many throw bent pins as

Silvia Foti

an offering. I dug out my bent nail, the one that had brought me luck on this case after all.

"I need to toss this in a nearby stream. Got one handy?"

The Wizard thought for a moment. "Go to Buckingham Fountain with your nail, and toss it in as an offering of thanks to the spring spirits resting in Chicago's Buckingham Fountain."

I smiled at his idea. "Yeah, I'll do that."

In some Tarot decks, the Fool follows a butterfly, which the Greeks called Psyche, a symbol of the soul. I'm following that butterfly now, and have an inkling of what lies in the next stage with The Magician.

The End

 Silvia Foti writes from Chicago, where she resides with her husband and two children. She is president of Love Is Murder, a multi-genre conference for writers and readers, and the Chicago chapter of Sisters in Crime. The Diva's Fool is her second mystery novel.